Jneuin x

Calca Annie Francis~

The Day My Life Changed   (lark)

*Other books by Annie Francis-Clark
writing as J. A. Gordon*

The Day My Life Changed

ANNIE FRANCIS-CLARK

DERWEN PUBLISHING
PEMBROKE · DYFED

First published in Great Britain by Derwen Publishing 2013.

Derwen Publishing
3 Bengal Villas,
Pembroke, Dyfed
Wales, SA71 4BH

A CIP catalogue for this book is available
from the British Library.

ISBN 978-1-907084-24-9

Design and production by David Porteous Editions.
www.davidporteous.com

Printed and bound in the UK.

1

The Day My Life Changed

It started just like any other day – week day, that is – with Tony's Smartphone going off at 6.30 and me opening one sleepy eye to see the back of his impressively gym-honed body going into the bathroom. I heard the buzz of his razor and then the hissing sound of the power-shower accompanied by lots of throat clearing as he soaped himself and washed his hair and then stood under the hot flow rinsing himself making the spitting noises people do when they come out of the swimming pool. I heard the wet slap of his feet on the marble tiles as he left the shower and crossed the floor to the mirror above the basin where there was a silent pause as he cleared the mist so he could see to brush his hair. Then there was the soft 'Spppppt' of his cologne spray and even five yards away I was treated to a whiff of *Czech and Speake 88*, the cologne of the successful, self-assured man.

I turned over and opened both my eyes and was in time to see the front view of his naked body coming out of the bathroom. Even after ten years of marriage it had the power to make me catch my breath. He was still a little tanned from our holiday in Sicily and the muscles of his slightly damp chest glowed in the lamplight under their dusting of dark hair. Tony passed the bed and went to the wardrobe, pulling out one of the china blue shirts I had chosen for him since they really brought out the steely tones of his eyes. He put on the

5

shirt and opened one of the drawers hidden within the wardrobe, selecting a pair of navy shorts which he stepped into without sitting on the edge of the bed thus giving me a perfect opportunity to observe his long, lean legs as he eased himself into his underwear. After that, Tony's little reverse striptease was less exciting and I didn't bother to watch him putting on his trousers, tie and jacket but I saw the finished article as he turned and looked in the full length mirror at the side of the bed. He smiled at his reflection as he smoothed his short black hair and I had to agree with him – he was one hell of a handsome man.

Tony went downstairs humming to himself. I got out of bed and went to the bathroom, almost tripping over the wet towel he had left in the middle of the floor. I didn't bother to pick it up – I'd do it later. For now, I would just brush my teeth and comb my hair. The mist had cleared from the mirror and I saw myself looking back.

I was a mess. Dark circles accentuated the puffiness under my eyes and my skin looked pale under the blotchiness. Five cycles of IVF had done nothing for my looks nor my self-esteem. I was grateful that I was still wearing my nightdress so that I would not have to view my swollen breasts and sagging belly. Defiantly, I reached for the bottle of *Chanel No. 19* sitting next to Tony's cologne and sprayed a little behind each ear – I might look a fright but I could still smell gorgeous. Raking the comb through my tangled hair I decided that my roots needed doing and my nails too. Somehow, all these things had become too difficult recently.

Back in the bedroom, I pulled on a pair of tracksuit bottoms, a sportsbra and a long sleeved T-shirt. I couldn't find my favourite pair of clogs so I padded silently downstairs, barefoot. Going towards the kitchen I could hear Tony's voice over the comforting background noise of John Humphreys on Radio 4. 'Yes, yes. Today, I promise'. I thought he might have been talking about the radio programme and gave him a forced sunny smile as I drew level but he just quickly finished the call without saying more and put the phone in his pocket.

'Would you like any breakfast, darling?' I said.

'No, I don't think so, thank you. I'll have something at the office', Tony replied.

'What time will you be home tonight?'

'Oh, usual time, about seven'.

My husband picked up his case, kissed me quickly on the cheek, sniffed questioningly at my neck and left via the kitchen door. I heard the graunching of the garage door as it made its slow electronic ascent and then Tony's car crunching over the gravel drive at the side of the house.

As on so many previous, similar days, I was alone. The hours stretched out before me like a grey nothing. What would I do? My heart began to race uncomfortably as I reviewed my situation and ticked off the facts: I had no job, no prospects, no appointments, no child, no-one I wanted to call and invite for lunch. What would I do with all the time between now and the sound of Tony's key in the door?

Thinking back to the years of my life as a corporate princess when there were never enough hours in the day and I managed to do several impossible things before breakfast, I could hardly comprehend how I had come to be a woman in a tracksuit whose only attempt at grooming was a bit of perfume which was too strong for so early an hour. My descent into the sort of woman my younger self would have found an object of pity had been so gradual and insidious yet so complete that the realisation of it was a kick in the stomach and I suddenly needed to hang onto the granite worktop for support.

My mind was working overtime – memories came flooding into the foreground; myself as a bright young graduate, then as the promising possessor of an MBA, then a fledgling consultant, my first overseas trip, all those business lunches and dinners where people were interested in what I had to say and what I advised. I thought of all those clients who felt my views were valuable, all those meetings where someone else, a minion, poured the coffee and handed round the sandwiches, all that money I'd earned that was mine to spend as I wished without needing to justify it to anyone. I remembered the flat which I had furnished and decorated just as I wanted it – buying it had been one of the proudest days of my life.

Then there had been my social life – filled with interesting, fulfilled, outgoing, successful people of whom I had been one. How was I now no longer a part of that world? How had I become that most socially despised and useless creature – a childless housewife?

Of course it all started when I stopped work. We'd been trying for a baby for two years when the doctor suggested IVF and the drugs really didn't agree with me. The first round was unsuccessful but Tony wanted a family and so did I, so we went for another cycle and this time I felt worse so the doctor said I needed to rest. It was Tony who had said that I didn't need to work, his salary from the Bank was more than enough for our needs and I could, if I wanted, stay at home. At that point, I was so tired and emotional from the drugs, the pressure to conceive and the disappointment of having an empty womb that I allowed myself to be persuaded. It all seemed so easy – I would leave work, get fit and healthy, conceive, produce a baby and live happily ever after.

Some of my colleagues and friends had tried to tell me that it might not work out quite so perfectly but I was deaf to their advice and merrily (yes, merrily) handed in my notice and gave up a job that most women would have given their eye teeth for. The first few months of my new life were fun as I'd never before had the time to go to art galleries and matinees. I excelled myself in the culinary arts and made wonderful dinners so Tony came home to a house filled with enticing smells and a calm, happy wife.

In those first months, freed temporarily from the pressures of IVF, I rediscovered my body as a source of pleasure and Tony and I made love in every room of the house, including the garage (me up against the car, since you ask). But, as my life as a working woman receded, I put my sharp suits away and wore casual clothes, I let my hair grow, I stopped painting my nails. Gradually, there seemed to be no point in buying a new dress or a handbag and I, empress of retail, lost the desire to pound Bond Street or even trawl the malls. The lunches I had had with former colleagues or female friends petered out - we ran out of things to talk about, we had less and less in common and I felt intimidated by their confidence and continued connection with the glamorous world I had so easily abandoned.

Given that by that stage I was feeling, at the least, equivocal, about having left work, it was almost a relief to embark upon the next round of IVF and I willingly began the drug regime. This time the drugs affected me differently – I was not as tired as I had been which I attributed to no longer being subjected to the pressures of the working day – but I put on weight. Any and every woman knows how frightening this is; that first day when the trousers which had been loose no longer hang freely and a belt needs to be worn on the next hole, how suddenly there are little pockets of flesh hanging over the back of your bra and you even look fatter in the face.

I'd like to say that I was secure enough in my sense of self that this did not bother me over-much but I would be lying. It bothered me enormously and, as I got fatter, Tony got promotion and access to the Executive Gym. He went regularly as he said it was a great place to network with senior management and his hard, athletic body seemed to mock my soft, pillowy one.

Needless to say, I did not become pregnant after this third round and I seriously considered looking for a job. Good wife that I was, I discussed this with Tony before I took any steps and, in the dining room over the remains of the excellent dinner I'd made, he held my hand, looked into my eyes and told me that he loved coming back to a warm, tidy house, a home-cooked dinner and clean, perfectly ironed shirts. He told me that he loved me and that I did not need to go back to work.

I didn't look for a job.

But I agreed to the IVF only on condition that I would be able to spend some of the summer with my sister and her family in Devon. Tony conceded this with some reluctance as he knew that Jane, a farmer's wife, found him and his world a little too precious but off I went for the whole of August and came back renewed.

It had been exhilarating to walk along the lanes in my wellingtons, breathing the clear air, to sit at Jane's kitchen table helping Adam with his homework and Laura with her colouring while Jane scraped carrots and reminisced with me about our Hampshire childhood. I remembered who I was, reconnected with my confident self and rejoiced that she and I were back on intimate terms.

My rediscovered self-esteem was short-lived; I wanted to delay the next IVF cycle as I felt so well but Tony insisted that we start it as soon as possible as it had been the price of my visit to Devon – he said that a baby would be the crowning glory of our love and I couldn't argue with that.

So, it was back to the drugs and the nausea, back to joyless love-making and back to the bloated, unhappy me who felt like an alien in her own body. I felt so strange that I often thought *I must be pregnant* and I bought so many tests that I had to vary my visits to the local pharmacies, choosing sometimes the anonymity of buying them at the supermarket or going further afield. But no matter how many times I sat on the downstairs loo, little plastic strip in hand, heart in mouth and head pounding, it stubbornly refused to show the required blue line and I would throw the wee-laden test to the floor in disgust.

Tony was very patient all this time, not berating me for my failure to conceive and consoling me whenever a test proved negative. He was busy at work but he wasn't late home every night and sometimes we'd just sit together on the sofa, arm in arm, after dinner and watch something silly on the TV.

As I was only 36, Doctor Carmichael said it would be safe to have another round of IVF and Tony was all for it since we could afford it and plenty of women had conceived in their fifth cycle. I think I was still too befuddled by the hormonal disturbances of the previous cycle to object and I subjected myself again to the stimulation of my ovaries, the harvesting of the eggs and the indignity of the implantation process but this time I was so sick that I thought I must be having twins and almost convinced myself that all was working out as I had planned two years before when I left work.

I wasn't having twins. I wasn't having one baby. I wasn't having anything and my disappointment and desolation brought me to the pretty pass I found myself in that day. I felt broken, dead inside and helpless. All around me were the trappings of a well-to-do middle-class home – from the *Poggenpohl* kitchen to the limed oak floorboards, the *Philippe Starck* furniture, the wardrobes full of designer clothes and the double garage, everything about my home and my life screamed style and wealth but I felt suffocated by it and longed for something different.

With shaking hands, I made myself a cup of coffee in the *Gaggia* machine, put two sugars in it and sat at the brushed steel and glass table trying to decide what to do. The clock told me that it was 8.00 a.m. and I thought I had eleven hours to change things. I swallowed the hot, sweet liquid and felt more energised.

Without really knowing why, I went back upstairs into the largest of the three spare bedrooms and opened the door of the built-in cupboard. The remains of my working wardrobe were illuminated by the spotlight which came on automatically. Hanging there on their lilac satin hangers were my *Max Mara* skirts and jackets, my *Hobbs* dresses and my *Prada* suits. In the next section, in racks, were my kick-ass shoes. Next to them were my statement handbags. I picked up the nearest garment – a black linen fitted dress which I used to wear with a bright white jacket to meetings when I wanted to impress. I caught sight of the label and the fact that it was a size 10 and used to be a little loose on me brought me to tears. I dropped the dress, releasing a ghostly whiff of *Chanel No. 19*, and sat on the edge of the bed and howled.

I don't know how long I sat there and cried but I sobbed and sobbed and kept on saying 'What's happened to me? Where have I gone?' over and over again as if these questions were a mantra. I knew I had no answer at that point but I hoped that the continual asking of the questions might bring some enlightenment.

Eventually, I felt exhausted and empty. I curled up on the bed and rocked myself backwards and forwards as if I were comforting a child. Mum used to do that with me when I was little; she held me tight and told me that nothing could hurt me as long as she had me in her arms and that made me cry again. Mum was gone and couldn't help me. The only person who could help me was me and I decided something in my life needed to change.

A voice which came straight from the advice columns of a 1950s women's magazine told me what I needed to do was to pull myself together and make the best of things; instead of being a woman in a tracksuit I needed to make myself attractive to my husband and, instead of being a wet blanket, I needed to take control of the household and make him keen to return after a hard day's work to his perfect wife in his perfect home.

I got up from the bed, went to the bathroom and almost tripped over the towel Tony had left on the floor. I picked it up and, as he never used a towel more than once, put it in the huge wash-basket. I ran a bath and put lavender oil in it to soothe my frazzled nerves and settled into the warm water inhaling the fragrant steam in deep gulps.

After I'd bathed I felt a bit better and was calm enough to blow-dry my hair properly and put on some make-up. I was going to walk down to the local shops and get the ingredients to make a nice dinner and I would present a confident face to the world if it killed me.

I went boldly to the wardrobe – the one containing the clothes that I actually wore, not the one where I kept the clothes I didn't wear – and sifted through what was a possibility as an outfit suitable for a stroll in early autumn down to the shops for an overweight woman in her late thirties.

Defeat stared me in the face. There were jeans, hanging in the plastic bags in which they'd returned from the cleaners but I knew if I wore them I'd feel as if I'd cut myself in two. There were shirts but I knew that my heavy bosom would strain the buttons. I looked in the drawers and pulled out a stretchy, long sleeved T-shirt. Yes, that would do and the dove-grey colour suited me. I looked at jackets and found a black woollen one which was semi-fitted and gave me a waist where none existed. Eventually, after discarding several alternatives, I decided on a black pull-on skirt whose elasticated top I disguised with a wide, plaited belt. I pulled on thick, opaque tights and knee boots and looked in the mirror for the result.

If I held in my belly and arched my back, I looked like a normal woman. By 'normal' I mean someone who could go into a clothes shop without feeling overwhelmed with fear and self-loathing and who could look forward to a shopping trip with pleasure rather than mental anguish. Emboldened, I went back to the wardrobe where I kept the clothes I didn't wear and picked out one of my favourite handbags – a purple *Bottega Veneta* tote – and slung it over my arm.

Feeling reckless now, I hurried out of the house before resolve failed me. The cool autumn air struck my face and I picked up pace to keep warm. This was the first time I had ever walked to the shops. I normally went in my zazzy Mini-Cooper and parked behind the Post-Office. It was a three minute car journey, depending on the traffic, but it was a fifteen minute brisk walk and I enjoyed it. I revelled in the feeling of cold air in my lungs and looking at the piles of copper leaves in suburban gardens. I enjoyed seeing people go about their everyday business at a steady pace rather than the frantic rush that characterised everything in the City.

I arrived at the little shopping precinct with bright cheeks and in a better frame of mind. First stop would be the butcher as the choice of meat would determine what we'd have for dinner. The butcher was as cheeky as all of his trade and I emerged from his shop with a smile on my face and a, 'lovely piece of fillet for a lovely filly,' in my basket. Next was the greengrocer where I bought floury potatoes and very fresh-looking broccoli before going to the delicatessen to get the Emmenthal and Gruyere cheeses needed for a proper Gratin Dauphinois, one of Tony's favourite dishes. Then on to the wine merchant where I bought a bottle (just the one as it was very expensive and my desire was to have a romantic dinner with my husband, not to get him dead drunk) of *Romanee Conti*.

I passed the florists' and saw they had beautiful red roses in a big display in the window. The roses were long-stemmed and so velvety that I wanted to stroke them and stick my finger into their deep, rich hearts. I stood outside and contemplated buying a dozen so I could put them on the table in the dining room as a centre-piece but I felt their naked sensuality would be out of place among the cool minimalism of the room and, anyway, it would look as if I were trying too hard.

Walking reluctantly away from the roses, I noticed how different this shop looked from its neighbours. Alone among all the stylish, modernised, boutique shop-fronts serving this affluent enclave, this shop needed a coat of paint, a new door-frame and someone who cared enough to remove the dead flies from the bottom of the window. It looked sad and down-at-heel and I wondered just for a moment how the owner could be aware enough to buy such lovely flowers but not to notice how dingy the shop had become.

But it was nothing to do with me and I was a woman on a mission; I turned on my heel and went home.

2

The Day My Life Changed for the Worse

The actual meal would not be difficult and the trick would be to put the fillet in the oven only just before seven so it would be cooked but not overcooked by the time we came to eat it. I prepared the Gratin as it was a bit fiddly and then turned my attention to the really difficult part.

What on earth was I going to wear? I needed to look attractive and sexy without its seeming that I'd tried and without looking hard or tarty. I used to pull this off as easily as anything but was a size ten then.

I went to the wardrobe containing the clothes I wore and looked at everything with a hypercritical eye. Too long, too short, too dressy, too casual – I was beginning to panic – but then I saw the answer – my miracle dress. With a whoop of joy, I took it from the wardrobe and removed it from its plastic cover. Yessssss. This would do it – the soft black jersey was very forgiving and the crossover bodice could be adjusted to provide a view of however much cleavage I felt to be appropriate.

All I required now were the shoes and the right underwear. At this point I needed to be really honest with myself. Did I or didn't I? Was I or wasn't I? This stumped me so much that I had to sit down on the edge of the bed to think about it. Did I really want the evening to end in sex with Tony? I really wasn't sure and this was strange as we'd had such a torrid time earlier in our marriage but I thought about all the times we'd had 'duty sex' when I was trying to conceive and how it had blunted my appetite. Then I thought about Tony coming out of the shower that morning and a longing stirred deep inside me.

That was the answer to the underwear question. I went to the drawer where I kept my 'best' things and pulled out a pair of bottle green silk knickers and a matching bra trimmed with black lace. Luckily I had some sheer black hold-ups also trimmed in black lace so everything was matching and harmonious and, if I pulled in my tummy, I looked ripe but not seriously over-ripe.

Shoes were the next thing. Heels were, of course, a necessity but if I went too high I ran the risk of looking like an ageing hooker so I chose a lovely pair of *Emma Hope* black suede court shoes with a medium heel which gave me height and lengthened my legs while preserving my dignity.

I was pleased with all of this preparation and began to feel excited at the thought of a lovely dinner followed by a standout session with my husband. I showered quickly, brushed my teeth and decided to put my hair up as this exposed the nape of my neck; Tony used to come up behind me and kiss me there when we were first married and it sent delicious shivers up and down my back. He hadn't done this for some time and I missed it so I wanted to send a signal that I was open to this caress.

I put on my make-up with extra care; *Lancome* foundation with a bit of loose powder on top just to set it, a bit of grey eyeshadow and smudged black liner to give a smoky eye but not the full Dusty Springfield look and then a nude lipliner all over the lips with a bit of gloss on top. I added mascara and a tiny dusting of shader under my cheekbones then checked the result. In soft lighting I'd pass for a self-assured woman who could be up for it if you played your cards right. Perfect.

Having dressed, I decided that a couple of inches of bosom was about right and then added a bit of shader into my cleavage for more depth and allure. I put on my shoes and clipped on the pearl earrings I'd worn on our wedding day. They were a present from Mum and I wanted to feel her near me.

Then I realised I'd forgotten something. Perfume. Another tricky decision. Tony liked *Shalimar* but I'd worn that all through the IVF years and something about it now reminded me of disappointment and procreational sex. I wanted recreational sex so I needed to smell different. I opened a drawer in my dressing table and viewed the options: *Aromatics Elixir* – lovely but too warmly comforting, *Y* by Yves St Laurent – too businesslike, *White Iris* by Trish McEvoy – too summery, and then I saw the answer at the bottom of the drawer – *Mitsouko* by Guerlain – feminine without being a pushover and the essence of intelligent, smoky mystery. I sprayed some behind my ears and a little into my cleavage and went downstairs.

At the bottom of the staircase, on the hall mat lay several envelopes and packages. I picked them up and took them into the kitchen. There were some letters for me and some for Tony. I put them into separate piles and then sat at the table to open mine. I picked up the first one and, for a moment, studied the name and address. Tony and I had been married for ten years but it hadn't occurred to me in all that time to think about my name and now that I stared at the envelope it was almost as if I were looking at the name of a stranger when I read 'Mrs Rowena Boxer'. Yes, that was me but it also wasn't me. I began to feel confused so I picked up Tony's letters to see if I could sort them in any way and was surprised to see he had a letter from his pension fund. They usually wrote to him in the spring so I hoped it wasn't bad news.

I put both piles of letters on the granite counter and looked at the clock. It was six p.m. and my husband would be home in an hour. I went to the dining room and set the table with the good cutlery, glasses and linen. I put two candlesticks on the table and replaced the half burned candles with new ones.

I opened the wine and put it to warm next to the oven. Then I ran upstairs to check my hair and make-up and, as I came down again, I felt a flutter in my stomach – a teenage flutter, the kind you get when you're getting ready for a really important date and I realised just how much I, Mrs Rowena Boxer, wanted to make love to my husband.

At six forty-five I put the fillet in the oven and didn't know what to do with myself until the pivotal moment when I would hear Tony's key in the lock. He'd said he would be home at seven so I wouldn't have to wait very long but I couldn't settle to anything, I just paced the kitchen like a tiger in a cage.

Seven o'clock came and went. Seven fifteen came and went and there was no sign of Tony. I took the fillet out of the oven and moved the *Romanee Conti* to a slightly cooler place. At eight fifteen I finally heard Tony's car on the gravel, followed by the sound of the garage door and I hurriedly put the fillet back in the oven and raced to the dining-room to light the candles. By this time I was in quite a state and my hair was descending from its former chic chignon into tendrils around my face which was hot from the oven and wearing an irritated expression because Tony was an hour and fifteen minutes behind schedule but hadn't bothered to ring to warn me.

From the kitchen, I heard his footsteps on the path and tried to calm myself as I waited for him to open the door. I heard the key in the lock and him walking down the hall, pausing momentarily as he passed the open door to the dining-room. 'Good, he's seen the candles and the table', I thought. He would be pleased that I'd made such an effort.

As soon as he entered the kitchen I knew something was wrong. His face was a queer mixture of beaten spaniel and cocky, schoolboy bravado. I went to kiss him and smelled alcohol on his breath. His clothes gave off that 'I've been in a bar with a lot of boozy friends' smell and I wanted to say something about how he could have rung.

He looked at me closely. 'Jesus Christ, Ro', he said, 'What's going on? The dining-room's lit up like it's Christmas and you're done up like a dog's dinner'.

'I'm glad you mentioned dinner', I said with false brightness, 'Because I've made your favourite – Gratin Dauphinois with fillet and I got a really nice bottle of red to go with it'.

Tony sat down with a thump at the kitchen table and put his head in his hands groaning. I wondered if he was ill – if he was having some sort of weird stroke and said, 'What is it, darling, are you ill? Can I get you something?'

And then he said the words which changed my life in an instant. He said, 'No, you can't get me anything and I won't be staying for dinner. I won't, in fact, be staying because I'm leaving you, Ro.'

I thought I'd misheard. I thought it was some silly joke that he'd come up with to divert me from his lateness and lack of consideration but, as I stared quizzically at him and he held my gaze with a steely glare, it began to dawn on me that he wasn't joking.

'What?' I said, wrinkling my nose in emphasis, after what seemed like an age but was probably only ten seconds.

'You heard me', he said, 'I'm leaving you, Ro. I'm leaving you for another woman and I wanted you to hear it from me first. I didn't want anybody else tittle-tattling to you about what's been going on'.

The words 'what's been going on' echoed painfully round my head for a while before I thought to say, 'What *has* been going on?'

'In common parlance, Ro, I've been having an affair', Tony said slowly, enunciating each word carefully as if I were either deaf or stupid.

'For how long?' I managed to whisper as I clung to the counter for support.

'Long enough', he said defiantly.

'What do you mean 'long enough',' I said.

'Long enough for her to get pregnant', he said and I felt as though he had taken a knife and slashed through my guts so they were dripping viscously onto the expensive limestone tiles but I wouldn't, I *would not*, let him see how much he had hurt me.

'Pregnant? Congratulations', I said with more composure than I felt. 'Who is it?'

'Tasha', he said and he rolled the word appreciatively around his mouth as if it were the *Romanee Conti* and looked up at me with a lascivious smirk which told me all that I needed to know about the true nature of his relationship with his leggy P. A.

'How unimaginative', I said, 'And how commonplace. It never ceases to amaze me how lazy men are and can't even leave the office in search of a…..' I couldn't find the words and then I could, 'Cheap fuck.'

'How dare you', he said, anger making his face hard. 'How dare you say such a thing about a sweet, innocent young girl whose only mistake was to fall in love.'

I almost laughed at his stupidity but I too began to feel angry and I screamed at him, 'Get out, get out. Get out of my sight'.

'Alright, I'm going', he said and picked up his car keys. 'You can stay here', he added as he got to the front door, 'For now'.

And then there was the sound of his *Porsche Boxster S* speeding away into the darkness.

3

Falling

My hand was shaking so much I dropped the glass on the floor and moved my foot out of the way of a jagged shard only just in time. I wiped my sweaty palm on a piece of kitchen roll, opened the cupboard above the sink and took out a thick tumbler which I filled with the *Romanee Conti* and knocked it back. Somehow it felt good. So I did it again and smiled to myself that there was no Tony to give me a disapproving look. Feeling emboldened and skittish, I opened the side door into the garage and went to the pot on the top shelf where I kept my cigarettes and lighter. No more sneaking out to the garden, I could smoke in the house if I wanted. I took the wine bottle and my cigarettes and went upstairs where I sat on the matrimonial bed, the bed I'd so recently wanted as the scene of an orgy with my husband, lit a fag, lay back and inhaled.

As I watched the smoke rise to the ceiling, it occurred to me to consider what should I do now? I had no idea how I felt – numbness had set in and it was as if I were watching it happening to someone else. I thought I should cry and wail and storm and rage but I couldn't find those feelings in me. I lit another cigarette and, seeing the wardrobe door open, had a little laugh at the thought that Tony's immaculate *Hugo Boss* and *Ermenegildo Zegna* suits would now bear a trace of corrupting smoke. I wondered if I might, actually, impregnate them with the alien taint if I smoked in the bedroom enough before he came to collect his clothes and thought it was a good idea. I remembered the story of the Tory MP's wife who, on learning of his infidelity, cut the arms from his suits and sold his beloved car for a song and felt that my idea was more subtle and better so I lit yet another cigarette and stood in front of the serried ranks of beautiful suits and jackets on their cedar hangers and blew smoke all over them.

Then I had another brilliant idea. I went to the cupboard where Tony's shirts were kept and looked at them- crisp and perfect, ironed with love by me, just waiting for him to put his muscled torso into them. Tony normally wore white shirts to work; he said it was right for an executive in his position but I knew he really fancied himself as a bit of John Hamm in 'Mad Men' lookalike and he fostered this with the shirts and the tight fitting Italian suits. He was right though, he was positively mouth-watering in his nine-to-five gear.

I stubbed out my cigarette with the others in Tony's toothmug, picked the ten white *Hilditch & Key* shirts from the cupboard and put them on the bed. I knew what else I needed but couldn't at first think of where to find it and then I had a brainwave. I went to the cupboard in the smallest bedroom and rifled through my folded sweaters until I found what I wanted.

Taking my sweater and Tony's shirts to the utility room, I looked at the programmes on the *Neff* washing machine. All the garments were cotton, so something hot but no too hot should do it. I selected a 60 degree wash and put everything in the drum and closed the door. Washing powder was not necessary so I just pushed the button and had the satisfaction of seeing Tony's pristine white shirts begin their journey arm in arm with my new scarlet sweater.

I was feeling reckless and powerful by now so I went to the garage and picked one of the bottles of *Louis Roederer* champagne Tony had been saving for a 'special occasion', subtext, wetting our baby's head, and decided it would be cold enough to drink if I added ice to it in my glass. And it was –

it wasn't *quite* as good as if it had been served to me in a cooled crystal glass by a waiter in a long black apron but it was still pretty good and I sat in solitary splendour in the dining room knocking back the precious bubbles on top of the expensive, heavy, *Romanee Conti.*

Somewhere in me there is a Girl Guide leader and she has a very specific voice, a bit like Dawn French when she's playing the Vicar of Dibley. When I was half way down the *Louis Roederer*, Dawn made an appearance in my head. 'Steady on Ro', she said, 'Don't you think you should have something to eat?' She was right, of course, she's always right, so I went to the kitchen and sliced some of the fillet (how I did this without at the same time slicing myself, I'll never know) and ate it with some of the potatoes which had browned almost to a crisp while I'd been drinking and smoking more than was good for me.

I looked at my watch – ten thirty – too late to ring Jane – so I got up from the table leaving my dirty plate, knife and fork, wine glass and saucer doubling as an ashtray and went upstairs to bed. I smiled to myself on the way up the stairs knowing that what I had just done was irreversible, that Tony would never forgive me for polluting his clothes, dyeing his shirts pink and leaving his immaculate house in a mess but, as I took off my miracle dress and silk underwear and lay on the bed, it occurred to me that I didn't give a monkey's.

....

I woke with a pounding headache and a dry mouth which tasted more horrible than I could ever recall and then I remembered the red wine, the vintage champagne, the burnt *Gratin Dauphinois* and the cigarettes. I lifted my head from the pillow and was horrified to see that I had gone to bed wearing my make-up. Even in my strange state, I knew this was the mark of the incorrigible slut and I felt I had to clean my face.

I got to the bathroom but, before I could slather myself in

cleanser, I felt bile in my mouth and then I was sick in the basin. There was no time to get to the loo. It made me feel worse to see the contents of my stomach lying there, silently berating me for my excesses but then I thought that whatever was happening was justifiable as my husband had just left me for a younger woman who'd managed to do the one thing which had eluded me – become pregnant by Tony.

The previous day's events all came flooding back and my weakened physical state meant I could hold it in no longer – I sank to the floor and lay on the marble tiles and sobbed as if my heart would break. The pain was so intense that, at one point, it felt as if I were having a heart attack and I had a fleeting image of being found there on the floor, dead, in my own vomit and that made me cry even harder. I felt ghastly in my head, in my stomach, in my heart and in the depths of my womanhood. I felt like a stray dog which had been kicked to within an inch of my life and I lay, naked, on the cold, unforgiving floor and howled until my throat hurt.

Dawn came to the rescue. 'Sit up Ro', she said and I did as she suggested. 'Now try to stand up', she said and I did, hanging onto the basin for support, 'Now see if you can manage to take a shower', and I obediently stood in the stall and turned on the water. It was cold enough to start with to make me gasp but it soon warmed up and I reached for my *Jo Malone* White Jasmine & Mint shower gel and actually washed myself all over with it, using a wash cloth to scrub my face clean.

I reached for one of the big, fluffy white towels from the rack and draped myself in it. It smelled of stale cigarette smoke which made me gag but it dried me anyway. I put another smelly towel round my head and went in search of something to wear. What does the newly deserted wife choose? Should I go for a defiant, who-gives-a-toss brittle glamour? Or should I go for sackcloth and ashes? I decided that, given my extremely delicate stomach, I would go for that old favourite – comfort – and chose a black mid-length stretchy skirt and a long polo necked jumper also in black. I found my beloved *Ugg* boots under the bed and put them on. This gave me a feeling of being a little bit more in control and I was strong enough to go back to the bathroom and clean my teeth and pull my hair into a short ponytail. I looked in the mirror and looked quickly away – mirrors and I were not on speaking terms. The 'Croydon facelift' hairdo made me look like a chav and my extreme pallor made me look like a half-dead chav. Who cared, though? Certainly not me.

I went slowly downstairs picking my way over the treads very carefully as I didn't want to trip nor did I want to make too much noise since the pounding in my head was quite bad enough. I got to the kitchen where my nose was assaulted by a potent mix of old smoke, red wine, burnt potatoes and dried out meat juices. I ran to the sink where I brought up some startlingly yellow bile and stood there clutching my belly as I dry heaved and watched the bile disappear down the plughole with the stream of water from the cold tap.

'This won't do, Ro', said Dawn and I had to agree with her. I needed to pull myself together. Coffee was what I needed. I went to the cupboard and opened the tin containing the ground coffee. Empty – apart from a few fragrant grains. I couldn't bear the sound of grinding beans so I opened a packet of camomile tea bags and boiled the kettle. Even the smell of the camomile steeping in the boiling water in my cup was overwhelmingly strong and I had to take very small sips so I didn't gag again. I sat down heavily at the kitchen table, grateful to feel its weight against my body but cursing the cold, unforgiving Perspex of the chair under me.

I felt old, tired, empty and washed up. I wasn't even forty and yet there seemed nothing left for me. My marriage was in tatters, I had no job, no security and nothing to love. I looked around me at the shiny trappings of my husband's success – he was everywhere in this house, his taste, his choice, his money. I was nowhere. Where were the feminine touches? Where was the colour? Where were the curves?

Everything was hard and cold, linear and right angled. I hadn't been allowed to have anything patterned or, God forbid, floral, in the house. I hadn't even bought the red roses yesterday. I'd been pleased last night that I hadn't completely shown my hand with the flowers but now I thought I would like to have something soft and yielding to reassure me.

I walked into the dining room and surveyed the detritus of my meal. God, I'd been messy – there were red wine stains all over the table and copious spots of candle wax now unevenly dotted the glass interspersed with bits of disaggregated fag ash. My dirty plate, the but-filled saucer and glasses were still there along with the cutlery and it was all too much – I couldn't clear it up now. I needed to clear my head, I needed some fresh air.

I put on my *Burberry* trench coat and anchored my cashmere scarf around my neck in a Fulham knot, picked up the nearest bag I could find – my black *Mulberry* Bayswater bag – and locked the front door behind me. I couldn't take the car, I wasn't fit to drive, and I set out for the shops. I had no idea what I wanted to buy but I just wanted to be out of that house with its stale smoke and its broken dreams for a while.

I walked slowly as if I were a very old lady. I felt that the few people who were around were staring at me but I was past caring. I may well have looked drunk but I knew that, even in my diminished state, I was still an expensively dressed drunk and, in this upwardly mobile neighbourhood, such things mattered.

I got to the shops somehow. Did I want something to eat? My stomach rebelled at the thought of meat and potatoes but it gave a half-hearted 'Yes' to an almond croissant so I bought two from the artisan baker and, remembering that potassium is good for those in shock and that oranges contain potassium, I bought a bag of cheery looking clementines from the greengrocer. The clementines were wildly overpriced because they had some of their leaves but I bought them anyway because they looked so nice and I needed their colour in my dark life. I then realised I was outside the florists and there were still some of the beautiful roses in the window along with the dead flies.

I hadn't been in the shop before since flowers hadn't featured much in my life with Tony so I didn't know what to expect. I opened the door. An old-fashioned doorbell tinkled above my head. There were large, dark green, metal jugs of blooms ranged on the opposite wall; beautiful big lilies whose white petals shaded to deep pink opening their inner depths to view, majestic bird of paradise flowers whose complex structure and resemblance to exotic plumage made me want to smile, tall blue thistles, surprisingly large, bright scarlet carnations and other things whose names I didn't know but all dazzling in their fragile and oh-so-transient beauty. The display was a testament to someone's taste and devotion to flowers so how come the rest of the place was so down-at-heel and why wasn't anyone there to serve me?

At that moment, a teenage girl came in, saying, '*Ciao*', and closing her mobile phone as she crossed the room towards me. She had a sullen, closed look which said, 'I don't like working here, I am meant for better things and I particularly don't like serving boring bitches like you.'

'Yes?' she said.

'I'd like some flowers,' I said.

She looked at me as if I were very stupid and as if she wanted to say, 'Well I didn't think you'd come to read the gas meter,' but what she actually said was, 'Which?'

I wanted to scream at her that I was the customer, that my money paid her wages, that she should pay more attention to the state of the shop, that a clean shirt and a smile wouldn't go amiss but what I said was, 'Some roses, please,' and hated myself for having said 'Please.'

'How many?' she said.

'A dozen,' I said and she looked at me blankly before I added, 'Twelve,' by way of explanation and she began to walk towards the window to get the roses.

She picked up the large metal jug and humped it over to the counter on the wall opposite the floral display. 'They're very expensive, three pounds apiece,' she said in a voice she probably reserved for speaking to the terminally stupid.

'So?' I said, glaring at her and shrugging my shoulders which made her give me a look with a tinge of respect in it; I was not as boring as she thought. She picked out twelve roses and began to wrap them, badly, crushing their heads in too much tissue. I couldn't bear to see them so abused so, to her astonishment, without a word, I elbowed her to one side and took them from her and wrapped the blooms carefully and with reverence before counting out the thirty six pounds and making for the door.

'Anythink else I can help you wiv?' she said in a mocking tone.

'Yes,' I said, turning towards her from the door and finding within me something of my former killer corporate personality, 'You can clear those fucking dead flies from the window, they give people the wrong impression – anybody'd think you don't care.'

I saw her jaw drop in a most satisfying way before I turned and left. Outside, I looked up at the flaking sign above the shop. 'Ted Johnson's Florists, estd. 1966,' it said. Whoever Ted Johnson was, he had an eye for beauty but he was probably ancient and he'd lost the plot commercially. What a shame, I thought as I started out for home.

4

Falling, falling, falling

It took me ages to walk home; I suddenly felt very tired as the alcohol left my body and my blood sugar levels plummeted. When I reached the door, I was reluctant to go into the house even though I was completely wretched physically and at rock bottom mentally but I had nowhere else to go so I unlocked the door and went in. The red light on the Answerphone was flashing and I rushed to listen to the message in case it was Tony telling me that he'd made a big mistake and was on his way home to try for a reconciliation.

It *was* Tony but his message was curt and told me only that he would be coming on Saturday at mid-day to pick up his clothes and I was to remember to take my car for its service on Thursday. There were no words of regret, encouragement or love – nothing on which I could pin any hopes and nothing which would explain why he felt it was acceptable to throw ten years of married life down the drain. Had I really wasted ten years? Had it *all* been a failure? Did he ever love me?

I took my shopping to the kitchen and filled a large glass vase with water before clipping most of the leaves from the roses and then arranging the long-stemmed beauties so that each was fully displayed to best advantage. They looked lovely and I decided I would keep them in the kitchen to brighten the room while I worked there. I made myself some more camomile tea, sat at the unwelcoming table and ate my two almond croissants from the bag. I sipped my tea and went back to the question I had posed to myself earlier. Did he ever love me?

I thought back to when we met – I was 25, he was 23 and I was in so many ways more successful and mature than him. *I* was the one with the terrific job and the money and the sophisticated tastes and he was drawn to me because I could teach him a lot about the workings of the corporate world. I was drawn to him because of his good looks but also because he had an easy charm and he made me feel special. We spent most of our time in those days drinking in any number of high end bars with long zinc counters, laughing at most things. We were young, good-looking and on the way up and we fitted one another's idea of the perfect partner. Hindsight is a wonderful thing and, looking back from the viewpoint of the intervening twelve years, I saw that Tony had never loved *me* in the sense that he wanted the best for me, even thought it might not have been the best thing for him, he only loved the idea of having a smart, sassy, sexy wife who could hold her own in most company and he fell out of 'love' with me when I ceased to fill that role. With a rush of disgust it occurred to me that I had been a doll to him – his own personal Barbie whom he could mould and groom and manipulate; Tony had constantly analysed and criticised my choice of clothes, my tastes in décor, music and even my preferred foods, subtly substituting his choices for mine. He had also, I realised, subtly criticised my friends and my former colleagues –'You're not still seeing her, are you? Hah ha hah ha', such that I'd gradually become more isolated and *dependant on him*. The irony was that, having created the bendy dolly he wanted, he had so crushed my spirit that I was no longer the fabulous woman he met and he moved on. I felt very angry and I couldn't believe I had allowed my love for him to blind me to what he was doing.

I suddenly thought all of this might not have happened if Mum had been alive. Mum had always encouraged me, seen the best in me and urged me to make the best of myself. It was Mum who was proud of her clever daughter and wanted me to go to University and been delighted when I got a First in Economics and Business Studies. I know that she loved both Jane and me equally but I had a special bond with Mum since her father had prevented her from going to the grammar school and she made sure that I got the education she had missed. Jane was never academic and neither was our brother Michael so I was the one on whom Mum pinned her hopes and I didn't let her down – my postgraduate MBA and rapid rise in the world of business had been high points in her life but, just when I was about to get the job of European Sales Section Head, Mum was diagnosed with lymphoma.

I wasn't living at home by then so, although I knew she'd been having terrible night sweats, we all thought it was the menopause and she didn't mention the lump in her groin until she started to lose a lot of weight. When we were told it was lymphoma we all hoped it would be Hodgkins, the non-fatal kind, but it wasn't and the fact that it was then that Dad chose to leave her was the reason why none of his children had spoken to him since.

Mum was very ill when Tony and I married but she made a real effort to dress up and look the part of the blushing bride's happy mother on the day. She gave me the pearl earrings when she was helping to arrange my veil and we had a bit of a weep because we both knew she wouldn't live to see a christening. How prophetic that was.

I knew if Mum were still alive, she'd fold me in her arms and tell me it was going to be alright, that it was okay to fail in marriage and I would make the best of the rest of my life. But Mum wasn't here and I wondered why I hadn't yet rung Jane who was the next best thing to Mum in that she knew me inside out and loved me in a true sisterly fashion.

I thought for a minute or two and then had to admit to myself that I hadn't rung Jane because I was ashamed to. The thing was that Jane had had the standard life – leave school at sixteen, get a dead-end job, meet someone, get married and have children – the sort of life which would have bored my younger self rigid. But it had all worked out for Jane with her lovely husband and family and her idyllic life, baking and making things and here was I, the supposedly successful one, all washed up and nothing to show for the last ten years other than a broken heart and a big arse.

I couldn't ring Jane at that moment because I didn't want her pity, nor did I want to hear the strain in her voice as she tried to suppress the hint of triumph in her words. Yes, Jane loved me as a sister, but there was a definite competitive edge in our relationship and, if Jane felt vindicated now by her choices, I was not feeling strong enough to justify mine. Nor would I ring Michael whose wife, Marianne, was the original gym bunny who thought it was actually illegal for women to eat chocolate. No, I would just have to tough this one out on my own until I was on a more even keel.

I sighed as I came to this conclusion and then realised with a start that Tony would be coming on Saturday to pick up his clothes including, I assumed, his precious shirts, so I went to see what had happened in the washing machine.

It was carnage. My scarlet sweater had shed so much colour it was a pale shadow of its former self but the sparkling white shirts were ruined. They were pink but not the sort of pink which says, 'I am a proudly pink shirt', they were more that pale salmon-pink which used to be the colour of old ladies' corsets. The thought of this made me laugh but I didn't know how I would face Tony having done this to his shirts. I could lie, of course, I could say that I was so upset that I put them in the machine without knowing that the sweater was there but he knew that the wardrobe was full of clean shirts so why would I be washing clean shirts? I didn't want to lie, anyway; Tony had obviously been lying to me for quite some time and there was enough falsehood in our relationship without my adding to it.

I then had a good idea – I would pack all Tony's clothes

myself so he wouldn't see the shirts until he unpacked them. This would also mean he would spend as little time as possible in the house and that suited me so I put the shirts in the dryer and went to make myself another cup of tea.

When the shirts were dry, the colour was even more 'old ladies' corsets' and I knew he would never wear them – not even for gardening had he stooped to do such a thing (which, for your information, he hadn't, ever) – but I felt I needed to iron them to foster the impression of their having been ruined by mistake so I stood for over an hour at the ironing board doing Tony's shirts for the last time. It was a job I had done with love as he insisted no-one else did them just as he liked. 'Ha', I thought to myself, 'I wonder how the lovely Tasha will manage? Will she be able to iron them without putting a crease all the way down the sleeves?' Then I recalled a conversation I'd overheard at the Bank's Christmas Party the year before when one of the Investment Managers, Douglas Cheung, a frighteningly clever young economist from Hong Kong, said Tasha was easy on the eye but she needed to peer down her blouse to be able to count to two and I wondered what she and Tony talked about.

Then it occurred to me that they probably didn't talk much – they probably spent their time in bed, crawling all over one another and making the baby I had so longed for. I started to cry and couldn't stop and there I was, iron in hand, my tears falling, dripping down my nose and hissing as they hit the hotplate. I put the iron down and went in search of a tissue for my nose. I couldn't find any in the kitchen so went to the downstairs cloakroom for some loo roll and I was in there, sitting on the closed seat, blowing my nose, when I smelled burning.

I ran back to the utility room to find smoke billowing from the ironing board and a big hole in the shirt I'd left there; in my distress I'd put the iron down flat on the board not in its rest. Too bad. Tony wasn't going to wear these shirts anyway and I quite liked the clean smell of the burning, it was a fitting accompaniment to the bonfire of my life.

I went and found another bottle of the *Louis Roederer*, put some ice in a tumbler and drank a deep draught of the fizzy mixture. Then I sat at the kitchen table, feeling the glass cold against my arms and drank the rest of the bottle. I felt numb and rudderless, as if I'd been cast adrift in the middle of a huge ocean and I had no idea what I needed to do to find land but after about ten minutes the alcohol hit my bloodstream and made me skittish again so I spent a happy half hour with the iron, burning patterns on Tony's already ruined shirts.

After another bottle of *Louis Roederer* I was capable only of dragging myself upstairs and collapsing on the bed.

When I woke it was dark and there was a pile of drool on the pillow next to my open mouth. I lifted my head to investigate the extent of the damp patch and wished I hadn't moved. Nausea washed all over me and I felt the acid almost eating away at my stomach. I had to get off the bed and go to the bathroom as I urgently needed to pee but I felt so dreadful I wondered if I'd be able to make it. I lay on my back, trying to breathe slowly and deeply to calm the clanging in my head and work out how many steps it would take to get to the loo while hoping the urge would go away. It didn't, of course, and, in the end, I just gathered what was left of my courage and stood up, as the alternative, to pee the bed, was too horrible to even contemplate.

Once I'd emptied my bladder, I could concentrate on the rest of my symptoms: headache? Tick. Sore throat? Tick. Aching limbs? Tick. Sore chest? Tick. Runny nose? Tick. 'Oh hell! Oh sodding, sodding hell', I thought, 'I'm coming down with flu'. The nausea eating away at my belly was the only symptom I could pin entirely on the champagne – the rest was down to a virus. This was hardly good news but I realised that my immune system was in shock along with the rest of me and I needed to have a hot bath and get to bed to sweat it out.

While the bath was running, I undressed very slowly so as to disturb my pounding head as little as possible. I put some eucalyptus oil in the water and lay there for a soak. I closed my eyes and breathed in the clean aroma of the oil as it cut through the fog in my head. When the water grew cool, I opened my eyes and, turning the tap with my left foot, let in more hot water. I tried not to look at my body as I knew it would upset me but there was no avoiding it. It was there, it was a fact. It was no longer the firm, springy, joyous playground it had been when Tony and I were first married – it lay beneath me now sagging, white, bloated, puffy and worn out by the hormonal excesses it had endured.

I began to cry again and let the tears fall. I don't know how long I stayed there, sobbing into the bathwater but I topped it up with hot several times before I could be bothered to get out and wrap myself in one of the smoke infused towels. I went to the sink to clean my teeth and was confronted with the dried out remains of my vomit from the night before. I'd meant to clean it up but had forgotten and I couldn't face it now so I took my toothbrush, went to the guest bathroom and cleaned my teeth there.

I had the brief thought that a hot toddy with lots of whisky might be the thing to bring out the flu but my stomach made it very clear that whisky would not be welcome so I went to bed, but this time I went to one of the guest rooms as I couldn't get back into the bed that Tony and I had so recently shared and where his pillow still reeked of him.

I put on my warmest pyjamas – a cashmere pair I'd rashly bought for myself one Christmas, much to Tony's annoyance – and got into the cold bed. My nose was running and I needed to blow it so I had to get out of bed and get a box of tissues from the bathroom which I put on the bedside table and tried again to settle down to sleep but I found, if I lay down fully, it was really hard to breathe. This meant I had to get out of bed again and get the pillows from the other guest room and put them at my back so I was almost sitting up as it was the only way I could breathe through my nose. Eventually, I fell asleep, too exhausted by alcohol, the flu and the disintegration of my life to stay awake enough to worry about whether I could breathe.

I woke to daylight and a hot sweat that involved my head, back and chest. My breathing was rasping and laboured and my nose was full of gunk. I have never felt worse physically than I did then. When Mum died I was inconsolable but I was in good health so this total bodily pain and discomfort was new and frightened me a bit. I sat on the edge of the bed and wondered whether I should call the doctor or an ambulance but I decided I would have another hot bath first.

I lay in the hot oily water letting the eucalyptus work its magic on my nose and my nerves. I felt I had to have some purpose to get me through the day and decided I would, even if it killed me, pack up Tony's things and tidy the house for when he came at the weekend. Then I remembered my car was due for its service and I needed to get it to the garage by eight thirty. I had no idea of the time so I had to get out of the lovely bath and get dressed no matter how ill I felt.

I pulled on my knickers from the day before and the comfy sports bra that was fast becoming my underwear of choice. Then I found my tracksuit bottoms and my *Uggs* and a big, thick sweater. Once I was wearing all of these, I had another really hot flush and had to sit down on the edge of the bed until it passed but at least I could see from the clock that it was only seven forty-five and I would have time to clean my teeth and pull my hair into a ponytail before leaving the house. I didn't look in the mirror while brushing my hair as I couldn't bear to see the depths of despair and defeat in my own eyes; it would only upset me more. I put on my trench coat and left the house.

When I got to the garage, Derek the mechanic, was worried about me but his kindness only highlighted my situation and I thought I would just collapse there and then and lie on the oil-stained concrete and howl and tell him that my husband didn't love me, had never loved me and my world had come to an end. Luckily, my red eyes and nose and my general

36

ropiness could be put down to flu so I contented myself with telling him I was okay really and would go home to bed. Derek got one of the others to drive me home and said my car would be delivered back to the house when it was ready. I sat in the car with the young mechanic who had the radio on loud and wondered why the important men in my life, Tony and my father, who were supposed to love me, were far less reliable than the men who looked after my car.

When I got indoors, I had a big cup of peppermint tea to clear my nose and a slice of toast and honey to soothe my throat before tackling the job of packing. I got down the big *Ralph Lauren* duffle bags Tony used when he was travelling and set about eliminating all traces of him from the bedrooms. This involved packing away his clothes including his underwear and his ski stuff. Then I packed all his stuff from the bathroom not forgetting his tongue-scraper and the spare heads for his electric toothbrush. I got the ruined shirts from the utility room and folded them carefully so, from a distance, they looked like a weird Hawaiian print, and I put them in the bottom of one of the duffle bags so he'd find them last.

I knew Tony was gone for good – there was no way back for him from his decision to leave me and no way back for me from his betrayal – so I might as well pack all his other stuff as well. There were big cardboard boxes in the garage, still stacked, folded flat, against the wall from when we'd moved in six years before. Reassembled, they were ideal for my purpose. I took several of them into the kitchen and, over the course of the day, between needing to blow my nose every few minutes, I filled them with Tony's books, his CDs, his DVDs, his car magazines, his old photo albums, stuff from his old flat etc., etc.. When I'd finished, the hall was filled with his suits, coats, the boxes, his skis and the duffle bags. It was cluttered and a mess but, apart from the garage, I had cleared him from the rest of the house.

I awarded myself a toasted cheese and onion sandwich and a glass of red wine. It was six o'clock and the long, dark evening stretched ahead of me. The rest of the wine looked tempting and I knew I could dull the pain and pass the time by drinking myself into a stupor but I didn't relish the thought of how I'd feel the following morning so I put the cork back in the bottle and put the bottle back in the cupboard. I felt relieved I was still sufficiently in control of myself to be able to forego the wine and *to want to wake up in the morning*. Without really thinking about it, I'd decided that I wanted to live.

5

Fallen

I passed the evening in true Bridget Jones style (but minus the booze); lying on the sofa under a blanket watching a succession of romcoms starring those tragic female icons Jennifer Aniston and Katherine Heigl. I can't say that they cheered me up but they did pass the time and I made my way up to the spare room well after midnight. I still felt awful but I had the passing thought that the spare room wasn't really 'spare' any more, it was becoming my bedroom.

I woke the next day still suffering from the sore throat, headache and runny nose. When I saw myself in the bathroom mirror I thought I had never looked worse; the dark circles under my eyes were now black and I had one of those horrible, big red spots on my chin – you know the kind I mean, those which never come to a head but ooze clear stuff instead and take ages to go away. The really sad thing, though, was that I just didn't care. I was past caring.

I showered and dressed in the most comfortable and comforting things I had – big knickers, sports bra, velvet tracksuit and my *Uggs*. I scraped my hair into a ponytail again, contemplated trying to disguise the circles under my eyes and the big zit with *Touche Eclat* but decided there wasn't enough *Touche Eclat* in the world to be effective and I would just go barefaced.

I had toast and an egg for breakfast but couldn't taste a

thing through my bunged up nose. Several cups of peppermint tea revived me a little and then a shot of strong espresso gave me the caffeine kick I needed to tidy up the house in readiness for Tony's visit the following day. It would never have been pleasant to empty my makeshift ashtrays with their ageing cigarette stubs nor to pick the bits of dried sick from the bathroom sink but my stomach was still rebellious and I felt horribly brackish while I was doing it.

I was slow, too, and it took me until the early afternoon to get the house in order. Then I had a bit of tinned soup and went back to the sofa for another forbidden activity – daytime television. I lay under my blanket with a cup of camomile and watched hitherto forbidden programmes about antiques, house conversions and living abroad but none of them distracted me as much as the films I'd watched so, after looking at the news (all bad), I had another long session with female stars who are unlucky in love but this time it was Sandra Bullock and Hilary Swank who helped me get through the evening.

I slept badly, tossing and turning, wondering what I'd say to Tony, what he would say to me and, most important, what I could possibly wear for the encounter which would enable me to feel dignified and in control of the situation or in control of myself, at least.

I showered and washed my hair then blow dried it carefully. I tried the *Touche Eclat* on my dark circles and on the huge zit but it just made me look very chalky under the eyes and emphasised the size of the spot so I scraped it off and sprayed myself with a good dose of *Chanel No. 19* instead. I put on Mum's pearl earrings and decided I would wear the silver grey boyfriend jumper Jane had given me last Christmas with black leggings and my ever faithful *Uggs*. After I'd dressed, I didn't look in the mirror as I wanted to *feel* that I looked alright and didn't want to present myself with evidence to the contrary.

I went downstairs and had some cereal to try and calm my

growling stomach but I was jittery and nervous at the prospect of seeing Tony. I couldn't get my head round the thought that he would be coming here, to our home, and I would not be able to kiss him, nor take him into my arms and ask him about his day. I felt sick again and had to rush to the downstairs loo to bring up my breakfast.

When I came out, there was post on the mat and I saw there were several letters for Tony so I put them on the growing pile on the counter in the kitchen. It was half past ten. He would be here in about an hour and a half. If he were on time, that is. Would he keep me waiting as he'd done the night he told me it was all over between us? I realised with a jolt of shock that that night had been as recent as Tuesday yet it seemed like a lifetime ago and, in many ways, it was – on Tuesday I had been a woman with a husband and an ordered life and now I was alone and totally at sea.

I put on the television and sat down to watch cookery and children's programmes just to drown out the voices of defeat in my head.

Then I heard his car on the gravel. I stood up in order to face him.

My stomach lurched and somersaulted like a washing machine and my heart pounded. I told myself I could handle this and I clenched my fists in determination but it was no good – by the time I heard his key in the door, my knees were jelly and I had to sit down again.

It was unfortunate that *The Bugs Bunny Show* had just started and I was sitting facing the television when Tony came into the sitting room. The look of disdain on his face will stay with me for a long time.

'Jesus Ro', he said, 'You're a complete mess. Look at the state of you. What are you doing watching….?' He spat out the word '*Cartoons*'.

He came and stood between me and the TV. He was wearing tight jeans, a white T-shirt and the black leather flying jacket I'd given him not long after we met. I wanted to rip it from his back and stamp on it. I also wanted to punch him in the face but I didn't know how and I wasn't sure he wouldn't punch me back.

'Your stuff is in the hall', I said, 'Take it and go'.

I'd imagined that we'd have a conversation – that he would thank me for having packed his things, that we'd talk about how matters could best be arranged and we might agree it could all be as amicable as possible but his rudeness and his lack of concern for me, his wife of ten years, made it impossible. I just wanted him to get his stuff and take his handsome face and muscular body and get out of my life so I could lick my wounds in private.

'Alright, I will', he said, 'But don't think that's the last of it. We'll need to sort the house out'.

He went into the hall and I heard his boots clunking over the boards as he went backwards and forwards to the car with his stuff while I watched *Bugs Bunny*. Then the door slammed and I wondered whether I should go after him with his letters but another wave of nausea made me decide against it.

I don't know how I survived that night, the following day and the next few days. They are a blur to me. I was sick, I couldn't eat, I couldn't think of anything other than the fact that Tony was with her and that he had never loved me. I was in a trance induced by lack of sleep, lack of proper food and, most important of all, lack of love.

At one point, late on Monday evening, my trance was interrupted by the phone ringing. I didn't answer it but Tony's voice came over the Answerphone, loud and clear. He had obviously just found his shirts and was none too pleased. 'You bitch', he bellowed, 'You twenty four carat bitch. You'll pay for this. Mark my words, you haven't heard the last of this'.

Tuesday passed in a similar way in my crying and wanting the pain in my heart to be gone. Then on Wednesday there was a letter addressed to me and the franking marks told me that it was from a firm of Solicitors.

I made a small cup of strong espresso and opened the

letter. It was from a top-notch West End firm. The thickness of the paper and embossed heading screamed 'expensive'. I held my coffee cup in one hand and the letter in the other but they were both shaking as I read Messrs Bolton, Greene and de Latymer's words.

The letter was written in that constipated, poker-up-backside style lawyers use when they're trying to intimidate the opposition and it was quite clear that I was now very much the opposition; Tony must have been in touch with them the day after he'd found his shirts. The letter said that Tony wanted a divorce and that, due to 'the condition' of his new partner, he did not want to wait the usual two years' separation but to divorce as soon as possible. 'Good,' I thought, 'I'll make him wait', but then I read the rest of it and nearly dropped the coffee cup.

The letter went on to say that Tony had the right to divorce me as a result of my 'unreasonable behaviour' but that, if I played ball with him as regards the house and contents, he would allow me to divorce him on the grounds of his adultery. In the meantime, he would pay the mortgage and give me an allowance for three months or until I found a job, whichever was the sooner.

I didn't know which bit of this hurt me more – the 'unreasonable behaviour' or the fact that he expected me to go out and get a job in only three months when he and five cycles of IVF trying to conceive his child had reduced me to a nervous wreck. But what was I going to do? I had no income and, as far as I could see, few prospects unless I could pull myself out of this pit of misery and lack of self-esteem. Where was Dawn when I needed her? She had been absent for some time, probably ministering to more worthy causes than me. Yup, my confidence was so low that I actually believed Dawn French was the Vicar of Dibley and she had abandoned me for other parishioners.

I had to get some food and thought that while I was out I would check the balance of Tony's and my joint account which he normally kept topped up so that there was a running balance of about £1,000 for housekeeping. I put on my trench coat and scarf and made myself walk to the shops where I bought a few groceries using my debit card and then I went to the ATM, put in my PIN and pressed the button for an onscreen balance. The digital ink on the screen said that there was £50.23 in the account. I thought there must have been a mistake so I retrieved my card, inserted it again and asked for a printed balance. Still £50.23.

Obviously Tony was determined to make this as difficult as possible for me. How was I going to live? I must get a job but the thought of trying to get back into the corporate world with its 'kill or be killed' philosophy brought me out in a sweat.

I stumbled home somehow and did what any woman in my circumstances would have done – I put on my pyjamas, made myself some hot chocolate, sat on the sofa and watched both Bridget Jones films back to back. Then I rummaged in the cupboard and found 'One Day' starring Anne Hathaway. Her cod Yorkshire accent may have been a disaster but her unrequited love for cold, handsome Dexter was a parallel with my life and I sobbed my heart out for most of the film. From there, it was an easy step to the remastered version of 'Love Story' and then back to 'P.S. I Love You' which I'd watched earlier in the week but her despair so matched mine that it was therapeutic and, anyway, Gerard Butler was in it in a tight white vest.

At about nine-thirty p.m., I went to the kitchen to make myself more hot chocolate and saw the pile of letters addressed to Tony. I idly turned them over while the milk was heating and picked up the one from the bottom – the one from the pension people. Somewhere at the back of my mind was the thought that, after ten years of marriage, I would be entitled to at least a part of Tony's pension. He hadn't seen the letter, nor had he asked for his post so I put the kettle on and, while my hot chocolate was cooling on the counter, I steamed it open.

I felt like a naughty schoolgirl engaging in a silly prank and knew it was unworthy of me but he had treated me so badly, as if I were to be discarded like an old, worn pair of shoes, that I felt justified. Well almost.

The letter was a response to his request for information and gave the value of his pension pot as £450,000. This was such a shockingly large figure that I had to sit down. How had he amassed such a sum? I thought I knew all about our finances. I thought we were a team.

I sat at the table sipping my chocolate and remembered the times when he had told me that his bonus from the bank was less than expected and did I mind if we kept my car for another year? I had put my arms round him and consoled him for his disappointment and said that, of course, I didn't mind keeping my lovely car for another year. Maybe he had lied to me. Maybe he had had much bigger bonuses than he admitted and he had put the money into his pension to make the most of the tax relief. How long had he been lying to me? Had our whole marriage been a sham?

Whatever was the answer to that, the existence of this fat pension pot put my attitude to the letter from Tony's lawyers in a different context; he'd said that we needed to sort out the house – yes, we did – but we also needed to share out the pension.

I switched on my laptop and Googled everything I could find about financial settlements on divorce and discovered that my situation was stronger than I'd thought. I could be entitled to up to fifty per cent of the joint assets but, because of my relatively young age and qualifications, it would more likely be thirty per cent. However, given the pension pot, that thirty per cent had suddenly become much more valuable. The difficulty, though, was that I knew now Tony would fight me every step of the way and it would take time to get this sorted out through the courts. How would I support myself and how would I pay for my own legal fees?

I looked at the other letters. Among all the junk mail, I

could see from their envelopes that there were two from the *Porsche* dealer, one from Tony's club, one from a holiday company and one whose logo and name I did not recognise.

Without thinking too long about it, I steamed it open. It was from a hedge fund company and, insofar as I could take it all in, Tony had a goodly chunk of money in there too – several hundred thousand pounds' worth of investment. More lies, more deceit, more pain but more money to go into the joint assets pot. I threw the junk mail and the letter from the cruise company in the bin – the latter made me think too much that the lovemaking on our recent holiday must have also been deceitful on Tony's part; I didn't know he was being unfaithful but did Tasha know we had sex three times a day on that cruise? Granted there was not much else to do while we were at sea, but I had thought of it as a sign that our marriage was in good shape.

I made detailed notes of the contents of the two letters and then put them back in their envelopes hoping they would dry out overnight. Then I went to bed and again slept badly, tossing and turning, thinking of all the times Tony had deceived me and wondering if anything about the last twelve years of my life with him had been true.

The following morning I woke with a shocking pain in my belly and a warm oozing feeling between my legs. I got out of bed carefully and saw that the sheets were scarlet. I was also dripping blood onto the cream carpet.

My periods had been unreliable ever since I started the IVF and I hadn't, in fact, had one for about three months, so in one way I was relieved that things could be getting back to normal with my cycle but the pain was really bad and I was bleeding a lot.

I made my way to the bathroom and kitted myself out with one of those big towels that I used to think you needed only if you'd had five children but which was the only thing to keep this flow under control and then took two painkillers. I went downstairs to make tea and found the hot water bottle in the pink cashmere cover Mum had given me years ago for these very situations. She knew how bad the pain was and how nice it is to put the soft warmth on your tummy. The fact that Tony had hated the colour only made it more dear to me. After changing the sheets and cleaning the carpet, I sat in bed sipping my tea with the bottle on my middle and then went back to sleep.

I woke at about two in the afternoon. I didn't feel a lot better but I needed to get some food and so I dragged myself out of bed, into my track suit and took the car to the supermarket where I used my credit card to buy some cheese, bread, apples and butter – all good nourishing stuff and not as expensive as the food I'd usually bought there. It was quite busy in the car park when I came out and there was a queue at the ATM where I checked the balance of the joint account again. It was still £50.23 and I almost knocked over the guy behind me as I lurched away in horror from the screen.

I drove home in a panic. How had I let myself get into this position where I'd become dependant on Tony? What had happened to my hard-won, career-girl outlook? I'd had a bit of money from Mum's estate but I'd happily spent it on the house, investing her money into what I thought was my future. I was almost crying with exhaustion, pain and rage when I got home and narrowly missed driving into the gate post. I got out of the car, shaking, and walked up to the front door.

I scrabbled around in my bag for my wallet to get my key and couldn't find it. It had to be there so I looked deeper into my bag and started taking stuff out to see if I could feel the hard edge of the leather wallet in the bottom of the bag. My panic returned with a greater intensity. My wallet wasn't there. I suddenly thought that the guy behind me at the ATM had been standing very close and my bag had been over my shoulder pointing in his direction. He must have taken it. I was locked out and all my cards had gone.

At that moment, I felt a terrible warm rush between my

legs and knew I was bleeding very heavily. I banged hard on the door with frustration, not wanting to believe that this latest misfortune had happened and then the path came up to meet me, my knees gave way and I landed on the cold tarmac.

6

Bump

'Are you alright, dear?' said an elderly female voice as I tried to lift my cheek from the ground. 'Oh my, you've got a nasty gash there', she said and I managed to look up and make out that it was my neighbour, Mrs Owen, who was offering me her hand to help me get up.

'I was just passing and I saw you go down', she said, looking at me with some concern. I put my hand to my temple and it came away streaked with blood. 'It needs a bit of a wash, dear', she said. 'It's got bits of gravel in it'.

'I've locked myself out', I said. 'I mean, someone's stolen my wallet and my key was in it. I can't get in.'

'Won't your husband be home soon?' said Mrs Owen and was probably surprised that her question had the effect it did.

I was at rock bottom. I had no more fight in me, so I just sat on the path and cried and sobbed and howled my pain and desolation as I tried to tell her that my husband had left me, I had no way of knowing how I was to survive the next few months and that I was almost bleeding to death from 'down below'.

'Oh dear, you *are* in the wars, aren't you. Why don't I take you next door, clean you up and get you a nice cup of tea while you wait for the locksmith?' she said.

I hardly knew the woman; even though we'd lived in adjacent houses for six years, we hadn't said more than 'Good morning' but I let her help me up and she took my arm as she guided me up the path to her front door.

Mrs Owen's house was the other half of mine and was the mirror image but, even in my distracted state, as soon as she opened the door, it was quite clear that her house was about as different from mine as could be imagined. Where my house was all cool shades, blonde boards, cold metal, glass and angles, hers was warmth, carpets, patterns, polished wood, flowers and photographs of family dotted about on the furniture. For some reason this made me feel even more alone and more of a failure and I started to cry again.

'Sit down, dear', Mrs Owen said, guiding me to a chintzy sofa covered in big cushions. 'Will you be alright while I go and put the kettle on?' I nodded and she went to the kitchen.

The sofa was remarkably comfortable and I let the tension in my shoulders relax just a little. When my neighbour came back with a tray, I was able to say, 'This is very kind of you, Mrs Owen', to her without breaking down again.

'Call me Bubbles', she said. 'Everyone does. My name's Barbara but I've been 'Bubbles' since I was a little girl'.

'My name's Rowena', I said as she passed me a cup of strong tea into which she'd put two sugars and a lot of thick-looking milk. Normally, I'd have gagged at the thought of sweet tea with whole milk but I sipped it and my body was grateful.

'Just drink your tea slowly, dear, and when you're feeling a bit more like yourself, you can pop into the downstairs cloakroom and clean yourself up a bit', said Bubbles and I realised that she was mothering me and it had been such a long time since I had been mothered and I was in such need of it that I started to cry all over again.

'Just let it out, dear', said Bubbles very calmly as if women sat on her sofa and sobbed their hearts out twice a week. Then she produced a box of tissues from behind her and handed it to me, so maybe they did.

Eventually, I finished sobbing and felt strong enough to go

to the loo where I bathed the cut above my eye and changed my towel so that I wouldn't bleed all over Bubbles' nice sofa. I brushed my hair, washed my hands and felt a bit better.

Bubbles helped me find a locksmith in *Yellow Pages* and, even though it was Sunday, he said he'd be there in an hour. I couldn't yet cancel my cards as I needed access to the internet to do that and Bubbles was not one of those elderly people who'd become a silver surfer so we sat in her cosy room and waited.

She had a way of asking difficult questions which made them not seem nosy or impertinent and I found myself telling her everything, even that Tony's new woman was pregnant. She wasn't shocked and just said, 'Well, it's not new, is it? It's an old story, you're not the first, dear, and you won't be the last'.

By the time the locksmith came, I was calmer and, for some strange reason, felt less alone. The locksmith was quick and efficient and, yet again, I was grateful for a man in my life who could be relied on to be helpful. Luckily he charged me only £45 so I gave him a cheque from the joint account hoping that it wouldn't bounce but before I went back to my house, I invited Bubbles for coffee the following day – it was the least I could do.

I had cheesy scrambled eggs on wholemeal toast for supper and took my camomile tea and the hot water bottle to bed with me. I was asleep as soon as my head touched the pillow.

The following day I woke free of pain and felt stronger. I showered and washed my hair and put on a bit of make-up. The cut above my eye was livid but beginning to knit together and the huge zit on my chin had shrunk and was getting to the stage where it would soon form a scab. I was amazed at the ability of my broken body to repair itself and wondered if my heart would heal as easily. I tested the situation by imagining Tony and Tasha, some months hence, cooing over their new baby and it made me feel very sick so I knew the answer.

I had a bit of cereal for breakfast and tidied up the kitchen and sitting room ready for Bubbles' arrival. She rang the doorbell on the dot of ten thirty and I ushered her in through the front door. Her face was a picture of competing emotions; she wanted to be able to say something complimentary about my home - something nice and reassuring - but I could see that, to her, it was unwelcoming and not homely so all she could manage was 'Oh, it's very modern isn't it?'

I left her perching on the not very comfortable sofa and went to make coffee. When I came back she smiled at me and it was the first genuine smile of friendship I'd had from anyone in a long time and I was in danger of beginning to cry again. 'How are you today, dear?' she said and I told her that I felt a little better but I really needed to start thinking of how I would get a job. 'What sort of job, dear?' she said and I told her what I used to do while she made approving noises and said I must be a clever girl. It was hard to tell her that I felt I couldn't go back to that world now – I was too raw. Then she said the most amazing thing and I wondered why I hadn't thought of it myself.

'Well, dear', she said, 'You don't want to get too good a job, do you? Not just yet anyway', and tapped the side of her nose.

I looked at her with respect. Of course she was right – if by some strange chance, I actually managed to get a well-paying job commensurate with my qualifications, Tony would argue that I could easily support myself and I would probably get less than even thirty per cent of the joint assets.

'Why don't you look for a nice little job to start with, just until you get your confidence back, dear?' said my new careers adviser, who had to be eighty if she was a day but was clearly still in possession of all of her marbles.

'Why not look in the 'Situations Vacant' in the local paper, dear?' she said and the former highly-paid executive in me almost snorted in derision but I didn't really know how to go about getting a 'nice little job' so I nodded at her and said I would.

She left at about a quarter to twelve having asked me to her house for coffee on the Wednesday but her parting shot to me was, 'And you can tell me then what you've done about looking for that nice little job'.

'Bloody hell', I thought, 'The woman's a life coach as well!'

I realised that she had skilfully drawn me out about my life and my problems but I knew little about her other than having seen the family photos dotted about her home and I made a mental note to try to find out more about my new, octogenarian, best friend when I went to see her in two days' time.

In the meantime, there was work to be done. I spent an hour doing more internet research on divorce settlements and local firms of Solicitors trying to work out how I could fight my corner against Tony while having no money to feed myself, never mind pay the legal fees. I was sitting at my laptop chewing all of this over and over when I suddenly remembered that Tony had kept a supply of cash in the house 'for emergencies' and wondered if he'd retrieved it before he told me he was leaving me.

I got the loft ladder down and made my way carefully up the rungs, opening the trapdoor to the roof-space when I was half way up the ladder. I didn't like going up there as there were spiders and cobwebs which had the horrible habit of brushing your face when you weren't expecting it but this actually was an emergency.

Once up there, I found the light-switch only to discover that the bulb had gone so I had to climb down the ladder and get the flashlight from the garage. Then I had to get back up the ladder carrying the heavy flashlight which I placed just inside the trapdoor opening as I levered myself back into the roof-space. There were cobwebs everywhere and I shuddered a little but I thought I knew where the money would be, if he hadn't taken it. It would be in his old school trunk – the one he had used when he went to boarding school. I saw it across from me – the words 'A. G. Boxer' written in bold black paint on the side. I crawled over to the trunk and undid the clasp on the lid cutting my thumb on the sharp, ancient metal as I did so. This was one piece of Tony's kit which I'd forgotten to take down to the hall. My thumb bled onto the school photographs which were at the top of the trunk and I sucked it to try to stop the bleeding. I took out the photographs and the old cricket sweaters which were underneath and there was a smallish parcel wrapped in thick plastic secured with several rubber bands. I couldn't see through the plastic but I thought it was likely to be the money.

I crawled back to the trapdoor and threw the parcel onto the landing then I gingerly stepped onto the ladder with the flashlight in my hand. I made it safely to the floor and picked up the parcel. Much rested on its contents and I decided I needed a cup of strong coffee before I dared open it.

I took the parcel to the kitchen and placed it on the counter while I made my coffee. Then I put it on the kitchen table and slowly unwrapped it.

It was a big wodge of fifty pound notes. My heart was pounding as I counted it out. As a woman whose basic currency is debit and credit cards, I wasn't that accustomed to actual cash and I knew (from a friend who once tried to pay a taxi driver with one) that fifty pound notes were something of a rarity so I was shocked at how seemingly a small parcel of notes could add up to £14,000.

Emergency money? Some emergency. How did he acquire fourteen grand in cash? Was this yet another secret bonus? Was it money he'd won? Had he paid tax on it? Had he even come by it honestly? All these questions coursed through my mind and I needed another espresso to calm me before I could even begin to think this latest turn of events through.

OK, I thought, the first thing is that Tony will want this money and the second thing is that I need it more than he does. Will he dare ask me for it though? Why didn't he remove it from the house before he left? He must have known that he was leaving me and he could have taken it anytime before the previous Tuesday evening, so why didn't he?

Maybe he only left that night because the lovely Tasha nagged him beyond endurance. If so, good luck to her because I'd never had the guts to nag Tony. Then I remembered the hurriedly finished call on his mobile that morning – 'Today, I promise', he'd said. Maybe he'd been promising for some time to leave me and she was piling on the pressure. Well, she would wouldn't she – she wanted a life with the father of her child. In a way, she wanted my life – the designer house, the sexy husband and the sexy car.

So, assuming that I was right about that, what would he do now, when he wanted to retrieve the money without alerting me to what he was doing rooting around in the attic? He would wait until I was out and then use his key to get into the house without my knowing.

Then I realised he couldn't do that. The locksmith had changed the front door lock and I had the only key. Nor could he get in the back door if I bolted it before I left the house. I let out a whoop of triumph and said 'Up yours, Tony,' while giving a one finger salute to the empty air.

Now I had to have a plan for dealing with Tony's lawyers and their suggestion that I play ball with them. Well, they wanted a quickie divorce presumably so he could marry Tasha and legitimise their baby. I remembered that, although Tasha thought it was quite alright to screw a married man, she came from a conventional family in Surrey and they might not want a little bastard from the wrong side of the blanket as a grandchild. The beauty of this was, the longer the divorce dragged on, the more Tasha would nag and the more desperate they would get. But I mustn't be seen to be unhelpful, I must appear to co-operate. The pension fund and hedge fund letters were obviously helpful to me so I must get photocopies of them – the details I'd noted down were probably not enough – and I must do as suggested by my strategic planner next door; I must get a nice little job which *showed that I was willing* but paid very little.

It was about two in the afternoon by now and I was hungry. I took this as a good sign as it was the first time in ages that I'd felt a proper healthy kind of hunger rather than just a horrible empty feeling in the pit of my stomach. I put the money – my fighting fund – back in its plastic bag but minus £100 I needed for immediate use and got in the car. I went to a little restaurant about two miles away and had Spaghetti Bolognese which I really enjoyed. The owner looked askance at my fifty pound note and very pointedly took it and peered at it in the light of the window, scanning it for the watermark, then he felt the quality of the paper very carefully, rubbing it between his fingers and I had a moment's queasiness at the thought that Tony might have been involved in some scam, that the note was forged and I would end up in custody.

In the end though, the Italian must have been reassured and he gave me two ten pound notes and some coins in change. I took my new found wealth to the little supermarket next door and bought the local evening paper. It was the first time I'd ever done this and it felt almost illicit as if 'Times' readers like me weren't actually allowed to read such a publication.

Feeling replete after my good lunch and quite buoyed by finding the money and having a plan for how I would deal with the divorce, I put the paper on the counter when I got home and had a nap on the sofa. When I woke it was dark and I realised I'd slept for a couple of hours. This was good. I felt rested and calm. I had a cup of tea and picked up the paper. It was the usual local news – a cat rescued from up a tree, a local couple's diamond wedding anniversary with a picture of them in the midst of their huge, smiling family (lucky them), an announcement of the closure of a factory, etc., etc,. It was all so dull that I nearly gave up but once I'd got past the 'Entertainment' and 'Items for Sale' (wedding dress, size 10, not used, £200 o.n.o. – poor girl, I felt for her) pages, I found the 'Situations Vacant' section. There were three pages of jobs and some of them were unexpectedly bizarre. I was intrigued by the advert from the local authority for a grave digger, the police wanted a dog handler and a factory which made the sort of things you buy in joke shops – whoopee cushions, red noses and the like – wanted someone to join the production line. Interesting though these jobs were, they were not, even if I actually managed to get one, the sort of job I could take as Tony wouldn't easily accept that he'd damaged me so much the best I could do was to make plastic dog poo all day. There was a fine balance between 'a nice little job' and a downright silly job. So far, I hadn't seen anything which would qualify as a nice little job.

I had another cup of tea and thought about watching 'Truly, Madly, Deeply' instead but there was the one page I hadn't yet seen so I turned over and it hit me straight away. There at the bottom was an eighth page advert for a 'Sales Assistant – Florist' and I greedily scanned the rest of it looking for the details which would tell me more about the employer and the website where I could make my application. There was nothing. No website, no place from which to download a form, just a phone number – a landline number. The advert was eye-catching in its size and because the small amount of actual information was surrounded by so much expensive empty space, I wondered if it was a joke but it really stood out among the rest of the tightly worded small ads and I thought this message must be deliberate in its terseness. I glanced away and then looked at it again. It was actually quite elegant and I liked its attitude whose subtext was 'We have a job here. You may or may not want it, but we don't care either way'. There was no doubt about it, it had captured my attention and piqued my interest. And, anyway, what could be more of a 'nice little job' than working in a flower shop?

I knew that my mind would race with all sorts of questions – which shop, where, how much money, what were the hours and, above all, wouldn't they refuse me because I was overqualified? So, I settled down to another evening of tragic film heroines but, halfway through *Ghost*, I felt it was too cloying and I surprised myself by watching *Gladiator* instead.

I slept soundly and was well enough for scrambled egg on toast, then I sat at my laptop and spent all morning composing my reply to Bolton, Greene and de Latymer. I had to keep reminding myself that I was as well-educated as them and knew something of the ways of the world but it was hard not to feel very vulnerable in this unfamiliar situation. I strengthened my resolve with the thought that I knew stuff about their client's finances that he probably hadn't told them and this, and several strong, sugary espressos, helped me write a businesslike letter of which I felt quite proud.

I printed my letter out on our thick, headed writing paper and thought I might get in the car and deliver it by hand. There was a big world out there and I wouldn't have minded a drive into London, going past Harrods and Harvey Nichols and watching the busy shoppers. It made me think that I might, one day, rediscover my aptitude for retail. I was on my way upstairs to have a shower when I suddenly had another thought.

My letter was too good.

I came down the stairs again and sat on the sofa to think this through carefully. If I sent Messrs Sue, Grabbitt and Runne this well-written, cogently argued, literate letter then they would say that I was capable of getting the kind of job I'd had and of earning the same good salary. It would not occur to them that it's one thing to sit in your PJs in the solitude of your own home and spend the whole morning writing one letter but entirely another to perform in the alligator-filled swamp which is modern corporate life. OK, maybe they knew that as well as I did, but it was their job to argue the opposite and I was not going to give them the ammunition to shoot me down.

I went and had the shower anyway, dressed, put on a spritz of *Chanel No. 19* and went back to my laptop. This time I put myself into a different frame of mind. I took myself back to the moment Tony told me he was leaving me for the pregnant

Tasha and how I'd felt and this time I wrote a very different letter. It was the letter of a broken woman and written in a tone of dignified regret; it was the letter of a woman who had no fight left in her, who could not stand in the way of her husband's newfound happiness because she had no resources left. She did, however, say that she would try to find a job as they suggested and could Tony please pay the allowance as soon as possible.

When I felt I had struck exactly the right note in every word of the letter, I printed it on the cheap paper we kept for writing to trades-people and put it into one of the cheap, brown envelopes we kept for the same purpose then I found a stamp and went to the corner of the next street and posted it.

I felt drained and exhausted when I got back home but, just as I was about to collapse on the sofa, I realised that I'd done nothing about the job advert and I would need to account to Bubbles the following morning for my actions (or non-actions). There was something very compelling about my elderly neighbour and I really didn't want to admit to her that I'd lost an opportunity. I looked at my watch. It was quarter to five.

I raced to the kitchen and found the paper, scrabbling quickly through it to the 'Situations Vacant' page. There was the number. It was now ten minutes to five. I prayed that they didn't knock off early and that they wouldn't say that they'd already filled the vacancy.

With surprisingly sweaty palms I picked up the phone and dialled the number.

7

A Few Surprises

The phone rang out at the other end. I counted twenty rings before a tired sounding woman answered with 'Yes'. This floored me a bit. I expected someone to pick up the phone, say the name of the company and 'Can I help you?' In other words, I expected a professional response to a ringing phone and I'd had my reply all worked out on this basis so the simple 'Yes', flummoxed me.

'Er, I'm, I'm ringing about the job', I stuttered.

'Yes', said the woman.

'The job in the paper…..the vacancy for a Sales Assistant?' I said lamely, tailing off to nothing.

'Oh', said the woman, 'You'll need to speak to Mr Johnson. Hang on'.

'Oh crikey', I thought, 'It's the shop near me. It's where I bought the roses. Bloody hell. Do I really want to work there with the peeling paint and dead flies?'

'Yes', a male voice said over the line. Did they ever say anything else at this dead-end company? What had happened to their telephone skills? I didn't want their crummy job. I didn't want to sell flowers to spoiled rich bitches like me. I had a post graduate qualification, I used to be somebody.

But I had to see Bubbles the following day and explain myself and, to be fair, I'd had to agree with her strategy so, I swallowed my pride and said, 'Hello Mr Johnson. My name is Rowena Boxer and I'd like to apply for the job you have advertised in the local paper'.

'Oh', he said. He wasn't making this easy for me.

So I had to make it easy for him. 'Is there an Application Form to fill in?'

'Not that I know of', he said. He sounded old and, like the woman, tired. I felt sorry for him. There was clearly something very wrong here. The shop was a mess, they had no website. Basically, they didn't have a clue. But, but, but... .the truth of it was that I, Rowena Boxer, smart, clever, former high-flyer, now broken woman, needed this job.

'Maybe I could come for an interview?' I said.

'Well, Chrissy's away at the moment but I suppose I could see you', Mr Johnson said.

'Will tomorrow at three in the afternoon be alright?' I said.

'OK', he said and I had the thought that he was going to put the phone down without telling me where to come so I quickly asked him for the address and then he put the phone down without saying goodbye.

I sat down with a thump on one of the uncomfortable kitchen chairs. That was without doubt one of the weirdest phone calls I'd ever had. OK, so he wasn't approaching this in a professional manner but I could. I went to my laptop and spent over an hour updating my C.V. It wasn't easy coming up with an explanation for my years at home without going into very personal details I'd rather keep to myself so I said that I'd been pursuing private interests. I didn't think Mr Johnson's interview technique would require more of an explanation than that.

I printed the C.V. and put it in my *Mulberry* handbag ready to take with me then I had a really panicky thought. What in heaven's name was I *going to wear* to this weird interview? What does a horribly over-qualified but (to be honest) under-experienced woman wear for an interview for a job she doesn't really want but in fact needs? All my clothes were expensive and, if Mr Johnson realised that, he'd wonder even more why someone with my C.V. wanted the job. Then again, he'd sounded so world-weary on the phone, he may not be up to recognising *Burberry* and *Mulberry* when he saw them.

I went to the wardrobe where I kept the clothes I wore and stared at its contents for some time before I came up with an outfit. I decided that the best thing I could do was to try to fade into the background and thought that, if I wore black from head to toe under my trench coat, it would be difficult for him to gauge the quality of my clothes. So, I put a black cashmere polo neck sweater, my pull-on skirt, opaque tights and my soft suede boots on the bed ready for the following day. I would wear Mum's pearl earrings for luck but omit my one and a half-carat diamond engagement ring and *Cartier* watch.

Feeling strangely excited because I was actually taking steps to make my own future, I decided I would go for a little drive anyway so I got in the car and drove round to look at Mr Johnson's shop. It was closed, of course, and there were no lights on. The peeling white paint looked ghostly under the street lamp and there was nothing in the window other than the dead flies but I could see that inside the shop there were still rows of beautiful flowers in their dark green jugs. Whoever had the eye in the company was still doing the buying.

I went home and had some tomato soup for supper before settling down to watch two George Clooney movies. I was in bed by ten thirty and asleep by eleven. I had the alarm set for eight thirty and woke with a clear head. I showered and washed my hair, blow-dried it and put on a bit of make-up. I dressed and went downstairs for egg on toast while I watched the news and then it was time to go and see Bubbles.

'You look nice, dear' were her opening words to me and I felt a huge rush of gratitude. We went into her sitting room where she had the fire going. The metal pipe feeding into the grate was a give-away that the burning coals were really burning gas but it was a cosy touch on a grey day.

'How are you, dear?' Bubbles asked me when she brought in the coffee on a tray with a sparkling white cloth. I told her all about my letter to Tony's lawyers and about my interview. She listened carefully to me while I was relating all my thought processes about the letter but, when I told her about the interview, she clapped her hands with delight and said, 'That's my girl! Well done.'

I felt another rush of gratitude and wanted to cry. This woman, my elderly neighbour, a virtual stranger had given me more care and encouragement in three days than Tony had given me in ten years. I blinked back the tears as I didn't want to disturb my mascara and remembered my wish to know more about her.

'Thank you', I said, 'But what about you Bubbles? What was your job? When you were working, I mean?'

'Oh, goodness me', she said laughing, 'If I told you, then, as they say in the films, I'd have to kill you. More coffee?'

'Seriously?' I said looking at the slight, white-haired woman in front of me.

'Seriously', she said. 'I'm sorry, dear, but I can't talk about it and I can't tell you why I can't talk about it because that would be the same thing as telling you about it, wouldn't it?'

I nodded but I so wanted to know what this remarkable woman had done in her life that it was hard not to press her. I had to respect her silence though; it was obviously a mark of her professionalism that she couldn't and wouldn't indulge my curiosity with stories that would probably make my hair curl.

I looked at her with renewed interest and now saw the ramrod straight back, the steel in her eye and remembered the panther-like, soft fall of her feet. I pictured her in WWII, in a beret, packing a pistol and a cyanide capsule. I saw her walking into cafes in foreign cities, wreathed in smoke, meeting men in homburg hats and exchanging information on which hundreds of lives depended. Or maybe she'd worked in the code breaking section? I would never know but I saw that; although she was old enough to be my Gran, she was much more fascinating than my contemporaries obsessing about house prices and whether their spoiled brats would pick up the nanny's terrible accent.

'Tell me about your family then, please', I said and her face lit up.

'Oh, well, there are four of them. All grown up, of course', she said. 'There's Dominic, he's the eldest, he's a dentist, then there's Alison, she's a Carmelite nun, then there's Caroline, she's in the RAF and then there's Marcus who's an artist', she continued, reeling her children off on her fingers as she went.

'Wow', I said. I was impressed by her children's achievements and the sheer range of jobs they'd chosen. One daughter in the Air Force and the other a Carmelite nun – these children had clearly been encouraged to be strongly individual - I bet Bubbles never worried about her offspring talking like the nanny.

'Tell me about Caroline', I said, 'Is she nursing in the RAF?'

'Oh no', said Bubbles, 'She's flying missions into Afghanistan, bringing the wounded back to hospital here'. She said this very calmly but with great pride. At this moment, I wanted her to be my Gran, I wanted to have done something to make her as proud of me as she was of her daughter. Again, I wanted to cry because my Mum was gone, my Father was a pillock and I needed someone to care for me.

Then I had another thought. What if I'd had my dearest wish? What if I'd become pregnant by Tony and had our baby? Would our child have had the kind of upbringing that produces both RAF pilots and nuns? The answer was a resounding 'no'. Tony's and my baby would have been swathed in designer stuff from birth and I would have been on the competitive Yummy Mummy circuit where your child's every stage of development is scrutinised so that someone can boast that her child is the first to talk or walk or play the violin and everything and everybody must conform to a perfect, glossy magazine template. This would have been bad enough if our child had been a boy but it would have been twenty times worse if it had been a girl; heaven help any girl child of Tony's if she'd turned out anything other than blindingly beautiful. Why had I not seen that before?

'Are you alright, dear?' said Bubbles, 'You looked a bit lost there for a moment'.

'I was just thinking that I'm really relieved not to have had Tony's child', I said, 'I don't think he would have made a good father'.

'Why do you say that, dear?' said Bubbles.

'Because he wouldn't have allowed our child to be an individual', I said, 'I mean that he would have been ruthless in imposing *his* ideas and norms and wanted to produce a copy of himself'.

'I see what you mean and that was where my husband was such a good Dad', said Bubbles.

'In what way?' I asked, intrigued to know what kind of Dad had the insights and courage to let his children be themselves, even if it was unconventional.

'Well, he was an engineer but he was blinded in an accident but he managed to see what interested all the children and to encourage their interests even though he couldn't actually see them, if you see what I mean', said Bubbles.

'Oh. I do see what you mean!' I said, 'Maybe he listened to them more because he couldn't actually see them'.

'Yes, you're probably right', said Bubbles, 'I'd not really thought of that before. It's funny how a stranger can make you look at things differently isn't it, dear?'

'My goodness, yes,' I said and meant it with all my heart.

8

Chrissy

My time with Bubbles went very quickly – we seemed to have a lot to say to one another – and then I had to go home, have some lunch, freshen up and get ready for my interview. I felt nervous. I felt as nervous as I would have done had it been a real job I was applying for. The irony of this made me laugh but my need for the job was very real and I didn't want to flunk it through being ill-prepared.

Johnson's didn't have a website so I took the old-fashioned route and looked them up in the phone book. *Yellow Pages* told me that there were actually seven shops dotted about the area and I was surprised that it was such a big business. Maybe there had been someone at one time in the company who had a head for retail but that person wasn't there any longer and they were trading on customers' goodwill. My business head said that that might work for a while but it was a recipe for disaster in the long term and somebody needed to get a grip or Ted Johnson estd. 1966 wouldn't be established for much longer. I couldn't help myself – I began making a mental list of all the things they needed to do to bring themselves up to 21st century standards and I'd already got at least ten urgent items before I stopped myself. It was not my company, it was not, in either sense of the phrase, my business – I would do my best at the interview and leave it at that.

I put on my coat, picked up my bag, squared my shoulders

and set off for the office building whose address Ted Johnson had given me. It was not very far from my house but I'd never been to that trading estate before and I wanted to make sure that I wasn't late. The traffic was light and I got there in good time so I sat in the car for ten minutes looking round.

The sun had come out and was casting shadows. It was quite a run-down place. I guessed that the buildings had been put up in the 1950s and I knew from my Economics studies that building materials had been in short supply after the war so that explained the utilitarian designs and the disintegrating street furniture. There were people coming and going from the small manufacturing units and it looked as if all the buildings were occupied which said a great deal about the resilience of this area's economy. There was a white van over in one corner of the car park selling fast food and hot drinks and the discarded wrappers and drinks cartons decorating the ground showed that the workers used it regularly as their canteen. I 'tutted' to myself at their laziness and thought that, like the dead flies in Johnson's shop window, the litter made the whole place look uncared for.

From the name plates outside the office building, it appeared that Johnson's had half of the second floor and I was surprised again that they had so much office space when they seemed hell bent on going out of business. It was five to three now so I got out of the car and entered the two storey office block. The hallway was covered in ancient, none-too-clean, carpet tiles. There was a dusty smell in the air and the distant hum of conversation interspersed with the whirr of copying machines. I felt as if I'd stepped into a time machine and gone back to the 1980s.

I started up the stairs and was irritated to find not only an empty crisp packet but also a *KitKat* wrapper on just the first flight. I picked them up in disgust and stuffed them into my *Mulberry* Bayswater thinking that it was the first and last time my beautiful bag would be contaminated with such rubbish. I climbed up the next flight to the landing and was faced with two doors. The one on the right bore the name 'Johnsons Florists Limited'.

I knocked on the door and waited. No-one came so I knocked again. Still no-one came so I tentatively opened the door. There was a big window opposite, framed in that horrible bare metal beloved of fifties' architects but it was so much lighter in there than I'd expected that I had to shield my eyes for a moment. There were about twelve work-stations – desks with (I couldn't believe my eyes!) electric typewriters - and some with adding machines but only five of these were occupied. There was a very old photocopier in the corner next to a partitioned section which, presumably, was Mr Johnson's office.

The occupants of the desks all turned in unison to look at me. I felt as if I might as well have landed from Mars. They were women in late middle age, all wearing man-made fibres and all with the same permed helmet of hair. One of them, the one nearest to me, spoke.

'Yes', she said. I nearly laughed. It just had to be that one word, didn't it? And she'd obviously practised it a lot because she managed to make it sound like an accusation.

'I've come to see Mr Johnson', I said, trying not to sound too off-put by all the others staring at me.

'Will he know what it's about?' said Mrs Unhelpful.

'Yes, he will', I said more firmly than I felt, 'He's expecting me. I have an appointment with him for three o'clock'.

I heard a titter from further into the room but couldn't see from whom as the light from the window was obscuring her. I decided to ignore it.

The woman who'd spoken to me seemed glued to her chair and I wanted to pick her up and throttle her for being so obstructive. Had it not occurred to her that I might, I just might, be an important visitor? Someone who could have some influence over her future?

'It's alright Olive, I *am* expecting Mrs Boxer', said a male voice behind me.

I turned and came face to face with a tall man in his late sixties. He had broad shoulders and a shock of pure white hair. His eyes were cornflower blue and his skin blotched with too much sun but it was obvious that he'd been a very good-looking man in his prime.

'I'm sorry I'm a bit late', he said, holding out his hand and giving mine a strong shake. He looked searchingly at me and said, 'How do you do'. I liked him instantly. I had no idea why this charming, courteous, slightly olde-worlde gentleman surrounded himself with these polyester-clad witches, but I wanted to find out.

'Come in', he said, leading the way into his office and, just as he got to the door, he called out, 'Olive! Tea!' over his shoulder.

He sat at his desk and motioned me to the chair opposite. The sun was no longer in my eyes and I could make out the large battered desk piled in one corner with what appeared to be invoices. There was also a pile of magazines whose covers featured glorious colour pictures of exotic flowers and that day's *Telegraph*.

'So you want to be a shop assistant, Mrs Boxer', he said, 'I am assuming that it's Mrs Boxer'.

'Yes, I do,' I said, 'I saw your advertisement and it really attracted my attention and, yes, you are correct, it is Mrs Boxer'.

'Forgive me, Mrs Boxer', he said, 'But you don't look like the kind of woman who really *wants* to be a shop assistant. Have you brought your C.V. by any chance?'

I put my bag on the corner of the desk nearest me, opened it and put my hand in to pull out my C.V. but the crisp packet and *KitKat* wrapper were uppermost in the inner pocket and landed with a crackling sound on the desk. Mr Johnson and I looked in surprise at the litter.

This was not going as I'd expected. I'd expected to be in the driving seat but I'd got off on the wrong foot with Olive and her crew and now Mr Johnson must think that I stuffed myself with junk food. I froze.

'Oh dear', said Mr Johnson, 'Did you not have time for lunch? Can I get you a sandwich?'

'No, no. Thank you. The wrappers aren't mine. I found them on the stairs on the way up here and I don't like to see litter so I picked them up', I said.

'Fair enough', said Mr Johnson, 'Now may I see your C.V.?'

I dipped into my bag again and handed him the document. He unfolded it, took some spectacles from his desk drawer, plonked them on his nose and then read it carefully.

'Very impressive, Mrs Boxer. Very impressive indeed. You will, no doubt have anticipated my next question. So why does a highly educated woman want to work in a shop?'

My response came from absolutely nowhere and completely broadsided me. I burst into tears and for several long seconds was unable to speak through my gulping sobs.

Mr Johnson took it all very well. He sat there impassively as I tried to tell him that I was in the middle of the breakup of my marriage and that I needed a job. I fished in my bag for a tissue but couldn't find one and Mr Johnson reached in his pocket then handed me one of those hankies (the white ones with the striped border) that you give your Granddad at Christmas. I wiped my eyes and nose with it and was amazed that it smelled of really nice cologne; I could have believed that he might use *Old Spice* or something else that had been around in his youth but this was definitely not *Old Spice* or anything of its kind – it was modern and fresh and I liked it.

When I'd calmed myself a little, he fixed me with his blue gaze and said, 'I expect you'll want to launder that hankie and give it back to me, won't you?'

I nodded and he said, 'Good. You start work Monday at the Chipstone shop. The hours are 8.30 to 5.30 with a half-hour lunch break. Your day off is Thursday. You will be paid £11,000 per annum on a monthly basis.'

'But, but, but, how do you know I'm right for the job?' I stammered.

'I don't', said Mr Johnson, 'But the fact is you're the only person who's applied for it. If you don't really want it, that's fine, but if you do, be there at 8.15 Monday morning and Chrissy will open up for you and show you the ropes.'

'I do want it, I want it very much, Mr Johnson', I said.

'Good. And my name's Ted', said Mr Johnson.

'And Chrissy is....?' I asked

'Chrissy is on holiday with the children, it's half-term and they've gone skiing in Italy', said Mr Johnson as he opened the office door and showed me out. I was crossing the outer office when I heard him call out, 'Mrs Boxer', and, to the sniggers of the menopausal harpies, he said 'Welcome to Johnson's Florists, I hope we'll be happy together'.

I stumbled down the stairs and sat in my car for quite a few minutes before I felt calm enough to start the engine. The truth of the matter was that the 'interview' with Mr Johnson, Ted, had deeply unsettled me. Yes, I had achieved what I set out to achieve and the eleven thousand a year was exactly what I wanted in terms of being able to report to Tony's lawyers that I now had a job but there was something under the surface of the whole thing that was disturbing. There was an elephant in the room, visible and understood by others but unknown to me. The thing was, when Mr Johnson, Ted, gave me his hankie and looked into my eyes, he didn't just look into my eyes, he looked into my soul and he let me know that he understood my grief.

I drove home and thought how pleased Bubbles would be that I'd secured the 'nice little job' but I was hungry now and the urgent thing was to have something to eat. I overcame a lifetime's aversion and parked the car at a nearby McDonalds where I had a chicken salad and coffee. Both the salad and the coffee were good so I celebrated my new job with some doughnuts, which were also quite good in a very naughty way, before I went home.

When I got in, I rang Bubbles and told her about the job and she was so delighted that I thought I'd start crying again but I asked her to lunch on the Friday to divert my mind from too much emotion.

I spent Wednesday and Thursday tidying up the house and the garden and the physical exertion did me good; I slept well and I felt that I was carving out a new identity for myself. It was miles different from my old life but I was beginning to see my old life had been built on lies and the appearance of things rather than their substance. Several times in those two days I had the conversation with myself that there was nothing wrong in selling flowers – flowers brought colour and beauty into people's lives – and I was very pleased that, on one occasion, Dawn made a re-appearance in my head and wholeheartedly agreed with me.

The lunch with Bubbles on the Friday was a triumph. We went to a local pub and had fish and chips and a bottle of Sauvignon Blanc and laughed almost all the way through the meal. She was excellent company – well read, knowledgeable about current affairs and politics but always interested in another view and I liked her more and more. I insisted on paying for the lunch as she'd rescued me when I was locked out and, as I said, I was now a working woman.

On the Saturday, using some of Tony's cash, I went to *Gap* and bought a few simple tops and trousers which I felt were appropriate for my new role and then I had a lovely, long bath luxuriating in the scented bubbles. While I was lying in the warm water, I realised that I didn't actually miss Tony. What I missed was having someone to care for. This was another revealing thought and it felt uncomfortable to have to conclude that maybe I hadn't really loved Tony, not as I'd loved Mum. Yes, yes, I know loving a husband isn't the same as loving your Mum but I know my Mum would have done anything for me and I would have done anything for her but would I have done anything for Tony? I couldn't work out the answer and Dawn merely said it was up to me to decide so I went to watch the *X Factor* instead, knowing it would get me so angry it would drive all thoughts of Tony out of my head.

It rained all night and woke me several times so I was a bit groggy when I woke on the Sunday but, after breakfast, I drove to the shops and bought the *Sunday Times*. I couldn't resist it, though, and made a special detour to Chipstone so I could look at my shop. In the autumn daylight, it still looked forlorn but I blew it a kiss and told it the cavalry was coming and I would soon be looking after it. A rainbow chased me all the way home.

I spent the rest of Sunday in my cashmere pyjamas reading the paper and vegetating on the sofa watching the TV. I kept telling myself that I would soon be working five days a week and I should get my rest while I could.

At eight in the evening, I laid out my clothes for the following day: black, straight-leg trousers, silver grey long sleeved T-shirt and matching boyfriend cardigan. I would also wear my soft black boots to see if they were comfortable enough for standing all day. I wondered what I should do with my hair and decided I'd wear it up so I put out a big clip in readiness for the morning.

I fell into bed both excited and exhausted by what the following day might bring but my last thought as I fell asleep was that, despite Mr Johnson's having asked her, Olive the unhelpful had failed to appear with the tea.

The next day the alarm went off at 6.45 and I showered and washed my hair, dried it and put it in the clip. Then I dressed and put on a bit of foundation and lipstick, a slick of eyeshadow and mascara and just the merest hint of *Chanel No. 19* behind my ears. I couldn't eat breakfast as I was like a cat on a hot tin roof but I made a strong espresso and put it in a big cup with lots of milk.

At 7.45, I got in the car and made my way to Chipstone, parking my Mini behind the library and thinking the £7 per day charge would eat into my new salary. I was very nervous of meeting Chrissy, who was obviously Mr Johnson's daughter; she'd just come back from a skiing holiday with her children, would probably be gleaming with health and have that sort of smug happiness that infuses people who're secure in their nuclear family. I thought that Mr Johnson, Ted, would have had time to tell her all about our 'interview' and she'd probably either feel sorry for me or despise me for marrying the wrong type of guy. I developed this idea and decided that Mr Johnson's daughter would be tall and skinny with endless legs, blonde hair and blue eyes and I'd have to hate her on sight.

I got to the shop at ten minutes past eight and stood outside the front window. Chrissy was due to appear at eight fifteen. I wondered from what direction she'd come and I kept looking from left to right for a tall, striking, blonde woman with a bit of a tan. I looked at my watch, eight-nineteen, no Chrissy. Jeepers, what was keeping the woman? Was she at the gym? Having a row with the nanny? Did she not appreciate that I needed quite a bit of training on the till and on the book-keeping side before I could be let loose in the shop?

Some minutes later a Rolls Royce crossed in front of me followed by a man on a bike and a woman with a pushchair almost ran over my foot so I was looking very much to my left when a voice from behind me said 'Hello. Are you Mrs Boxer?'

I turned and looked into blue eyes which were the same as Mr Johnson's but much younger and filled with unfathomable sadness. 'I'm Chrissy' he said and held out his hand.

9

Back to Business

I took his hand, shook it and said, 'How do you do'.

'That's funny,' he said, 'Dad says that'.

'My Mum used to say it', I said, 'She hated it when people say 'Pleased to meet you''.

Chrissy smiled at that, a lovely boyish smile which I was happy he'd bestowed on me but it didn't reach his eyes.

He unlocked the shop and I followed him in. There was a musty smell and the air felt damp. 'I'll just pop into the back and put the heating on', Chrissy said, 'We can't have you getting cold, can we?'

He went through a little door at the back of the shop and I heard him pottering about for a minute or two and then there was a whoosh followed by a blast of air from the heater I was standing next to but hadn't noticed before. Chrissy returned wiping his hands on a clean hankie which he then stuffed back into the pocket of his jeans.

'OK, Rowena, is it alright if I call you Rowena?' he said and I nodded. 'Dad tells me that you have two degrees and a fabulous career history so forgive me if this sounds a little rude but why do you want a job as a shop-assistant?'

I was ready for this question this time and, anyway, I didn't want to start my new job with a red nose and puffy eyes.

'I'm in the middle of a divorce and, having been at home for a few years, I want to ease myself gently back into the world of work,' I said.

'Well, I suppose that means you'll be here for just a few months, then?' said Chrissy, 'And then we'll have to start all over again'.

I had my answer ready for this too and said, 'It depends. I have quite a few ideas about how your business could be made more profitable and up to date and I'd be very pleased to talk to you about them. Why not use my expertise while I'm here?'

He looked nonplussed at this and shifted from foot to foot while he thought about it. 'More profitable?' he said and scratched his head as if he'd never heard of a business being more profitable before and then 'More up to date?' and that too made him confused.

'Yes', I said, 'There are many ways your processes could be made more efficient and your shops more attractive. I don't know too much about the rest but take this one, for example. The dead flies in the window have been there for at least ten days and it gives the wrong impression. You're selling beautiful flowers and they need the right setting. This place needs a coat of paint and you could do with bouquets in the window so that people can see how best to put the flowers together, you could get some different...'

'You have thought about it, haven't you?' Chrissy interrupted me, 'But the thing is maybe we like it as it is. Maybe Dad and I rub along just fine in our old-fashioned way and we don't want to change'. He was defensive and I wondered of I'd been offensive but, surely, everyone in business wants to move forward and be profitable, don't they? That was my thinking anyway, and everything I'd learned for my MBA told me it was the way to go.

'I'm sorry if I've offended you', I said, 'I just wanted to be helpful'.

'No, *I'm sorry*. I shouldn't have jumped down your throat like that it's just.....' he tailed off and I waited for him to finish his sentence but he went over to the till and said, 'I need to show you how this works'.

The till was easy – it was the same model that I'd used when I had a Saturday job in *TopShop* when I was fifteen – you do the maths for how old that made it. Then he produced a little invoice/receipt book from under the till which had top copies and flimsies connected by a piece of carbon paper which you moved every time you wrote out a receipt for a customer. I thought back to when I'd bought the roses and recalled that the girl who'd served me hadn't written out a receipt and wondered if this was one of the reasons she was no longer there.

'What about the stock?' I said.

'What about it?' Chrissy said, looking flummoxed again.

'I mean, what about replenishing the stock. When does it happen, who does it, who prices the flowers?

'Oh, I see', said Chrissy as if I'd just brought down the Ten Commandments. 'OK. What happens is that Dad and I buy the flowers from New Covent Garden about three times a week and we top up the stock as necessary. Obviously, sometimes, it's topped up more frequently – Christmas, Valentine's Day, Mother's Day, they're the big busy times in our trade. Dad and I price the flowers, and the prices are on stickers on the jugs, see here', he said pointing to small paper stickers at the back of the jugs on which were written in black marker pen the price per stem or for multiples of five and ten, 'But, if they're getting a bit towards the end of their shelf life, you can knock them down for a quick sale'.

'Do I keep the shop key?' I said.

'No. I come and open up and lock up and take the contents of the till. We don't leave any money here overnight', Chrissy said.

'And what about credit and debit cards?' Little Miss Efficiency asked him.

'Oh yes, this is the machine', he said, producing one of the many types of card readers from under the counter. He then showed me how it worked and gave me a laminated card which had a troubleshooting list and several phone numbers for when the card reader wouldn't work or there were problems with a customer's card. So far so good. I felt that I was getting to the end of his patience though. He'd just come back from holiday and should have been refreshed but he looked tired and strained and I didn't like to keep firing questions but I wanted to make a success of this job and I needed the basic information before I felt ready to be unleashed on an unsuspecting public.

One final thing', I said, 'How often do you need me to reconcile the books?'

'Well, you need to cash up at the end of each day. You have a £50 float and I collect all the money as I said but you'll need to make sure that the till roll, card takings and the cash all add up every day'.

'OK', I said, 'And now one final, final thing'.

He laughed a little bit at that and rolled his eyes but the smile still didn't reach them.

'Shouldn't I have a Contract of Employment?'

'Yes, you should', he said mock grudgingly, 'Olive sees to all of that, and the wages. She'll be along to see you sometime soon'. He paused and then looked a little bit pleased with himself. 'Er, there are a few important things you *haven't* asked me about'.

'Oh really? I can't think of anything else', I said.

'The loo is in the back', he said with a smirk, 'And there's a kettle so you can make yourself a cup of tea'.

'Oh yes', I said raising my eyebrows in what I hoped was a comic, self-deprecating way but might just have made me look slightly crazed.

'And you lock the back door and take the key with you when you go to lunch', he went on and I nodded, mock penitent.

'And, if you're coming by car, you park it at the back', he said, triumphant now that he'd knocked Little Miss Efficiency down to size. But it had all happened in good part; we'd been jousting he and I, we'd been testing one another out for size and he liked it that he'd found a worthy opponent but he liked it even more that he'd managed to find his lance and use it effectively.

Chrissy took a money bag from his pocket and put £50 in various denominations in the till. Then he turned to me and said 'I'll be back at about 5.45'. He moved towards the front door and then turned and said, 'Welcome' to me over his shoulder. He smiled the lovely boyish smile again but his eyes were still filled with sadness. Then he left.

I was alone in the shop. I felt as if I'd been hit by a truck. Something had just happened. I wasn't sure what but my mind was all over the place and my heart was going nineteen to the dozen. I went into the back and sat on the loo to try to gather my thoughts and my emotions but I heard the bell on the door and had to go back into the shop.

'Hello, dear' said Bubbles, 'I hope I'm your first customer'.

'Yes, you are', I said, 'How can I help you, madam?'

She bought ten blood red, long stem carnations and we debated whether the maidenhair fern or the aspidistra leaves would look better and decided that the deep, glossy green and simply shaped aspidistra leaves were a more fitting counterpoint to the frilly, scarlet fluffiness of the carnations. I wrapped the flowers and leaves carefully in layers of paper from the pile on the counter but thought that the white tissue was boring and old-fashioned; Bubbles and I had chosen an elegant bouquet and it would have looked much more dramatic wrapped in black tissue but I thought I would need to leave it a few days before I mentioned this to Chrissy.

When Bubbles had gone, I wanted to return to my musings about how my meeting with Chrissy had affected me – I wanted to understand what had happened – but my earlier feelings had gone somewhere else and I had to content myself with finding a dustpan and brush and sweeping up the dead flies from the window.

My next customer gave me a funny look as soon as she

clapped eyes on me, a kind of 'What on earth are you doing here?' look and then, as I wrapped her yellow roses, gypsophilia and eucalyptus, she saw my *Cartier Panther* watch. It was as if she'd been stung. She recoiled in shock. I wondered quite which law of the universe she thought I'd broken but, once she'd gone and I'd considered it, I saw she thought I'd upset the order of things and if I could afford such a costly timepiece, then somehow, the shop was charging too much for the flowers. As I thought they were charging too little, I made a note not to wear the watch to work again. I would wear Mum's old watch which was inoffensive and wouldn't scream 'designer' at customers who wanted to be the only rich bitch in the shop.

I had seven customers that Monday morning and took only £135. I had no idea how much were the business rates for the shop, nor the heating and lighting and the wholesale cost of the stock but the rent and my wages alone would surely eat up such a small turnover. Maybe it was busier towards the weekend and Chrissy had said that there were busy times of the year but my business brain did wonder how this company managed to be profitable.

There were even fewer customers in the afternoon but one man bought fifteen gorgeous long stem red roses and, when I covertly peeked to see if he was wearing a wedding ring, I wondered whether his wife was a very lucky woman or what he'd done that was so terrible it required this many roses in atonement.

By the end of the day I'd taken only £238. This worried me. I couldn't help it. All my education and training and instincts were screaming that this business had the skids under it and needed a big kick up the backside to bring it back into profitability. It was obvious they were doing little to no marketing, that there was no professionalism in their sales technique and I knew I could, with little actual cost or effort make such a difference that I was itching to get my hands on it all. My mind was full of great ideas and, to be honest, I wanted to be able to take the company on as a project as much for my own interest and challenge as I did for keeping a long-established family business going.

All of this was swirling round my head when Chrissy came to lock up at ten minutes to six. I saw him out of the corner of my eye as I was sweeping the bits of greenery and petals from the floor. He was walking quickly, hands in this pockets, but there was such a dejected set to his shoulders, broad like his father's, that I felt I couldn't intrude on whatever it was that was making him so sad.

When he came into the shop, he gave me a perfunctory smile and said he was pleased I'd been able to add up the takings properly. I said maths was one of my strong points and he said that was good because it hadn't been for my predecessor. He delivered these words deadpan, as if our earlier jousting session hadn't happened and I felt that I'd never be able to enquire about the elephant in the room; much as I wanted Johnson and Company Limited to put their business in my capable and willing hands, I would never get past their sadness and it would be impertinent of me to try.

I went home tired because it was all new and adapting to a new environment is always draining even if it seems simple on the surface. I had a bite of supper and went to bed early so I'd be rested for the following day. I was up and about by 6.30 and chose basically the same outfit as the previous day but, this time, with a lovely icy blue long sleeve T-shirt and boyfriend cardigan on the top. I was careful to remember to wear Mum's watch. Chrissy came and unlocked the shop but although we exchanged 'Good morning' and I made him a cup of tea while he unloaded the fresh stock, there was no banter between us. It was as though I'd taken him by surprise the previous day and he'd not had his barriers in place but they were certainly in place now. He didn't even smile at me and I wondered if I'd, unknowingly, said something to upset him but I didn't dare ask for fear of upsetting him again. There was such fragility to him, it frightened me. Even though he was tall and broad and, insofar as I could tell without his taking off his thick checked shirt, in good shape, he gave off this air of being very damaged and I didn't want to damage him further or remind him of what had caused the wounds in the first place. It was all a mystery and, after he'd left, I resolved to mind my own business.

Polyester Olive turned up at 10.00 while I was serving a very difficult woman who wanted me to reduce the price of some calla lilies we'd just had in that morning because, according to her, they were past their best. Olive stood inside the door and watched me trying to convince the woman that they were perfectly good and would last for at least a week. In the end the customer settled for three bunches of Alstroemeria which I reduced in price as they were coming to the end of their freshness. When she'd gone, Polyester Olive said, 'You need to watch that one. She's always wanting a bargain and she always wants the best flowers on the cheap'.

'I think they're very good value even at the full price', I said and meant it.

'Not everyone knows how much they cost wholesale', said Olive.

'Oh really', I said, my business head coming into play, 'What are the margins like then?'

'Not very good. Mr Johnson doesn't charge nearly enough really', she said but then was all brisk and busy, taking a document out of her bag and handing it to me. It was my Contract of Employment and she needed a signature but I told her that I couldn't sign it unless I'd read it thoroughly and she agreed that she'd come back on the following Monday.

That day I took a grand total of £173 and on the Wednesday it was £264. If this continues, I thought, I'll be out of a job quite soon as the company couldn't possibly keep going.

I had lunch with Bubbles on the Thursday and we had a really lovely time at the little Italian place I'd found before. We shared a bottle of Chianti with our spaghetti and spicy meatballs and I wasn't used to drinking at lunchtime anymore so I had a little nap on the sofa when I got home. It was getting dark when I woke up and I knew I wasn't up to going out again so I thought I'd indulge my curiosity a bit by looking up the Johnson and Company Limited accounts.

I somehow felt this was intrusive but I told myself it was all a matter of public record and therefore available to anyone. I found Companies House online and opened up an account with them then I typed in 'Johnson and Company Limited' only to find it was actually 'Johnson & Company Limited' and then I got stuck into analysing their most recent Report and Accounts.

There were several interesting things about the most recently filed Accounts. One was that they'd been filed late which made me think that the inefficiencies I'd already seen extended as far as statutory requirements. Another was that the turnover was, as I'd thought, very low for a business of that size but the third thing I noticed explained why Mr Johnson didn't seem too bothered about charging any more for his stock; the company owned all the seven shops and a warehouse on the trading estate I'd visited. This was all very valuable freehold property and was also, presumably, why the company had no bank borrowing or mortgages.

I went to make a cup of coffee and mulled this over. Obviously someone at some time in the company had had enough sense and enough money to buy all this land and not to get into hock to the bank. This was very shrewd and the value of that property must have increased several-fold over the years. Was it Ted Johnson who'd been the brains? If so, why was he so behind the times now and why was he not making the changes which would keep his investments safer than they were at present?

I sipped the hot, thick coffee and pulled up the Accounts for the previous year. It was a similar picture. The same valuable freehold premises but a poor turnover, profit and return on capital employed. I worked this last figure out in my head – it was second nature to me, hard-wired in my brain.

So there had been two lean years for the company and its fixed assets had prevented it from going under. What had happened the previous year?

The company's accounting period ran from 1st April to 31st March and I pulled up the Report and Accounts for the fiscal period which was three years previously but spanned two calendar years. I brought the coffee cup to my lips as I scrolled through the usual introductory stuff about the directors but what I saw for that year made me catch my breath. The Accounts for the years I'd already studied showed that there were only two directors: Edward and Christopher Johnson but the Accounts for the year I was now looking at showed two other directors: June Mary Johnson and Lucia Sophia Johnson.

I stared at the screen. Who were these women? It was likely that June Mary Johnson was Ted's wife, Chrissy's mother, but no-one had mentioned her and no-one had mentioned the other woman but Ted had said that Chrissy was on holiday skiing in Italy with the children, so was Lucia Sophia Johnson Italian, and was she Chrissy's wife? That would make sense but, if all was well in their world, why were Ted and Chrissy so mired in sadness?

On a whim, I Googled June Mary Johnson and Lucia Sophia Johnson and the first of the calendar years for which these Accounts had been prepared. Nothing. I then put the names in again for the following year and the headlines screamed at me from the screen. In big black banner type, the nation's newspapers had all reported the tragic accident along with grainy pictures of the scene.

'Three Generations Wiped Out' said the *Daily Mail*. 'Hit and Run Outrage', said the *Express* while the *Telegraph* and the *Times* were more restrained but the facts were the same. June Mary Johnson and Lucia Sophia Johnson had been crossing a road in South London one morning in early February with five month old Emilio Johnson in a pushchair when a large lorry going too fast had careered into them scattering them all to their deaths. The driver hadn't stopped and the people who'd witnessed the accident were either too shocked or too busy tending to the victims to take the lorry's registration number. It was mentioned more than once in the reports that the victims had been on a zebra crossing at the time and it seemed to make it all the worse.

I felt sick. It would have been bad enough to read about this tragedy if you didn't know the people but I knew them now and saw, with the clarity of a newcomer's eyes, just how terrible had been the effect on their lives. Chrissy had lost his wife, his child and his mother, Ted had lost his wife, daughter-in-law and grandson and the children, the poor little children – Edward aged six and Lucy aged three – had lost their mother, their grandma and their baby brother. There were poignant photographs of the funeral on the front pages of all the papers ten days after the accident and there were Chrissy and Ted standing next to the flower covered coffins, solemn and dignified in their dark winter coats and gloves but Chrissy had two small hands in his. Edward and Lucy looked as if they didn't know what was going on, they were shocked beyond comprehension and their little white faces were pinched and hollow-eyed as they clung onto their father's hands.

I couldn't bear to look any longer and I *did* feel that I was intruding. I shut my laptop down and went and had a long hot bath and a long hot cry. My own grief at the failure of my marriage was so recent and so sharp still that some of my tears were for me but most of them were for the Johnson family, the three generations which had suffered so much and whose losses were unimaginable. How did they get the news – how do you tell people that three of their loved ones have been wiped out? How did they cope? How did they deal with the inquest? I couldn't imagine how people could go through all of that and still be standing but then I thought of the two children. Yes, that was the answer – they had to remain strong for the children.

I got into my cashmere pyjamas and made some cocoa

because, after all that weeping, I wanted to sleep. I did sleep, but it was fitful and not restful. I was concerned, actually, that when I saw Chrissy at work on Friday, I would let it show in my face that I knew and I didn't want him to feel my pity.

I had the radio on loud while I was getting ready for work to try to drown out my thoughts but the accident and its long aftermath were crowding my mind all the time and I kept bursting into tears. I told myself to get a grip but I was still moist eyed when I drew up at the back of the shop. It was lucky, then, that it was Ted who came to let me in and replenish the stock. Chrissy had to take Edward to the orthodontist, apparently, and then to the school outfitters and wouldn't be coming that day.

Seeing Ted dragged me out of my earlier mood. His first words to me were 'Where's my hankie?' I laughed and told him that I still needed it as I'd got a cold now (this was to explain my red eyes and runny nose). We entered the shop and I made him a cup of tea as he'd been up since 1.30 that morning visiting New Covent Garden. He'd bought some amazing, very large calla lilies which were such a dark purple they were almost black and he had some stunning turquoise hydrangeas which I could see would be fabulous together with some eucalyptus leaves as a frame and a bit of elephant grass between the blooms.

'Wow, Ted,' I said, 'These are so beautiful', pointing at the lilies and the hydrangeas, 'Would you mind if I make up a bouquet with them and a bit of greenery and put it in the window?'

The smile he gave me would have lit the darkest corner of hell. It was dazzling and I felt so warmed by it that I almost started crying again but I swallowed it down and smiled back.

'*That* is a cracking idea, Rowena', he said. 'How nice it is to come across someone who really likes flowers and knows how to put them together.'

'Oh, um, thank you', I said. 'But I haven't any training or anything, I just like nice things'.

'My dear, I knew that the moment I set eyes on you. You obviously have a good eye', said Ted and I felt myself blush with pleasure at his praise.

When he'd gone I set to and made the bouquet tying it with twine as I was going to put it in one of the big green jugs. I then placed it in the middle of the window. I decided that if someone wanted to buy it, I'd add twenty per cent to the cost of the flowers to account for my labour and my creativity in designing the arrangement. It sold in half and hour so I made up another arrangement with green anthuriums, blue lizianthus and maidenhair fern. That sold quickly too and by the time I came to close up, I'd made up seven arrangements in the course of the day all of which had been sold. There were almost no flowers left in the shop and I'd taken more than £400.

'What did you *do*?' said Ted, as he walked into the shop and looked around at the empty green jugs. 'I'll have to get you some more stock from one of the other shops'.

'Er, I just made up the arrangement and sold it and then I made another and sold it and so on all through the day', I said.

'Rowena', he said and I loved it that he used my full name, 'Rowena, you are a marvel. I knew I was doing the right thing when I took you on.'

Strike while the iron is hot, is what Mum used to say so, as I was in Ted's good books, I thought I'd try another suggestion.

'Ted, you know those gorgeous purple lilies you bought this morning – the ones I sold with the hydrangeas', I said and he nodded, 'Well, the bouquet looked lovely but it would have looked nicer and been a better advertisement for the shop if I'd been able to wrap it in something other than boring old white tissue paper'. I finished my little speech and held my breath.

'What did you have in mind?' he said cautiously.

'Well, there are lots of different coloured tissues. Some arrangements will best suit one colour and some another but, if you want to try something a bit different, how about pink or yellow or black?' I said.

'It's very expensive, you know,' he said. 'It's a lot more expensive than the white stuff...'

'I didn't, but I might have guessed', I said, 'But the thing is, the coloured tissue looks more modern'.

'So you think we're old fashioned, do you?' Ted said and I couldn't tell if he was joking with me or not.

I decided that I must be honest with him. 'I think that someone in this company has a true flair for buying the right stock but, when it comes to displaying and marketing your stock, yes, you are old-fashioned', I said.

Ted stroked his chin and said, 'Well, I appreciate your honesty, Rowena, and I'll think about it. Leave it with me but please don't stop making up those arrangements, will you?'

I smiled and said, 'I'll keep on making them as long as you keep on supplying me with spectacular flowers'.

'Good', said Ted, 'I'll be bringing some more stock for you tomorrow'.

I wasn't sure whether he meant that he'd be bringing the flowers himself or that Chrissy would be opening up on the Saturday but it was Ted again and this time he had glorious big bright yellow calla lilies and orangey-red anthuriums which were crying out to be put together. There were more hydrangeas and some interesting thistles which I was itching to get my hands on and, all in all, I sold a dozen arrangements that day.

It was Chrissy, in fact, who came to lock up and gave me a mild look of surprise when he saw that I'd sold nearly every bloom in the shop. He looked even more surprised when he saw that I'd taken over £600 that day.

'Well done', he said but I felt that his praise was just a little bit grudging, as if he didn't want anything to change, as if he couldn't be bothered to do anything differently and, thinking about his dreadful loss, I couldn't blame him if it took all his strength just to get out of bed every day and keep going for his children.

10

A Period of Calm?

When I got home, there was a letter from Bolton, Greene and de Latymer asking me for the name of my lawyer. They told me that their client wished to put the house on the market 'as a matter of urgency' and Tony's Estate Agent wanted to come and look at the property 'at your earliest convenience'. As a sweetener at the end of the letter, they said that Tony would continue to pay the mortgage and outgoings until the sale and he would make me a payment of £300 per month for 'subsistence' for three months from the end of October.

Obviously, it was in Tony's own interests to keep the house going as he didn't want it to be repossessed and he needed to keep it warm and occupied since cold, empty houses sell less well so continuing to pay the outgoings was hardly generous and the £300 for three months was designed to appear to be helpful while trying to starve me into submission. Tony hadn't contacted me since his phone message so I didn't know when he planned on trying to retrieve his stash of fifties or, even, whether he yet knew that I'd changed the locks.

I was tired after my first week's work and I didn't want to think about all the issues in the Solicitors' letter, so I made some macaroni cheese, had a bath with lavender oil and watched TV for the rest of the evening.

The following day I got in the car and took myself for a little trip round to the six other Johnson shops. They were all in what would be called 'prime locations' – in well-established retail parades in areas which were either already prosperous or in the process of being gentrified. Not all were as run-down as 'my' shop, the paint was reasonably fresh on some of them, but none of them looked as if anyone there had had a new idea in some time.

I bought some groceries and the *Sunday Times* at the supermarket using more of the cash to pay for my purchases and came home. I had some lunch and then settled down in front of my laptop for the serious business of the day. I'd decided that I was going to continue with my role as the emotionally damaged, not really up to it, wife (hell, it was mostly true!) and not engage a lawyer but do the divorce myself. Even with the cashstash and my wages, I didn't see that I would have enough money to live *and* to pay a lawyer and I knew that Tony would fight me harder if he thought I was wasting assets. My plan was to research it all on the internet and see what I needed to do to begin proceedings. Then I would write to Tony's lawyers, tell them I'd done it and ask for his offer of financial settlement. It would, of course, not be acceptable but I had the copies of the two letters as my hidden aces and the fact that the lovely Tasha would be breathing heavily down his neck all the time, nagging him to speed it all up as she didn't want to be nine months' pregnant and huge when they married.

I spent over an hour looking at the information available on GOV.UK and saw that I had grounds on account of Tony's admitted adultery with Tasha and because the marriage had most certainly irretrievably broken down. I downloaded the forms and filled them in, looked out Tony's and my Marriage Certificate and worked out in which County Court I needed to issue the proceedings. It was something of a shock to learn that the cost of this would be £340 and I felt a stab of anger that I was the one who had to pay to bury the marriage that Tony had killed.

I put all the paperwork together in one of the cheap brown

envelopes, addressed it, wrote the letter to Tony's lawyers, put that in a cheap brown envelope and took them both to the postbox.

I had taken a very large step. It was frightening after all these years to think that I would soon be a single woman again and I wondered if I'd ever have the courage to re-enter the dating market. The thought of trawling bars and clubs looking for Mr Right filled me with horror. I had no experience of internet dating but had read about all the pitfalls – the online guys whose pictures look like a young George Clooney only because they've posted a picture of a young George Clooney, the guys who expect sex on the first date and then never want to see you again. My self-esteem was low enough without any of that, thank you very much.

It did feel good though that, in the short time since Tony had told me he was leaving, I had made such progress towards becoming my own person again so I went to the downstairs loo and took another big step forward.

I went to the sink and wet my hands then I put a large dollop of hand soap in my palm and massaged it all over my fingers. My wedding ring was a bit snug so it took a few moments before I was able to ease over my knuckle but then it was lying, forlorn, in the sink and there was only an indentation in my finger where it had been.

It was a nice ring – white gold with little diamonds set into the front of the band. I'd been delighted with it at the time but now it was just a reminder of ten wasted years. It was quite valuable, though, so what was the best thing to do with it? I couldn't decide at that moment so I just put it in the pocket of my battered old mac which I kept hanging on the door in there for emergencies.

Then I did another thing which showed I was making progress. I picked up the phone, called Jane and told her that Tony and I had split up and his new girlfriend was pregnant. She was devastated for me and I heard no suppressed triumph in her voice. She offered to come and stay with me for a while but I said I was OK and she needn't worry, I was fighting back. I told her that she could tell Michael if she wanted, I didn't want to ring and get Marianne. I was very grateful to my sister for her concern and her love and it made me feel I wasn't alone in the world, especially as she made me promise to come for Christmas. She said the children would be wild with delight at the thought of their aunt being with them. It was probably not true but it made me feel that there could be life after Tony.

Then it was time for bed and I climbed the stairs with quite a feeling of achievement – perhaps the old me was still buried in there somewhere.

On the Monday morning, I put on my black trousers and boots but this time I wore a bright white T-shirt under the silver-grey boyfriend cardigan. I put my hair in the clip, quickly slapped on a bit of make-up and a short burst of *Chanel No. 19*. As I left the house, I realised I was looking forward to my day at the shop. I thought of it now as my shop and I wanted to be proud of it.

Chrissy was already there when I drew up at the back of the shop. He was standing in the little kitchenette with a steaming mug of tea in his hand.

'Want one?' he said by way of greeting.

'That would be lovely', I said as I took off my coat and hung it up.

He went to fill the kettle from the sink under the window and a shaft of early morning sun caught his head as he bent over the tap. The cold winter light made his brown hair shine like a new conker and I felt a lurch in my heart.

'So what have you brought me today?' I asked.

'Dad said to get some really spectacular flowers for you to arrange so I got the biggest they had and the most colourful - some bird of paradise, some longiflora lilies and some protea', said Chrissy but he was not as enthusiastic as his father. Obviously, it was Ted who loved flowers and had the flair.

Chrissy handed me my tea and gave me one of his tight,

going through the motions, smiles. His barriers were on maximum security alert and I had the feeling that he was uneasy in my presence. I smiled back and thanked him before going into the front of the shop.

The bird of paradise flowers and the lilies were lovely but the protea didn't go with either of them and I wondered if Ted, with his more discerning eye, would have bought them. I could see, though, that they might look surprisingly good with some of the big Thistles left over from the weekend and picked up a few stems of each and began to arrange them in my fist. Chrissy ignored my actions and busied himself with the till then he put on his coat and with a muffled 'See you later' was gone.

I felt deflated that he wasn't interested in my efforts to make his business more profitable but then I thought about it and knew that my wanting to transform Johnson & Co was as much to do with wanting to prove to myself that I wasn't brain-dead as it was to keep the company going.

I made up the protea/thistle arrangement with eucalyptus leaves between the flowers and aspidistra leaves as a border. It looked good – unusual but rugged – and I put it in the window. The proteas were expensive and I'd used six of them but I wanted to see just how much of a premium I could charge for having designed and made the arrangement so this time I added thirty per cent to the retail cost of the flowers. This meant I was asking £50 for the bouquet.

I wrote 'Long Lasting – £50' in black marker pen on a piece of white card and placed it in the middle of the window in front of the green jug containing the arrangement. It was still early Monday morning and I didn't expect to sell it that day. I was pleased with it; it looked architectural and took the eye away from the peeling paint on the shop-front

I sold it at 11.10 to a woman who wanted a centrepiece for the table for a lunch she was giving for a local charity. She was delighted that the arrangement was unusual while still being seasonal and she didn't try to knock the price down.

I was still glowing with pride when Polyester Olive arrived at noon. She was wearing one of those padded coats which are just about acceptable on the young and slim but made her look as if she'd wrapped herself in the winter duvet. My heart sank as she came through the door.

'Hello,' she said. 'Have you had a chance to look at the Contract? Is it alright for you to sign?'

I had read the Contract of Employment and it was pretty much a standard form so there was no reason not to sign and I smiled my welcome to her while I said, 'Yes, it's fine. Shall I sign it now and you can take it away with you?'

She nodded so I went and got my *Mulberry* Bayswater bag from the back and took the Contract from it. Olive looked sniffily at my bag as if I had no right to be working in a shop if I could afford a bag like that. Frankly, I was surprised that she recognised a *Mulberry* when she saw one but then they were featured quite often in the pages of the red top newspapers. I got my pen out of the bag. Olive looked askance at my *Mont Blanc* too and I made a mental note to get a cheap pen. I also noted that I would *never, under any circumstances*, give up my beautiful Bayswater bag.

I spread the Contract on the counter and signed and dated it. I saw Olive looking at my left hand and that she'd noticed I was no longer wearing my wedding ring; another thing about me for her to dislike. I handed her the signed document and she put it in her bag but while it was open she fished about and brought out an A4 envelope.

'Ted, Mr Johnson, asked me to give this to you', she said, handing me the envelope.

I was too interested to know what was in the envelope to wait until after she'd gone so I opened it immediately and her avid gaze showed she was as curious as me.

Inside was a trade catalogue for a company which supplied the tissue paper and a sample card showing all the different colours. I was as excited as a six year old at Christmas. The colours were gorgeous – a broad spectrum from palest pink through pillar box red, vibrant yellow, bottle green and sumptuous blue all the way to a dusky black. I wanted them all.

'He says you can choose four colours', said Olive.

'Oh, how lovely. Please will you tell him thank you very much', I said as Olive turned to leave. I was pleased she was going – I felt that she didn't improve the atmosphere in my shop but then she stopped me in my tracks.

Olive, at the door of the shop, turned to face me and said, 'Rowena, I know we may not have got off on the right foot but I see that you want to help make the business a success and I know that you have excellent qualifications so you could be just what it needs but you'll have to tread very carefully'.

'I think I know what you mean', I said and wished I hadn't.

Olive's eyes flashed angrily at me as she said, 'Who told you?'

'No-one told me,' I said, 'I was looking at the Company Accounts online and I saw the names and from there it was an easy step to find the newspaper reports. I wasn't being nosy or curious. I just found it, that's all'.

'Alright, I believe you', said Olive and gave me a nice, genuine, smile, 'But you must understand that the other staff and I, we saw Ted and Chrissy go to hell and back and we don't want them distressed or upset any further by anything or anybody'.

'I do understand and your loyalty and support do you great credit', I said and meant it.

'Thank you', said Olive and I thought she meant it.

'There's something I'd like to know, though', I said, 'So that I don't say the wrong thing'.

'What is it?' said Olive.

'Who was the business brain? I mean, someone was shrewd enough to buy the freeholds of the shops and there isn't any bank borrowing but Ted, Mr Johnson, seems not to be bothered about making a profit and I assume Chrissy would have been too young to make those decisions', I said.

Olive smiled as if she were remembering something or somebody of whom she had been very fond. 'It was her', she said, 'It was June, Chrissy's mother, she was the one with the business sense. She was the one who had all the good ideas. She had a sharp business head on her but she was very careful with the money. 'Money's hard to make and easy to spend', she'd say so that's why our office is so old-fashioned but since she died no-one's been interested in making changes anyway'.

'It must have been terrible for you all', I said.

'It was the worst thing. It was unbearable to watch Ted trying to keep strong for Chrissy but I think Chrissy would have got into the grave with Lucia and the baby if he could've', said Olive and there were tears in her eyes. 'But he had to keep going for the other two, didn't he, the poor little mites, and so here we are, three years later, trying to act as if it's all normal and it isn't. It's like walking on eggshells all the time, trying not to say something that will bring it all back'.

Olive pronounced Chrissy's late wife's name in the Italian way – 'Lucheeya' – and I assumed that she must have been Italian and that was why Chrissy and the children had gone skiing in Italy – so that they could visit the other side of the children's family.

'Well, I'm pleased that we've had this conversation, Olive', I said, 'So that I don't put my foot in it'.

'Good. That's cleared the air, then', said Olive, 'And, you never know, you could be just the kick up the backside that the company needs'. She saw my surprise and added 'In the nicest possible way'.

I laughed and Olive left. As she went out of the door, I thought that the padded coat quite suited her, actually.

I turned to the tissue paper catalogue and sample card. The colours all delighted my eye and the difficulty would be in choosing just four. I could see that there would be practical difficulties in having them all – there just wasn't enough space on the counter for so many – but I would need to be disciplined in my choice. I took the sample card to the window and looked at the colours in the daylight. The bottle green was very sumptuous and classy and it was a must as was the black but I needed a contrast and I felt that the pillar box red and vibrant yellow were the best choices. I knew could really make a splash with these and I pictured customers going out of the shop with bouquets of big lilies and fern wrapped in yellow and green tissue, or black and green even.

Then I thought about the ghastly plastic 'ribbon' in garish pink and blue which was the standard way to tie the tissue at the base of the stems. I wanted raffia – it was stylish and modern but I felt that I needed to wait a little while and let Ted see that I was producing profitable results before asking for something else.

I couldn't stop my mind from running ahead though. I made a cup of tea and sat on my stool behind the counter thinking about how I would redecorate the shop if I had a free hand. I looked over at the dark green jugs and decided I liked them and how, if the window and door frames were painted a similar colour, they would help draw the eye of passers-by into the window and onto the flowers in the jugs. The flooring was tatty lino and my dream would be to have stone tiles or terra cotta at least but that would be ruinously expensive, I was sure. The trick here, I thought, was to make the shop look upmarket without spending a fortune. Paint was relatively cheap and made a big difference but floor tiles were too costly.

Another big question was the signage. 'Ted Johnson's Florists estd. 1966' was informative but it spoke too much of the old-fashioned attitude of the business. It needed something more arresting and, as the shop was full of flowers, did we need to tell people that it was a florist? Surely all that was needed was the name; 'Johnsons' would do fine and it needed to be in a modern font and, I decided, it needed to be in silver which would show up well against the dark green and was more chic than gold (and, anyway, we didn't want to look like a Harrods rip-off , did we?).

In my mind's eye I could see all the Johnson & Company shops kitted out in their new livery and they looked wonderful. Then I thought about the staff. I had no idea what the assistants in the other shops were like. Were they like the girl who'd served me here in my shop? If so, heaven help the business. Was it a training issue? Did they just not *know* about customer service? Did they hate their jobs? I thought about this and realised I wouldn't even know how to begin to broach this subject with Ted or, much more difficult, Chrissy.

My biggest asset in persuading them to make changes would be increased profitability so I made up two more expensive arrangements and put them in the window. I sold one for £55 but the other remained unsold at the end of the day. I didn't actually mind though since it would be there in the middle of the window for passers-by to see and would be a good piece of marketing for the shop's new creativity.

Chrissy came to lock up and I felt as if I were picking my way through a minefield. As I drove home, I realised just how involved I had become in the shop and in the Johnsons' world in such a short time and I wondered if it was healthy for me.

At home there was a message from Hattons Estate Agency asking me to call them as they wanted to view the house to prepare the sale details. In being so caught up with the changes I wanted to make to the Johnson & Co business, I'd forgotten that I might soon be homeless.

11

What Happens Now?

The Hattons guy came to view the house on my day off, Thursday. He was full of public school arrogance and jargon. I disliked him on sight. He walked briskly round with his nose in the air as if *he* were doing *me* a huge favour. I offered him coffee and we sat at the kitchen table while he made his notes for the 'Property Description'.

'How is the market at the moment', I asked.

'Quite buoyant for a house like this – the modernised, median range properties in recently gentrified areas are selling well to the A and upper B social ranges in their thirties and forties'.

I decoded this for a moment and said, 'Oh', in reply.

'Yes, you've presented it well – clean lines, cool colours, nothing *fussy*. We have quite a few couples who're looking for something like this and, because they're cash rich and time poor, they want something they can just move into. They don't want anything twee and they don't want a project'.

'How long do you think it will take to sell? I asked innocently.

'Not long. First impressions count a lot and my clients will take away a good first impression'.

We agreed that the photographer would come the following week so that the house details complete with slideshow could go online without delay. I closed the door on him and mulled over what he'd said. Would I be out on the street before Christmas? It seemed possible. Shit. My life as Bridget Jones, holed up in her tiny flat, drinking alone, night after night, was about to begin in earnest.

Then I had a terrific idea and laughed out loud at the simplicity of it. I put a wodge of fifties from the cashstash in my wallet, got in the car and made for the nearest big shopping mall where I went straight to the *Kath Kidston* shop.

Being used to the Zen-like qualities of my home, my eyes popped at the riot of flowers and patterns and I was hard pressed to choose but, still smiling, I made my purchases and, having put them in the car, as I walked swiftly to my next destination, I thought about where I would display them all.

At the *Laura Ashley* shop there were more delights and I had an hour's fun choosing the kinds of things Tony would never allow in *his* house. I was triumphant as I let myself in with my numerous shopping bags but I needed a cup of tea and a sandwich before I could set to work. As I sank my teeth into my ham on *ciabatta*, I planned it out in my mind.

The trick was going to be to fill the house with all this strategically placed coloured, patterned, girly stuff so that Hattons' cool couples who were used to drop dead minimalism would shudder so much that they couldn't see it was just superficial and removable.

I started just inside the front door ('First impressions count' he'd said) with a pair of *Kath Kidston* spotted wellies then I put handsoap and handcream in turquoise flowery containers in the downstairs cloakroom along with a couple of towels covered in jolly stars. Moving on to the kitchen, I let my creative powers run riot with an array of floral teatowels, polka dot jugs, patterned cake-tins, spotty mugs and bowls, and, my most inspired purchases, a bright yellow oilcloth for the glass table on which I placed a teapot covered in a glorious knitted teacosy in the style of an old brown radio.

I put all of this in place and clapped my hands with glee. Yes, this transformed the kitchen and yes, it would deter purchasers but, at another level, it pleased me more because I actually *liked it*. I had a glass of wine to celebrate and then went upstairs.

Frilled pillowslips had an immediate impact but when I added ruched ruby velvet cushions and a buttoned lilac silk throw to the master bedroom it was uncanny how it changed the whole 'vibe' of the place. I followed through in the other bedrooms and then went to the bathroom.

My dressing gown, hanging behind the door, went onto a padded pink silk hanger, the white towels were replaced by gorgeous eau de nil ones with a pattern of a humming-bird. This raised my spirits so much that I began to sing as I transformed this former temple to masculinity into a feminine domain by the addition of glass jars with coloured cotton wool balls, pretty containers for hand-soap and bath oils and, *pieces de resistance, toile de jouy* covers for tissues and the spare loo roll. I hoped that this last little touch alone would produce such a *frisson* that prospective purchasers would run screaming from the house.

I had another glass of wine before tackling the rest. I was really enjoying myself, not least because it was the first time in ten years I'd been able to have what I wanted.

In the dining room, I put a warm rug under the table and a linen cloth on it followed by a pair of mirrored candlesticks and a multi-coloured glass and chrome cake-stand. In the sitting room, I put a cream fluffy rug between the big sofas and rose-spattered cushions on them. I changed the stark, uncompromising modern pictures for pastoral scenes and put an elaborate gilt mirror over the mantelpiece.

It was finished. Gone was the cold, angular atmosphere. Gone was the brisk, testosterone fuelled feeling of my former home – it had been replaced by something warmer and softer. The god was gone, please welcome the goddess in all her glory.

The photographer, Trevor, was chatty and friendly, coming through the front door like a bracing burst of seaside air. He had a quick look round the hall and nodded to himself as he decided from which standpoint to take his pictures. He looked a little askance at the dotty wellingtons but took pictures from an angle which obscured them. Then we moved into the kitchen and he gave me a strange look.

'I don't get it', he said.

'Don't get what?' I said.

'This room. What's going on in here?'

'Er, it's the kitchen', I said, all innocent.

Then Trevor's face broke into a broad grin and he laughed while picking up the brown knitted 'radio' tea cosy and admiring it.

'I think I get it', he said, 'I don't mean to pry – it's none of my business – but you're getting divorced, aren't you?'

'Yes, and my husband wants to sell the house', I said as calmly as I could.

'And you don't want it to be sold?' Trevor asked.

'Not really. Not this way, anyway. Not without my having a say as to the timing of it and without knowing where I'll go', I said, managing to get the words out but there was a wobble in my voice.

'So you've filled the house with stuff like this to put buyers off?' said Trevor, pointing to the tea cosy and raising an eyebrow at me.

'Well, yes, I suppose that's right', I said lamely, marvelling at Trevor the photographer's advanced people skills and penetrating cross examination technique.

'I suppose he's gone off with someone from work?' said Trevor.

'His P. A', I said and he nodded in recognition of a common story.

'Pregnant?' he said and I nodded.

'Seen it all before', he said. 'You'd be amazed at what we see in this job – the full range of selfish behaviour from people squabbling before the body's even cold to divorces so bitter that one of them has the dog put down so that the other can't have it'.

Trevor said this very kindly and I relaxed a little. 'Don't worry', he said, 'I'll take the pictures so that all your... *alterations*...are in the foreground.'

'Thank you', I mumbled, through a constricted throat brought on by the need to cry because of his understanding.

When he'd finished, we sat in the kitchen over coffee and he told me about his real dream job – film director – and how he spent his spare time making low budget 'indie' productions with his friends. We were getting on like a house on fire and I was beginning to notice his nice grey eyes, clean hair and straight teeth when he mentioned his 'boyfriend'. I felt a stab of disappointment but was grateful not to have got my hopes up any further before having them dashed. Trevor gave me a hug and said, 'You'll be OK, I can tell. You're brave and clever and he didn't deserve you. It won't work out with the P.A. – it rarely does'.

I cried for ages after he left and when I met Bubbles for our lunch I was red-eyed and still tearful. She understood though and said it was natural for me to grieve; it was all still so recent.

The house details went online on the Monday. It was most confusing – the words said one thing – 'cool, elegant, modern lines' – and the slideshow pictures, all twenty of them – showed frills and flowers and curves and softness. Trevor had done me proud and, once I'd stopped laughing, I felt the lump in my throat again at his generous gesture.

Tony must have been looking at the property pages as keenly as me because the phone rang that evening at about seven o'clock. 'He probably gets home earlier to the lovely Tasha', I thought as I ignored the ringing. It went onto Answerphone and I heard Tony's voice, tight with anger.

'What the fuck d'you think you're doing, Ro? This isn't a game. That house is going to be sold full stop, even if I have to drag you out of there kicking and screaming'.

He sounded like the kind of person who'd have the dog put down out of spite and I felt intimidated by his vehemence but Trevor's words came back and calmed me. I slept badly though and there was a nasty deep crease caused by a rumpled pillow all down one side of my face when I went to work. Chrissy gave me a questioning look when he came to open up but I didn't want to explain and was very tight lipped with him. It was a quiet day in the shop but I was still tired and out of sorts when I got home.

Bubbles rang the bell almost as soon as I was into the house.

'He was here today', she said breathlessly – she'd obviously hurried over – 'Tony, your husband'.

I looked at her for more. 'Come into the kitchen, sit down and tell me what happened', I said, 'From the beginning'.

Apparently, Tony had parked his car in the drive and slammed the door so hard that he'd attracted Bubbles' attention. She went upstairs and watched from her bedroom window as he went up to the front door and tried to get in with his key. Obviously, it didn't work so 'with a face like thunder' he went round to the back but it was bolted so he couldn't get in there either. Then he came back to the front door and had another go but his key still didn't work and his frustration must have been rising all the time because he smacked the door hard with the flat of his hand before stomping off down the drive and revving his car furiously before driving away in a cloud of exhaust. Bubbles was very good at describing all of this and I pictured every moment in my mind's eye. I could imagine Tony's reaction – he wasn't used to things not going his way and didn't deal well with setbacks.

Bubbles and I had a glass of wine and a chat before she left me to get on with my dinner. I was on edge all evening waiting for the furious phone message but Tony must have realised that I wouldn't answer his call since the next communication was a letter from Messrs Bolton, Greene and de Latymer telling me that I must immediately remove all 'frivolous, extraneous and superfluous ornamentation' from the house and provide Tony with a key which fitted the new lock. In the meantime, 'pending my compliance' Tony wouldn't be paying me the monthly amount he'd earlier agreed.

I crumpled the letter up in disgust and threw it on the hall floor then, for good measure, trampled it underfoot for a minute or two while muttering 'Bastard, complete bastard' to the empty air. Halfway down a bottle of Rioja on an empty stomach, I felt more mellow and started to work out my strategy.

I thought about writing back and asking them to define 'frivolous, extraneous and superfluous ornamentation' as I'd liked to have seen the painful look on the lawyer's face when trying to describe all that wonderful stuff I'd bought but this would only anger Tony further without producing anything positive. No, I needed to seize the initiative. They expected a reaction but I needed to give them something more creative. Well, Tony would be getting more stick from Tasha as the days went by and my position strengthened every time she had to let out her belt. Now was the time to make demands. But what did I want?

It was simple, I wanted the house – mortgage free. Tony could have the rest. Given that I had put some of my own capital into the house and he had secret funds, I felt this was not unreasonable. First, though, I needed to smoke him out so I sat down and wrote to Tony's solicitor saying that I would not give him a key nor would I change the house but I was entitled to know what financial terms my husband proposed to offer and, 'given the urgency of the situation', I was sure 'that a reply would be forthcoming within the next ten days'.

I printed the letter on the cheap paper, put it in one of the brown envelopes, posted it and waited.

The reply arrived within days. Tony and his solicitor must have thought that I'd played right into their hands. It was quite a thick letter setting out in detail what they had calculated to be the 'matrimonial assets', Tony's huge contribution to these assets and my scrawny input. They had also (thoughtful of them) calculated my 'reasonable financial needs' and how these were to be met from my own salary and what Tony would agree for me to have from the matrimonial assets.

He was obviously not feeling generous when he and his lawyer cooked up the idea that I could be induced to write off ten years of marriage for a paltry twenty per cent of the assets, especially when the assets as listed were wildly short of what Tony actually had. To my delight, he hadn't disclosed either the pension pot or the hedge fund holding. Gotcha! He was hiding the bigger part of a million pounds from his lawyers. I assumed this would not go down well with them so I sat down again to write to them.

I marked my letter 'Without Prejudice' and told them that I wanted the house, mortgage free. I enclosed, without comment, the copy letters from the pension people and the hedge fund managers leaving the lawyers to draw their own conclusions about their client. I posted the letter (cheap paper, brown envelope, as usual), went home and treated myself to the bottle of *Louis Roederer* I'd earlier put in the fridge.

Then I waited.

12

Victory?

Obviously, it was going to take some time for them to reply to me. I imagined Tony's solicitors would need to see him to get him to explain the undisclosed funds and his lack of candour, then he'd need to work out how best to pay off the mortgage, so I didn't expect to have a reply in the next few days, even though Tasha would be pulling her hair out (I hoped, anyway) with frustration at the further delay in getting her heart's desire. Even so, I expected a reply within, say, a fortnight.

But two weeks came and went and there was nothing – not even an acknowledgement – and I had to sit on my hands to stop myself from writing or e-mailing to enquire whether they'd got my letter; the last thing I needed to do was to look *keen*.

It was stressful, though, all that waiting and the way I dealt with it was to go into survival mode. This, and the long, dark, cold, nights entailed eating lots of comfort food – shepherd's pie with a cheesy mash topping, sausages and mash with onion gravy, deep crust pizzas, macaroni cheese with bacon – you get the drift – all hugely comforting and fattening, and to sit in front of the telly in my jimjams, make-up free, hair in a scrunchy, watching old movies.

When the doorbell rang at 8.30 one evening about three weeks into my lonely vigil, I was so engrossed in my own little world that it scared the hell out of me and I jumped with fright. Thinking it was late and a bit cold even for committed Jehovah's Witnesses, I went to the door to preach to them about the comforts of one's own hearth and was horrified to find Tony on the doorstep.

He pushed roughly past me to get into the house. I followed him into the sitting room where the TV was showing 'Brief Encounter' and the coffee table was littered with the detritus of several evenings' worth of half empty hot chocolate mugs, some with clumps of marshmallow still clinging to them. There were bits of crumpled, used tissue on the floor in front of the sofa where I'd been crying at a film and hadn't bothered to clear them up when I went to bed – all in all, neither the room nor I was in a fit state to receive visitors.

Tony stood, tall and imposing, tanned (again?) and handsome in front of the fireplace. He put his fingers in the belt loops of his jeans (a gesture which he knew annoyed me) and looked at me through eyes filled with hatred and loathing. I stared back with what I hoped was a clear, fearless gaze even though my heart was banging as though it would break through my chest wall.

'I won't even bother to comment on either this room or you', Tony began, 'Suffice it to say that I hope never to set eyes on either of you again'.

'Suits me', I said.

'I don't know what you think you're playing at, Ro,' he said, 'But, to be honest, it's been a real eye-opener to me that you're such a complete cunt'. He spat out the insult.

'I don't know why you've come, but it's obviously not to enquire after my health so let's cut to the chase shall we?' I said.

'I've come for my things in the attic', he said and I knew immediately what he meant.

'Fine,' I said, 'Help yourself, you know how to get up there'.

He stalked out of the room and I went back to Trevor Howard and Celia Johnson, turning the sound up so that I wouldn't hear Tony rooting about above my head.

He was up there quite some time and I was two glasses into the bottle of Merlot I'd decided to substitute for hot chocolate before he reappeared. His face was a study in barely, suppressed rage. He strode over to the sofa and stood, towering over me, while I tried to appear cool and calm.

'You think you're so clever don't you, Ro?' he said through clenched teeth, 'But you haven't won, not by a long chalk. I'm going back to a beautiful young woman who loves me and who is carrying my child while you're making love to a bottle of wine. You're going to be a lonely old woman, Ro, and you deserve to be. Looking back, I never really loved you – you were cold, Ro, and unresponsive and', he went to the door and turned to throw this back at me, 'A lousy fuck'.

I listened to the front door slam, his feet on the drive and the roar of his car before I dared breathe out. He'd come for the cashstash, obviously but the remaining cash was tucked away, at her suggestion, in a biscuit tin in Bubbles' kitchen – she'd foreseen Tony would come for the money and had offered her services as a safe place to hide it. That woman was a genius. I breathed a sigh of relief that he hadn't got his hands on the money but then I started to think about what he'd said. Was I going to live out the rest of my life alone and unloved? The Bridget Jones fantasies of being found dead with my face half eaten away by cats flooded into my mind. Was I a lousy lover? I'd thought that our sex life had been, until fairly recently, in good order, but was I wrong? Or was Tony just trying to hurt me in the most fundamental way possible by attacking my womanhood?

The answer wasn't in the bottom of the Merlot bottle but I drank it anyway and another one afterwards just in case the second bottle was somehow more knowing than the first.

It wasn't and I had a shocking headache the following day to go with the sick at heart feeling that my marriage had been a sham all along – right from the word go. When I got to work, Chrissy must have been having his own problems as he clearly didn't want to engage in conversation with me any more than I wanted to speak to him so for that day and for some time afterwards, we pussy footed round one another, communicating in grunts and sign language.

I got the letter from Messrs Bolton, Greene and de Latymer at the end of November. It was quite short. Tony would agree to my having the house and contents, mortgage free, on condition that I applied for the decree absolute of divorce at the earliest possible opportunity. This was what I'd wanted. I'd won. The house was mine. I didn't need to move, I could have a lodger, if I wanted and I should have felt proud I'd managed to achieve this in the face of such opposition.

But it was ashes in my mouth. I felt old and tired, fat and ugly and, worst of all, unloved and unlovable.

And Christmas was coming.

13

The Festive Season

The *decree nisi* came through in early December and, as agreed, I applied for the absolute immediately. I would be single by mid January so this would be not only my last Christmas as a married woman but also my first Christmas without Tony for over ten years. It was a ghastly thought. How would I get through all that happy family stuff when my heart and my spirit were still broken? How would I manage not to scream or break down in tears when everyone else I laid eyes on would be full of festive cheer and *bonhomie*?

As the shops filled with seasonal goods and people preparing for weeks of frenzied socialising, I tried to concentrate on the blessings in my life – I would be going to Jane's, I *did* have some family, I'd got the house and I had a job. Sometimes, I thought of how unbelievably terrible it must have been for Ted and Chrissy that first Christmas after the accident and it was humbling and salutary; I didn't know how well or badly the run-up to Christmas was affecting them but life was, at least, busy at the shop.

We had holly wreaths and mistletoe circles from the first week in December. I asked Ted if this wasn't a bit early but he said the Christmas trade always starts in that first week and he knew his stuff because, almost as soon as I'd put them on display, the wreaths and circles were sold. Ted was going to the market nearly every day and bringing exciting things back for me to make into bouquets and arrangements. I really loved this aspect of my job and it helped to stop my mind from churning the same old thing over and over – how Tony and Tasha would be spending their first Christmas together, in love, looking forward to the birth of their baby.

One morning, a Friday in mid-December, Ted's market purchases included snowdrops and violets and I decided to put them together in little posies encircled by the violet leaves, wrap them in black tissue and tie them with the black raffia I'd persuaded Ted to buy. I was busy doing this when the front door opened and Chrissy came in followed by a pink whirlwind.

'What are you doing' she said as she ran up to the counter where I was working and picked up one of the violets. She was wearing a pink ballet skirt, pink leggings and a pink sweater and her dark hair was caught up in a bun at the back of her head.

'You've been to ballet, haven't you?' I said and she nodded, looking up at me with deep, brown eyes.

'Lucy, this is Mrs Boxer', Chrissy said, 'Rowena, this is my daughter Lucy. He said her name with some pride and I could see why – she was interested, intelligent and questioning without being at all brash or self-centred. I thought of all she'd had to go through and wanted to fold her in my arms and hold her for a very long time.

'Would you like to help me?' I said, 'Unless your Dad has other plans', looking at Chrissy for an answer.

'Would you like to stay and help Mrs Boxer for a little while', he bent down to ask her.

'Oh, yes, please!' she said with such enthusiasm that I wanted to cry.

'Alright, then, you can stay for an hour but don't annoy Mrs Boxer and please do what she asks you', said Chrissy as he went out of the door and left me with Miss Lucy Johnson.

I found a tall stool for her and a small pair of scissors. I showed her that I was trimming the violet and the snowdrop stalks so that they were the same height, mixing them, wrapping them in the leaves and then putting elastic bands round them. She listened carefully and watched me do it a few times before asking for her own flowers on which to practise. She had no difficulty with the scissors and had soon made her first posy.

'That's great, Lucy, really neat and you got them all the same height. I can see that you're going to be good at this', I said.

'Oh really, do you think so?' she said, eyes shining at my praise.

We worked harmoniously and enjoyably for over an hour, Lucy chatting about her ballet lessons, until Chrissy came back. He saw us sitting together at the counter, busy with our joint project and a shadow crossed his face. It must have hurt him to think that Lucy could have been learning about the world of flowers from her mother but her mother was dead and I was no substitute.

'Time to go, now,' he said.

'Do we *have* to, Daddy? I'm enjoying myself and Mrs Boxer doesn't mind, do you?' she said looking at me with those dark eyes.

'No, I don't mind, I don't mind at all', I said.

'OK, you can stay for another hour', Chrissy said and left us to it.

This time, we cut up the tissue and folded it so that it stuck up in points around the posies and then tied the raffia to keep it all in place. Lucy's little fingers were deft and she was better at tying the raffia than me so I gave her that job while I was serving the lunchtime customers.

Chrissy came back at about two and said that she really *must* come now and we both got down from our stools at the same time. I bent to say 'Goodbye' and she flung her arms round my knees in a big hug, nuzzling her face into my legs. Chrissy looked embarrassed but I patted her shoulders and said, 'I've really enjoyed having you here. Perhaps your

Daddy will bring you back and let you help me some other time'.

Lucy relaxed her grasp and looked up at me with a wide grin. 'Oh, yes, please!' she said as if I'd offered her a one way ticket to Disneyland rather than an unpaid job in her Dad's shop. Chrissy took her hand and they left. The shop felt as empty as my womb and I missed her as soon as they were out of the door.

Chrissy came to close up as usual that evening. As we were standing next to the till, I thought I ought, out of politeness if nothing else, to mention Lucy's visit, so I said, 'What a lovely daughter you have. She was utterly charming'.

'Yes, she is', he said, 'And she talked about you all the way home'.

I was delighted by this and smiled widely. 'Oh, it's quite normal', said Chrissy, 'She's like that with every woman of a certain age since….' he tailed off. My smile evaporated and I felt my stomach contract. I didn't know if he meant to insult me or was just trying to explain a situation which was emotionally charged for him and for his daughter. He saw my smile fade and his expression changed to one of concern.

'Oh, I am *so sorry*, Rowena,' he said. 'That came out all wrong. I didn't mean it that way. I didn't mean it to sound as if she didn't like you as a person. She *did* like you, she liked you a lot. I could tell that she did. It's just that….since, well, you know….' I nodded my head, 'Since the accident, she's been short of female company what with her Mum and her Gran…'

'I can't begin to imagine your loss', I said and wanted to wrap my arms around Chrissy and hold him until I could make it better but I contented myself with putting my hand over his on the counter and giving it a squeeze.

'They say time heals, but it hasn't yet', he said, 'It's just that we're more… used to it'.

'If I can do anything to help…' I said, but didn't know how to finish the sentence.

'Yeah, sure', he said as if he'd heard that a million times and no-one, no-one could do anything to help him in his grief.

I felt some sort of relief though after this conversation because at least we'd talked about it – we'd acknowledged the elephant in the room – and I was no longer the stranger who couldn't be trusted to know the deep, dark, secret. I hugged myself with this thought all the way home.

The following morning Ted came to open up. He seemed in a good mood. He'd brought a big box of poinsettia plants, their crisp green and red leaves offset by smart terracotta pots. I immediately unloaded them and arranged them in a row on the window sill.

'I knew you'd do that', said Ted.

'Do what?' I said.

'Put them there, like that. When I saw them, I knew because they're in smart pots and not nasty plastic, you'd put them in the window', Ted said, laughing.

'Am I so transparent?' I said, enjoying this warm exchange.

'No, I wouldn't say that. Not at all. What I would say is that you have an excellent eye and you're transforming this shop'.

I wanted to rush over and kiss him – on the cheek, obviously – but I just smiled broadly and said, 'Thank you. That really makes me happy'.

I meant it and then Ted dropped a minor bombshell. 'Would you like to come with me to the market on Monday', he said.

I didn't need to think about it, I answered in a moment, as eagerly as the girl who's just been asked out by the guy she's fancied for ages and who's been ignoring her. 'Oh, yes, Yes please!' I gushed.

'Good, be here at 2.00 o'clock Monday morning then', said Ted and watched, amused, as the smile faded from my face.

'They don't work nine to five, you know', he said with a bit of a smirk.

This was a challenge to my determination but if he thought I'd be put off by having to get up in the middle of a winter's night, he was wrong. 'I'll be here', I said.

Once he'd gone, I pondered this invitation and concluded that it was another acceptance; Ted must have felt I'd passed some sort of test and now he was moving me on to the next stage. I could have been irritated by this, I could have been angered by it – how dared Ted Johnson, who probably didn't have an 'A' level to his name, test me, First Class Honours graduate and holder of an MBA about business? I could have thought that but I didn't. I was delighted and excited. I *couldn't wait* to get to the market to see what was on offer and I relished the opportunity to have time with Ted so I could speak to him about the changes he needed to make to his business.

The biggest challenge about the trip wouldn't be getting up at 1.00 in the morning, it would be the usual, overwhelming challenge for any woman going into a new situation – what to wear?

Could I wear my *Burberry* trench-coat, dare I take my beloved *Mulberry* bag? I didn't want to look like a rich bitch who thought she was slumming it down with the plebs so the answer was probably 'no'. And it would be cold. It would probably be very cold. I pondered this all through the morning and then hit upon a solution – if Tony's old flying jacket was still in the loft, I would wear it with a warm polo neck sweater, trousers and boots. The bag was still a problem but I would deal with that when I got home. There were other, minor issues, such as whether to wear earrings, make-up or perfume but I shelved those decisions for Sunday evening.

The Saturday takings were the best yet – £1,180 – and I saw that Ted was impressed. We said 'See you Monday' when we parted and I went home to my house. I'd invited Bubbles round for supper and we had a really lovely evening sharing news and views so I went to bed feeling quite positive.

I woke in the dark to an odd feeling between my legs – warm and oozy. Still half-asleep, I turned over and felt something gush from me. 'Oh no, not again', I thought. I reached out to switch on the light and felt another rush from down below. I wasn't sure if I dared to stand in case I flooded the carpet but looking down at the sheets, my fears were justified – there was blood everywhere. Bunching my pillow between my knees to contain the flow, I staggered slowly to the bathroom where I had a wash and kitted myself out with two of the heavy duty pads which I seemed to need these days. I was too tired to change my sheets so I went to sleep in the former matrimonial bed in the former matrimonial bedroom. It already felt strange that Tony and I had slept there, together, for eight years but it was my house now and my bed and I could sleep where I wanted.

The following morning, I surveyed the 'Nightmare on Elm Street' that was my sheets. I couldn't face stripping the bed so I went downstairs and made myself scrambled eggs on wholemeal toast, took two paracetamol and a swig of iron tonic before wrapping myself in my dressing gown and falling asleep on the sofa with a hot water bottle.

I repeated the paracetamol and iron tonic when I woke at noon, replenished the hot water in my bottle, got a blanket and went back to sleep. I woke at four in the afternoon and made myself a toasted cheese sandwich before having a bath. I felt dizzy and had cramps but I knew I wouldn't call Ted to say I wasn't up to going to the market with him because I couldn't bring myself to fall back on that old excuse 'women's problems'. If he'd had a wife to whom I could have said that I was flooding, I might have, but he didn't so I would just have to make the best of it. I had more paracetamol, iron tonic and a mug of camomile tea then set the alarm for 1.00 a.m.

All thoughts of what to wear had gone from my mind while I was trying to deal with bleeding to death so when I woke on the Monday morning, I had to think quickly while I was having my shower. I dried my hair and put it in a clip before slathering a thick layer of foundation over my very pale face. Lipstick was too much for the middle of the night as was mascara so a well-kept corpse stared back at me from the mirror and the chunky black polo neck sweater I pulled on didn't help but it was warm and soft next to my skin. I put on very thick black tights and an old woollen skirt, my *Ugg* boots and, to top it all off, a grey overcoat which had originally belonged to Tony but been appropriated by me when he tired of it. A quick spritz of *Chanel No. 19* was the finishing touch and I was out of the door by 1.40 a.m.

Ted was already waiting at the shop. He had the kettle on and we had a very welcome cup of tea before getting into his car which was, mercifully, already warmed up by his earlier journey. I'd planned I would use this time alone with Ted in the car to talk to him about my thoughts for the business but I felt so rotten that it was all I could do to stay awake while he drove through quiet, dark, wet streets.

We got to the market at about 2.00 and I reluctantly got out of the warm, cosy car. Ted opened the boot and took out two bright yellow high visibility jackets and gave one to me. 'There's a lot of traffic going on in there', he said and I wondered what he meant but once we were in the actual market, it was a revelation; I had never imagined that this busy, bustling, twilight world existed. All around were noise and forklift trucks filled with flowers, plants and trees and smiling, chatty people, shouting greetings and comments to one another, eating sandwiches and drinking from steaming mugs, doing business in this brightly lit, modern building while most of the rest of the world was tucked up in bed. The array of flowers on display was staggering and my eye kept alighting on wonderful things I wanted Ted to buy.

But he was an old pro at this, I soon saw that. We walked slowly round, appraising everything while Ted was hailed by name from all sides. He introduced me to several wholesalers and, even though it was freezing cold, I glowed to think that he'd taken the trouble. Once we'd had a good look round, Ted turned to me and said, 'How about a bacon sandwich and a coffee?' to which there was only one answer.

We settled down on hard chairs in one of the cafes while I got on with the serious business of eating my sausage and bacon roll. Ted was halfway through his bacon, egg and tomato *ciabatta* when he said, 'So, Rowena, what shall we buy?' and I knew that this was another little test.

I chewed for a moment and then said, 'Well, what I've learned in my shop is that the clientele want stylish flowers and arrangements and they don't like clichés so I think we should go for things which are seasonal in some way but aren't the usual run of the mill or are presented in a different way'.

Ted nodded and said, 'Yes, I like the sound of that, so what should we buy?'

I too had liked the sound of what I'd said, you'd almost have thought I knew what I was talking about, but now he wanted actual recommendations rather than waffly generalisations. I took a big bite of crusty roll and crunched it for a while before saying, 'I like the new purple peonies, the quicksilver euphorbia, the silver dusted red roses, the white phalaenopsis orchids and the red euphorbia. I can make some striking arrangements with those and if we get some pussy willow, dogwood, hypericum and ivy then we can ring the changes'.

'You do know, don't you, that you've chosen some very pricy items?' said Ted.

I laughed and said, 'My Mum always told me that I had expensive tastes but my customers don't mind paying for something which looks new and fresh'.

I couldn't believe this all meant so much to me in such a short space of time but Ted had given me something much more than just a little job to tide me over, he'd given me a new sense of self-worth and I realised I cared very much for this business and wanted his approval.

'Well, you've done wonders with that shop so I suppose I ought to let you have what you want....and how about some of those very expensive, big amaryllis – the red and the white ones', Ted said and I wanted to throw my arms round him and hug him but I didn't.

'Great idea,' I said. 'And can we buy loads of those little

bits of hollowed out log and some cyclamen so that we can plant them and put them in the window?'

'Give a woman an inch and she takes a mile', Ted said, smiling, and I knew he was enjoying himself. So was I, even though it was still hours before I normally opened my eyes and my belly was still filled with cramp.

The rest of the day passed in a blur of tiredness and satisfaction. I was delighted to have the flowers and accessories I wanted and I set about making arrangements when we got back to the shop at half past six. I had four spectacular bunches to put in the window by opening time and sold them all at a good profit by mid-day. I was flagging by mid-afternoon and almost asleep at the counter by closing time.

Chrissy came, followed by a boy in school uniform. 'Edward, this is Mrs Boxer', he said and I looked down into two dark pools of sadness in a pale, oval face under a mid-brown thatch.

Edward Johnson reached out his left hand and said, 'How do you do', as formally as if he'd been a bishop. I put my hand in his and returned the greeting. His hand was cold and I wondered if his gabardine coat was warm enough to withstand the winter. I smiled at him and he smiled back but it was a forced smile and just looking at his little pinched face, knowing about his losses, brought a lump to my throat. He'd been six when his mother, grandmother and brother had been snatched from him and I wondered if there was ever a way a child could learn to cope with that much grief.

'You'll be breaking up for the Christmas holiday soon', I said, more brightly than I felt.

'Yes', Edward said dully, 'But they give us lots of homework, even in the holidays'.

'It doesn't seem fair,' I said, 'But I'm sure you'll do your best'. Edward gave me the tight, false smile again and I had the awful feeling that I'd somehow added to his pain.

I was relieved, though, that I'd checked myself in time and

not said, 'I bet you're looking forward to Christmas'. The Johnson family probably hated Christmas more than any other time of the year.

14

A New Year

Mum always used to say that a new year was an opportunity to make changes and so I sat in the living room on New Year's day and took stock of my life. Christmas hadn't been too bad, all things considered – I'd worked until mid-day Christmas Eve and then driven down to the West Country where I'd received a warm and considerate welcome from Jane and her family. We'd slept late and eaten very well and I felt that no-one was judging me for what had happened but it was hard to see Jane in all her domestic bliss and not feel like the odd one out.

To be frank, the best bit of the whole 'festive' season had been the Christmas dinner Bubbles and I had shared at her house. She cooked the stuffed turkey crown and I brought the vegetables and trimmings and we sat in her cosy dining room and drank good New Zealand Sauvignon Blanc and laughed and exchanged ideas and plans for the forthcoming year. Bubbles encouraged me to urge Ted to do a big makeover of the shops and, when I told her of the recent sales figures for my shop, she was lavish in her praise and I felt it really mattered to her that I was doing well whereas Jane was really more interested in the gory details of Tony's infidelity than my non-job at the florists.

I'd last seen Chrissy on Christmas Eve when he came to cash up and we'd had great difficulty knowing what to say to one another by way of 'goodbye'. I knew better than to say 'Have a lovely time' to him as it was obvious he couldn't possibly have a lovely time at this intense family-oriented period of the year and he, I assumed, knew I would be having my first Christmas alone so he couldn't wish me a happy Christmas either.

So we stood awkwardly at the shop door while he fished in his pocket for the keys.

'I'd better be going, then', he said, 'And you've got a long drive'.

'Yes', I said, 'Give my best to your dad and the children'.

'Thank you,' he said, 'Drive carefully'.

And that had been that. I'd wanted to hug him and hold him, tell him that one day it wouldn't hurt so much but it was not my place and, anyway, what did I know about that sort of loss?

Ted came to open up and lock up in the few days we were open between Christmas and New Year. He seemed subdued so I didn't want to intrude by asking how it had all gone. It was very busy in the shop on New Year's Eve with people wanting flowers and arrangements and table decoration for parties so, in a way, I was pleased that I was very tired and going home to an evening alone in front of the boxed set of 'Homeland' with a bottle of wine; Bubbles had gone to Bournemouth to see her 'baby sister', Margaret, who was also widowed, and would be away for a week. I missed her.

So there I was, slightly hung over, sitting on the sofa, reviewing my situation and, most pressingly, my finances.

They weren't good. My salary at the shop after tax and National Insurance covered the outgoings on the house – Council Tax, heating, lighting, telephone, insurance, etc., but I had to run the car, feed myself and at some point I'd need to have the outside of the house painted and go to the dentist, have my hair cut and pay for the occasional treat, etc, etc. The cash-stash was not inexhaustible and I faced a lean year ahead.

Should I advertise for a lodger? I thought the practical

implications through. It would need to be a female and, if she was in need of a room, she would probably be quite young. Did I want to be a sort of mother figure to a girl with boyfriend problems or, worse, one who was having a rip- roaring time in the bedroom next to me while I lay and stared at the ceiling, alone and unloved? No. Could I then, think about having a quiet civil servant or librarian as my lodger? Could I bear to have her nylon cardigans in my wardrobe? Could I bear to have her hanging round my kitchen in her quilted housecoat? No.

There was only one thing to do and it was a temporary solution at best but it was the only thing I could think of at that moment. I needed to sell my *Tiffany* diamond engagement ring. I went upstairs and retrieved the precious turquoise box and opened it. My ring, symbol of just how much I'd meant to Tony once upon a time, twinkled at me from its white silk nest. It was beautiful – very simple, just a drop dead perfect white diamond on a white gold band. I'd worn it with great pride ever since Tony had gone down on one knee and proposed to me, producing the ring in front of a whole restaurant of people who looked on indulgently while I cried with joy at the prospect of being his wife and the magnificence of the ring.

Well, that was then and this was now and I needed the money so I would take it to the jewellers on the High Street who said they bought 'precious items' and see what they would offer me. While I was at it, I'd take my wedding ring too – there was no point in keeping that either.

So, on the first Thursday of the New Year, I found myself outside 'Shapiro & Sons' with the precious items in my trusty *Mulberry* bag. I'd never done anything like this before and I didn't know what to expect but the first thing was to go inside the shop so I pushed open the fully glazed door a little clumsily as I was nervous.

'Can I help you?' said an elderly man from behind the shiny glass counter under which lay rows of rings and watches all glistening in the spotlights strategically placed overhead.

'Yes, er, that is, I have some rings to sell'.

He looked a little bit downcast as if he'd have preferred to sell me a ring rather than talk about buying one but he gathered his manners together and said, 'May I look at them, please'. His eyes lit up when I produced the *Tiffany* box from my bag. I put it and the other little navy blue box on the counter. Mr Shapiro (I assumed that was who he was, anyway) took the *Tiffany* box first and opened it with an anticipatory smile on his face. I smiled too as I thought of how his grin would broaden when he saw the size of the stone. He took the ring from the box and held it up to the light. He looked a bit puzzled. Then he went and looked at it under another light. 'Excuse me a moment', he said and disappeared into the back of the shop with my ring.

A few minutes later, to my relief, he reappeared and put the ring on the counter. 'I'm sorry', he said.

'About what?' I said.

'I'm not interested in buying it', he said, pointing to the ring, glinting on the counter.

'Is it the wrong time of year, or something?' I said, 'Do they sell better in the spring? Or maybe at Christmas time?'

'No, no, it's not that – it's the ring itself – it's fake, it's a cubic zircon'.

'*What?*' I leaned against the counter for support and felt something inside me unravel.

'But, but, but,' I gabbled, gasping for air as my heart did painful somersaults while Mr Shapiro got a chair and manhandled me into it.

'Take deep breaths,' he said, 'Keep breathing slowly and steadily,' and, yet again, the kindness of a stranger unhinged me. I started to howl and months of being brave and standing up for myself while I felt abandoned and unlovable came to the surface. 'Come into the back of the shop, dear', said Mr Shapiro, 'I'll get us a cup of tea'. He got me up from the chair and ushered me into a little kitchenette where he placed me in an armchair and put the kettle on. Then he thoughtfully went to get my bag and the rings.

While the kettle was boiling he opened the little navy blue leather box and took out my wedding ring. 'Let's see what we have here', he said and put the spyglass thingy to his eye, turning the ring round under the light.

'Quite different, quite, quite different. Genuine all the way through. A nice ring. He didn't stint here, at least,' said Mr Shapiro.

I expect he was trying to cheer me up, to give me a little bit of dignity to hang onto and I shouldn't have spoiled it for him but the words slipped out anyway.

'I bought that,' I said, 'I bought my own wedding ring. Tony, my……ex-husband, said he'd spent so much on our honeymoon and I…..bought…my…own…ring,' I sobbed.

'Drink your tea,' said Mr Shapiro, handing me a man-size tissue. I did as I was told and stopped sobbing. Anger was beginning to take over.

'That bastard!' I said, then apologised to Mr Shapiro but he smiled.

'I've heard it all before,' he said, 'In this trade you see happiness and sadness and in forty years I've seen a lot of both.'

'Does it happen often, then?' I said, curious about these depths of human nature to which I was being introduced by a kindly old jeweller.

'Oh, yes, a lot more than you'd think', he said, 'And the fakes are so good these days you need a good eye and some knowledge to tell the difference'.

'But the box?' I said.

'The people who take the trouble to make a good fake ring can make a good fake box', said Mr Shapiro patiently, 'And sometimes they have someone on the inside at the box factory so it's possible that your box is real'.

It was no comfort. Tony had palmed me off all these years

with a phony ring. I thought back to the time when it grew too small for me, when I was full of IVF hormones, and I'd said that I needed to take it back to have it enlarged but he'd said that he couldn't put me to all that trouble and he would drop it in for me. I'd thought he was being so loving and understanding but he was just covering his tracks.

'Bastard!' I said again and Mr Shapiro smiled indulgently at me.

'That's it,' he said, 'Anger is good. It gets you past the worst'.

'Thank you, thank you very much,' I said, 'You've been really kind. Why couldn't my ex have been more like you?'

'Oh you flatter me', said Mr Shapiro laughing, 'I expect I have my off moments too.'

'But you wouldn't buy your fiancée a fake ring, would you?' I said and he looked grave and agreed with me.

'So, do you want to sell this one?' he said, picking up my wedding ring. I nodded and he said, 'Would fifteen hundred suit you? Cash?'

It was far less than I'd expected to leave the shop with but, under the circumstances, it was a good price. I nodded, unable to speak in case I started sobbing again at this lovely man's generosity to a complete stranger.

I finished my tea while Mr Shapiro counted out the money and then left with my fake ring in the little navy blue box – Mr Shapiro said he ought to destroy the *Tiffany* box and I watched him smash it with a little hammer. It was curiously satisfying. But what to do with the ring? It was eye-catching and maybe someone would get some joy from it.

I walked past a shabby looking shop. The windows were full of pictures of dogs. They'd been abandoned. It was one of those badly funded local charities run by devoted volunteers unskilled in fund raising but great animal lovers. Tony hated dogs. Perfect.

I gave them the ring and a crisp fifty pound note and left before they made me their patron saint for the day. The following week, Mr Shapiro gave me a very good price for my *Cartier* watch and I gave a £100 to the charity – I had a lot of sympathy for the dogs – discarded by people they'd loved and thought had loved them and thrown out on their ear.

I had the house, for now, but unless things changed quite radically, quite soon, I would need to sell it and buy something much smaller.

15

Spring

There's no doubt about it, even in a London suburb, spring is a special time of year and I found this to be especially true in the floristry trade. January and February had been slow – people had no money for flowers once their Christmas credit card bills came in – but as soon as Ted started bringing in the hyacinths, the daffodils, the primroses and the tulips, they flew out of the door because people wanted that flash of colour after the dark winter days. Ted was taking me to the market about once a month now, asking my opinion and getting me known by the wholesalers. Chrissy was still distant and we were not nearly as comfortable in one another's company as were Ted and I. This bothered me as mine was by far the most profitable of their shops and I felt it was a bit unfair of Chrissy not to acknowledge it.

Then it was half-term and Chrissy was more distracted than usual. He seemed to be in a constant state of high alert, waiting for the next domestic disaster.

One morning while we were sorting his delivery, his phone rang and he had a short, fraught conversation with what I could hear was an adult female voice before slapping the phone down on the counter.

'Oh no', he said in a tired, defeated voice.

'What's the matter?' I said.

'It's Lucy', he said, 'That was her friend's mother,

reminding me that Lucy needs a fairy costume for Cressida's party on Saturday. Where am I going to get one?'

He looked exhausted and depressed as if he'd be a failure as a father if he couldn't magic a fairy costume from somewhere. I thought about it for a moment and then said, 'Well, if it can wait until Thursday, I can take her'.

Chrissy gave me a swift glance to see if I meant it or was just being polite so I smiled and nodded to reinforce my offer. He didn't smile back – he went into himself, deep inside somewhere, to consider whether he could or would trust me with his beloved, damaged daughter.

Then he smiled and said, 'Oh that would be such a help... and a relief, would you?'

And I smiled back and said, 'It will be my pleasure. I'm very keen on fairies and I know just the place'.

Chrissy knew that this was an attempt at light-hearted banter on my part and he actually joshed my elbow and said, 'Yeah, I bet you have them at the bottom of your garden.'

I felt the electricity from his touch for quite some time even after he'd gone.

The cleaner let me in to Chrissy's house on the Thursday morning: he wasn't back from swimming with Lucy yet so would I like to wait in the kitchen with Edward?

Edward was sitting at the table with piles of school books in front of him. He looked flustered when I came in but, with grave, old world courtesy, stood to welcome me and said, 'Oh, hello, Mrs Boxer. How nice to see you, how are you?' He was smiling politely but the smile didn't reach his eyes.

'I'm fine, thank you. What are you up to, some of the dreaded homework?' I said

'Maths', he said, 'I hate it', and I could see that he really meant it.

'Oh, I'm quite good at maths. Shall I have a look at it?' I said sitting down at the table next to him and picking up a pencil. He stared at my hand.

'You're left-handed', he said.

'Yes, and so are a lot of very clever people – Einstein for one,' I said. Edward smiled again and this time it was more genuine.

'I'm left-handed too,' he said.

'I know', I said, 'I noticed it when we first met. It's something to be proud of – some of the most creative people in history were left-handed.'

'That's not how some of the other boys see it', said Edward, 'It makes some sports awkward and some of the masters say it makes my handwriting odd'.

'Ah, I used to have the same problem until I learned to hold the pen like this', I said showing him how to hold the pen so as to rest it firmly between his second and third fingers and push the pen across the paper rather than pull it..

'Try it now', I said and watched him as he formed the letters of his name. He was a bit wobbly at first but then gained confidence and was making much better letters when the door opened and Lucy hurled herself at me from the other side of the room as I stood to welcome her. Her hair was wet and she smelled of chlorine as she clung to my middle.

'Helloooooo', she said, 'I'm so excited that we're going to get me a fairy outfit. I've been looking at them online and the one I like best is the Spring Fairy'.

'My daughter never has a problem knowing what she wants', said Chrissy laughing at Lucy who was now busy unpacking her swimming things from her little backpack and putting them in the washing machine.

'Are you ready to go shopping now with Mrs Boxer', he asked her and she nodded but I was a concerned at her going out into the still chilly morning with wet hair so I asked if I should see to her hair and was allowed into her princess pink bedroom where we spent a happy half-hour with the hairdryer and a brush before we got into my car and made for the costumiers. Lucy chatted brightly all the way, telling me that she was able to do without her water wings now but she didn't like swimming as much as ballet.

When we got to the costumiers, I parked the car and let her out of the child-lock door. She immediately put her small, warm hand in mine and continued chatting as naturally as she would to her best friend.

The fancy dress shop was one of those old-fashioned places where the costumes are properly made and not thrown together from garish, thin, man-made fibres and the people who served the customers were enthusiasts. They made a big fuss of Lucy and she and I were soon knee deep in little gossamer tulip skirts, satin bodices, sequined wings and sparkly tiaras.

With her dark hair and eyes and pale olive skin, she made a lovely fairy and although she wanted the Spring Fairy costume which was buttercup yellow, I thought she looked more striking in the mid-green Woodland Fairy outfit. It had a sort of shepherd's crook instead of a wand and the shoes were utterly delightful – little pixie boots in bottle green leather.

'I think you look wonderful in this one,' I said as she unselfconsciously preened in the changing room mirror.

'Oh, do you like it? I thought I wanted the other one but now I don't know, Mrs Boxer'.

'You can call me Rowena,' I said.

'*Ribena*? Your name is *Ribena*?' said Lucy, incredulous.

'No, Rowena. R-O-W-E-N-A,' I spelled it for her but it was a bit difficult for a six-year-old who hadn't heard the name before.

'Robina', she said.

'That's near enough,' I said.

She chose the Woodland costume and when it was packed in tissue in a big box we went to McDonalds for a late lunch so it was after four when we got back to the house. Ted was sitting in the kitchen with Edward. There were books all over the table. Edward looked pale and unhappy and Ted looked perplexed.

'Ah, the Fairy seekers return,' said Ted trying to be humorous.

'Oh, Gandy, I got the most lovely costume', said Lucy, 'Robina helped me choose it and then we went to McDonalds and had chicken nuggets'.

'While Edward and I've been tearing our hair out over geometry,' said Ted, still trying to be light-hearted.

'Oh, which bit of geometry?' I asked.

'It's the area of triangles', said Edward, 'I have to work them out'.

'May I look? I used to be good at geometry,' I said.

Edward passed the exercise book over to me and I was catapulted back to my schooldays when I fell under the spell of the logic and beauty of maths. It all came flooding back and I saw where the problem lay.

'Can I have a go?' I said and Ted willingly gave up his seat next to Edward so that I could help him.

'I'll get on with the tea,' said Ted while I explained the basics of triangles to Edward so that he had more of an understanding of what they were before we tackled working out their areas. Ted bustled behind me at the sink, peeling potatoes and Lucy sat at the table opposite me with her reading book, finger poised over the letters, tongue at the corner of her mouth, deep in concentration.

All of a sudden I was overwhelmed. This must be what it's like to have a family, I thought, and a dull pain crossed my chest. This is what I shall miss – this feeling of acceptance, belonging and love. I almost sobbed out loud and had to pretend that the strangled croak from my throat was a cough.

I needed to leave. I didn't want to be there when Chrissy got home – it would be too much like playing happy families and I couldn't bear it so, when Edward had grasped that the area of a right angled triangle is half its base times its height, I said I had to go. Lucy gave me yoghurt sticky kisses and Edward shook my hand and thanked me. Ted said, 'See you tomorrow morning,' and I got the lump in my throat again.

I mumbled, 'See you,' and got out of the house as quickly as I could. I drove home in a state, distressed because they were such a lovely family but they were not *my* family. When I got home, I sat on the loo in the downstairs cloakroom, scene of so many of my emotional dramas when the test stick failed to show that I was pregnant, and cried for half an hour. My tears weren't bitter, or angry or even for myself, they were regretful tears for the fact that life is so unfair and for the fact that Lucy and Edward needed a mother but their father was too damaged to start a new relationship.

I had to get a grip of my situation and of myself. I washed my face and splashed it with cold water before slapping on a bit of foundation, lipstick and mascara and going round to Bubbles' house for dinner.

I thought I looked OK but her first words to me were, 'Are you alright, dear, you look as if you've been crying,' and it was hard not to start blubbing all over again. I explained to her why I'd been crying and she put her hand on mine and said, 'Well, you never know what's going to happen, do you, dear? People are always able to believe that when they think something bad might happen but they're less inclined to think that something good will come along. Me, I'm an optimist and I say 'never say never'.'

'What a wise woman she is,' I thought and went home to bed in a much better frame of mind.

16

Blossom

Just about the time the trees broke through into flower, I noticed something interesting. One morning as I cast a bleary eye over my face in the bathroom mirror, I saw my skin had lost its wan puffiness and was looking quite bright and springy. I pinched my cheek to test this phenomenon and it didn't disappear. My eyes looked clearer too and, holy of holies, when I put my trousers on, I needed to move the belt in one notch. 'Wow, oh wow!' I said to the empty air when I looked in the full length mirror (something I normally avoided on account of not wanting to upset myself). All of a sudden, I looked quite different, as if someone had flicked a switch and a slightly older version of the young Rowena had been substituted for the other Rowena sometime in the night.

I peered in the mirror more closely. Crikey, yes, there they were; cheekbones. My cheekbones – I hadn't seen them for about six years. And there, unmistakeably, was my jawline. Bloody hell, I thought, I'm almost attractive. My hair, long neglected and just shoved into a clip, was still a disaster but the new me could handle a bit of eye-shadow and liner so I made the effort and really emphasised my eyes for the first time since Tony left. I put on a spritz more perfume than usual and went to work.

Ted had come to open up the shop. 'My, my,' he said, 'You're a sight for sore eyes. Why are you all dolled up? Are you going out tonight? 'Cos if not, I'll take you out myself.'

'Flatterer,' I said, and laughed and was pleased that he'd noticed. 'No, I'm not going out, I just felt full of the joys of spring this morning,' I added.

'Well, you look very nice,' said my new admirer and then got on with unloading the flowers.

Once he'd gone, I was alone for a while and began to wonder what it was about me that was different. Was it freedom? Was it that I was no longer subject to Tony's influence and subtle scrutiny? Was I eating better? It could have been any and all of these things but the real difference, I realised, was that I was finally free of all of those IVF hormones. The nasty flooding episodes I'd suffered had done their work and cleansed me of all the alien chemicals so that now I could be myself again. It was a cheering and empowering thought.

I found the phone book and looked up 'Hairdressers' and made an appointment for Thursday. This was extravagant and would eat into my dwindling resources but the new me wanted to be just that – renewed – and it required a thorough overhaul.

Chrissy came to lock up that night and raised his eyebrows on seeing my more glamorous face. He opened his mouth to say something but thought the better of it and the moment passed.

On Thursday I got to 'Hair Apparent' at nine a.m. and met 'Mr Robert'. I'd expected someone older and possibly quite staid but he was in his late twenties, hip and black. He was very handsome and I sucked in my stomach when he came over to greet me. He was tall and chiselled, quite like the gorgeous black doctor in 'Grey's Anatomy' and, going by his fitted sky-blue tunic with pockets for his scissors and comb and his clean, manicured hands with their pink nails set in contrast to his perfect velvet skin, he could well have been a surgeon. All of this went through my mind as I watched him cross the floor towards me and, if it had been a film, it would have gone into slow motion, the music would have come to a crescendo and he would have had a halo of soft lights around him. I fully expected him to have the same deep, dark chocolate voice as the soap opera hero.

'Hello,' he said, 'You must be Rowena, my nine o'clock.'

His voice *was* straight from a soap opera – but it was *Coronation Street* with a big dose of camp for extra authenticity as a ladies' hairdresser. I liked him immediately. With a flourish he took me over to a table by the window and seated me in front of a big mirror. A young girl appeared and put a cape over my top half. 'Thanks Kayleigh,' he said and took the clip out of my hair. This was the big moment.

Mr Robert took out his comb and raked it across my head several times, his face an impassive mask. He lifted the hair on either side of my ears and ran his fingers through it. Starved as I had been of close human contact for the previous six months, this was so pleasurable that I almost moaned. He made a slight sucking noise with his white teeth and reached under the table for a brush.

He brushed my hair over to the left of my head, then the right and ran his fingers through it again. I could have sat there all morning and wouldn't have cared *how much* it cost as long as Mr Robert went on exciting my scalp in this wonderful way.

Then he stopped and looked at me, looking at him in the mirror. Another big moment. 'OK,' he said, 'I'm guessing you want it shorter?' I nodded. 'And I'm guessing you want it layered?' I nodded. 'And I'm guessing you want some highlights?' I nodded. 'And I'd recommend some low-lights as well for texture,' he said. I nodded. 'Kylie will shampoo you now,' he said and another young girl, who could have been Kayleigh's twin, came and took me to the basin where she washed my hair and towel dried it.

Mr Robert spent a good forty minutes pulling bits of my hair through a cap, coating them with bleach and then wrapping them in foil. He made some of the highlights thicker than others 'for more texture' and did the same with the lowlights. Another girl, Kelly, brought me coffee and I sat comfortably with a copy of *Hello* magazine for an hour while the bleach did its work.

Kylie washed my hair, conditioned it and then it was time for the cut. Mr Robert placed me in a shaft of sunlight in front of the mirror and set to work. Another big moment. Was he going to cut off too much? Too little? Was he going to make my eyes look piggy? Was he going to make me look older? Was he going to give me a style that was too young for me? These thoughts coursed uncomfortably through my mind as Mr Robert clipped away with his scissors and brushed my hair this way and that and then he clipped away a bit more while clumps of striped hair fell to the tiled floor. Kelly brought me more coffee.

Then he was finished. 'OK,' he said, 'Keira will finish the style for you now.' Another, clone-like girl came over and wielding a hairdryer and brush, dried my hair then gave it some more body with straighteners and tongs. I hardly dared to look at the result. Robert came over to see.

'Blimey,' I said. I could not believe the difference. The colour was wonderful – he'd lifted my mousy hair to a dark blonde with choppy lights so that it appeared both thick and sun-kissed and he'd cut it into my neck at the back to shape it but left it longer at the sides to frame my face. I looked into the mirror in awe. A stranger looked back at me. An attractive stranger.

By the time I'd paid, tipped Robert, Kayleigh, Kylie, Kelly and Keira, I was several hundred pounds poorer but I skipped out of the salon with a light heart and went straight to the nail bar where I had my finger and toe nails painted bright pink in honour of the cherry blossom which was making the suburban streets and gardens so beautiful.

Bubbles held me at arms' length when I went to her house for supper and then she took me into the sitting room where the light was better and she looked at me from several angles.

Then she said, 'You look beautiful dear, really beautiful.' We had a big hug and I realised that her praise meant more to me than I could have thought possible.

Ted came to open up on the Friday morning and his eyebrows nearly disappeared into his hair when he saw me. He let out a long low whistle and then pulled himself up short. 'Oops,' he said, 'Was that an unwelcome sexist mark of appreciation from an old fool?'

'You're kidding!' I said, laughing, 'It's the most welcome sound I've heard in a long while…and you're no old fool.'

'You won't mind making me a cup of tea then,' said Ted and, as I put the kettle on, I thought that he and I had become really comfortable in one another's company. The elephant in the room had gone.

It was an entirely different thing with Chrissy when he came to lock up. He glared at me as though I'd done something dreadful and then he could hardly bear to rest his eyes on me. He grunted in response to my questions about the stock and couldn't get out of the shop quickly enough. What on earth was I supposed to have done?

In the car on the way home I suddenly remembered Daphne du Maurier's *Rebecca* – the black and white version with Laurence Olivier had been on not long before – and I wondered if I'd unwittingly done something similar to the second Mrs de Winter's gaffe with the fancy dress costume. But if I had, surely Ted would have noticed and tipped me off?

As soon as I got home, I went straight onto the internet and tried to find a picture of Lucia Sophia Johnson. It wasn't as easy as you'd think. There was plenty of news coverage of the accident and loads of heart-rending pictures of the bereaved family but the national papers hadn't carried any photographs of the deceased other than a small snap of the baby. I had to trawl the local papers before I found a picture of Lucia. She was small and dark with big brown eyes and black hair piled on the top of her head. She looked full of life and fun and I imagined Chrissy's life with her – adoring their family and looking forward to the future – and then it was all ashes – literally.

But the thing was, she was nothing like me, I was nothing like her – it wasn't as if I'd gone all out to try to look like her or anything so the elephant was still in the room. In fact, the elephant had company.

17

Easter

We were very busy in the shop with bowls of daffodils and basket weave bunnies holding hyacinths and jugs of pussy willow all redolent of spring, growth and fertility. My takings had gone through the roof and Ted was very pleased with me; he took me to the market once a fortnight now and I found the early mornings weren't nearly so bad in the better weather. I was sticking with my 'new look' and seeing Mr Robert regularly but the pink polish on my fingernails had had to go – it wasn't practical with all that cutting and wiring and raffia.

Chrissy was polite but distant – his barriers were firmly up – and I sometimes wondered if I'd imagined those few times when he'd been easy and open with me. We went through the motions and I tried to convince myself that it didn't matter that Ted thought I was the greatest thing since sliced bread but Chrissy seemed intent on ignoring me as much as possible.

Then, just before Easter, he opened up the shop for me and hung around a bit after we'd done the stock and the float. I had no idea what he wanted so I said, 'Would you like a cup of tea? Or coffee – I bought some really nice Colombian.'

'Coffee would be good,' he said, looking extremely uncomfortable and pacing the shop in front of the counter.

I couldn't bear the suspense so I said, 'Come on, out with it. Tell me what's the matter,' rather like Mum would have said to me when I was an awkward teenager.

'Er, it's Lucy,' he said. My heart sank.

'She's OK, isn't she?' I said, my face a mask of horror.

'Yes, yes, she is, she's fine. It's, er, it's her birthday,' colour returned to my face. 'And she's having a party and, er, she'd like you to come,' he said, all in a rush at the end.

'Oh is that all,' I said with relief, 'Of course, I'd love to come. When is it?'

'Monday, at the house at half past two.'

'Great. I'll see you then,' I said and he left.

Of course, I was pleased, flattered, touched even, that Lucy wanted me at her party but I was also really nervous about it. This was uncharted territory for me – I hadn't been to a children's party since my own tenth birthday and I imagined that things had changed quite a bit in the meantime. Would the parents be there? Probably, given that it was Easter Monday and they weren't at work. Would it be both parents or just gawping ranks of Yummy Mummies, curious to know what my status was in the set-up? And there was the perennial problem of what to wear? I groaned at the complexity of it all, thought that whatever I chose would be wrong and that, in the end, it didn't matter because the person who really counted was Lucy and she wouldn't notice what I wore.

On to the next thorny problem. Should I take a gift? Yes. What would be appropriate? This was a minefield. It would need to be something that showed I was more than a stranger to Lucy but less than a friend and definitely not something that smacked of intimacy with the family. Any item of clothing was therefore verboten. A doll would be a bit babyish, I thought, and something educational was too boring and distant. This issue occupied me for the rest of the afternoon, the drive home and half of the evening until I suddenly remembered Lucy unpacking her swimming things – her knapsack was too small for what she'd crammed into it and it could have been a hand-me-down from Edward. Yes, that was it; I'd get her a new knapsack.

As it was Easter Sunday the shops were closed, so I had to get there early on Easter Monday but I was delighted with my purchase of a pink waterproofed knapsack with lilac polka dots and a matching towel in lilac with pink polka dots. The shop wrapped my purchases in lime green tissue and put them in a sky-blue carrier bag with rope handles so I didn't feel the need to do more elaborate gift wrapping. I got a card with 'Now You're 7'on it and was home by eleven.

Now I could agonise over what to wear. It would be ridiculous to go overboard yet I didn't want to underplay it either. It was hard to know how to strike the right balance and all the more so because I had no idea who else would be there.

It was still quite chilly so I thought I would start with my black suede boots which were stylish but also comfortable and work up from there. I'd recently bought a winter-white below the knee skirt in honour of my weight loss and thought that, if I teamed it with a charcoal grey cashmere 'V' neck and a loosely knotted cashmere animal print scarf then, with Mum's pearl earrings, and some subtle make-up, I would look groomed and casually elegant.

I showered and blow dried my hair, got dressed and was going to put on some *Chanel No. 19* but decided that I'd wear *Mitsouko* instead. For added colour, I chose my purple *Bottega Veneta* bag and was ready to go. For some reason, I felt that this party was really important and I didn't want to mess it up.

There were several expensive cars parked outside Chrissy's detached Victorian house when I arrived and, approaching the balloon festooned front door, I heard the sound of girlish screams interspersed with adult voices. The door was open so I went in.

The noise was coming from the kitchen and I went down the long hall towards the hubbub. It felt very strange. Was I a friend of the family? Was I an employee helping out because they needed an extra pair of hands and they reckoned I, the recently divorced saddo, would have nothing better to do on a Bank Holiday Monday? I discounted this latter idea as I knew both Ted and Lucy valued me as a person but I still felt about as lonely as when Tony first left me.

Going into the kitchen, my loneliness intensified; standing around the granite topped island were handsome, stylishly dressed couples in their late thirties and early forties, wine glasses in hand, chatting animatedly to one another while small girls ran about chasing in and out of their parents' legs. I saw Lucy before she saw me – she was running after a girl with long red hair – and I didn't know whether to interrupt her or not. I couldn't see either Ted or Chrissy and I felt a complete idiot just looking into the room, not knowing how to enter it.

'Mrs Boxer,' said Edward, coming into the doorway beside me, 'Come in, I'm sure that Daddy will get you a drink.' I was so grateful to him for rescuing me that I wanted to hug him but I felt it would be going too far so I just smiled and said, 'Oh a drink would be nice.'

Some of the Yummy Mummies heads turned and began to look questioningly at me. I could see the thoughts going through their minds as they none too discreetly scrutinised me from head to toe– was I Chrissy's new woman? 'Chance would be a fine thing,' I thought and was surprised that I'd had that *thought*.

Then Lucy saw me and shouted 'Robina!' from across the room and forced herself through the forest of adult legs to get to me. I bent down to hug her and she buried her face in my neck.

'You smell different,' she said.

'Do you like it?'

'Yes, I like it, it's nice,' she said, 'And your hair is different. It's shorter and it's stripy now'.

'Oh, well, I wanted a change, and that's what the hairdresser gave me,' I said, acutely conscious that the Yummy Mummies were pretending not to listen but I could see them straining to hear every word and I knew that they were

144

thinking that I'd had a makeover because I was after Chrissy.

I straightened up and handed Lucy the carrier bag. 'I got this for you,' I said, 'Happy Birthday,' and bent down again to kiss her cheek.

'We're putting presents in the dining room for now,' said Chrissy coming in from behind us.

'Oh, Daddy, can't I open Robina's present *now*, please?' said Lucy, 'It *is* my birthday.' Out of the corner of my eye I could see the other presents, next to the party food, piled on top of the dining table. Lucy obviously hadn't asked to open any of them immediately and I could see the Yummy Mummies wondering why she only wanted to open my present. Chrissy was torn between wanting to agree to Lucy's reasonable request and not upsetting most of his guests. He looked to me for help.

'I tell you what, Lucy,' I said, 'Why don't we put it on the table with the rest of the presents for now and you can show me the garden? I'd love to see all the flowers coming out.'

'Oh, alright then,' said Lucy and put her hand in mine. Chrissy looked relieved and shot me a thankful glance.

We found Ted in the garden bowling a cricket ball to a boy of about Edward's age. 'You look nice,' he said to me.

'She smells nice, too,' said Lucy.

'She always smells nice,' said Ted as Chrissy appeared and handed me a large glass of white wine. He glared at his father as if he'd said something too familiar.

I chatted with Ted in the garden for a while then I thought I'd have to go indoors and face the adults in the kitchen. Gathering my courage, I went back indoors.

'Hi, I'm Rowena Boxer,' I said to a little group of parents huddled next to the fridge. They all stared at me and my outstretched hand.

'Mrs Boxer works for Daddy and Granddad,' said my new champion, Edward. The women looked relieved and the men looked bored. One man, a bit older than the rest, held out his hand to me.

Hello Rowena, I'm Gerald Foster,' he said and I smiled gratefully and shook his hand.

'What exactly do you do for Chrissy and Ted', Gerald asked and I felt the ground open up under me. Was I going to say that I was an assistant in one of the shops but I was only filling in until I got something better and that, actually, I was just as well-educated as anyone in the room but needed a little job because of my recent divorce? Was I hell. But what should I say?

'Er, er, I, I…..' I stammered.

Then Ted came to my rescue. Fixing the group with his most megawatt smile, he drew their eyes from me. 'Rowena makes herself indispensible to me. She is our new Commercial Manager,' he said.

I swallowed this lie gratefully and turned to Gerald and said, 'And what do *you* do?' Ted winked at me and left the room, followed by the others in the group.

'Oh, I'm in banking', Gerald said, reaching into the fridge to replenish my glass. As he closed the fridge door, he smilingly took a step closer to me treating me to a whiff of strong cologne and a closer look at his immaculate hair and perfect teeth.

'I'm Director of Corporate Services for Excelsior Bank,' he said, moving just that bit too close.

'Shit, shit shit,' I thought, 'This is getting hairy.'

'*Daaarliiinggg* – there you are!' said a female voice and a tall, slim, striking, blonde woman came into the kitchen and hooked her arm through Gerald's.

Gerald, unfazed, coolly took command of this new situation and said, 'Darling, may I introduce Rowena Boxer, she's Ted's new Commercial Manager. Rowena, this is my wife, Jessica.'

Jessica and I shook hands in that very female way when each woman wants to let the other know by the limpness of her fingers how little she wants to meet her.

'Rowena Boxer, you say?'

'Yes,' I said, 'Rowena Boxer.'

'Ahh, I get it! You must be Tony Boxer's *sister*. We met his lovely new wife Tasha recently at the bank's spring conference. Has she had the baby yet?' said Jessica and I would have sworn that she *knew*, she knew very well, that I was not Tony's sister.

'No, I'm not Tony's sister,' I said, 'I'm his ex-wife.'

'Oh, I *am* sorry. I appear to have put my foot in it. Do forgive me,' Jessica said.

I felt sick and somewhere behind my eyes tears were prickling but I wasn't going to let this woman know that she'd hurt me.

'No problem. I'm sure it happens to you all the time,' I said, pushing past her and Gerald, 'Now please excuse me, I need the loo.'

The downstairs loo was occupied so I went upstairs to find the bathroom. I didn't really need to go but I wanted to be alone to lick my wounds. I got to the landing and looked around wondering which door was which. One door was open and I went towards it. Edward was sitting on the bed in what was obviously, from the size of the bed and its plain linen, his room. It was eerily tidy. There was none of the haphazard untidiness associated with boyish interests – there were no posters, no cricket bats, no football regalia; it was almost Spartan in its simplicity. Above all, it gave me the feeling that it belonged to someone who was controlled because he was struggling to keep it all together.

Edward had one of those little gaming consoles in his hand but looked up from it when he heard my footsteps.

'Mrs Boxer,' he said surprised to see me.

'Please call me Rowena,' I said, 'Is the party not to your taste?'

'Not really. I don't like crowds all that much. And my friend's gone home now so I can't play with anyone.'

'I'm not sure that I like parties any more,' I said and then, not wanting to get into a conversation as to why I no longer liked parties, 'How's the maths going?' I added.

'Not so well. We're doing fractions now.'

'And you're not getting on with them?'

'I don't understand them. The teacher goes too fast for me and I've got lots of maths homework for the holiday,' said Edward throwing his game console down on his bed in despair. My heart went out to him. His life had been thrown into chaos with the accident and nothing could put that right but surely something could be done about his problem with maths?

'Edward,' I said, 'Would it help if I came on Thursday and had a look at the homework with you? Two brains are better than one.'

Edward turned towards me and there was a glimmer of hope in his face. 'Yes, it would, I think it would,' he said, 'Will you come, Mrs Boxer, er…Rowena?'

I wanted to cry – for him and for me – for the depths of sadness we both plumbed but I also wanted to make him smile. 'Yes, of course I'll come,' I said.

I found the bathroom, washed my hands and went downstairs. Ted was waiting for me.

'I meant it, I meant what I said,' he told me.

I wasn't sure what he was talking about – my head was filled with Edward's sadness and Jessica Foster's nastiness. I looked blank.

'You know, what I said about your job – about your being our Commercial Manager.'

I still didn't understand what he was getting at.

'Come into the sitting room,' he said and I followed him into the inner sanctum of the house. It had the feel of a room that was rarely used. The fireplace was empty, there were family photographs on the sideboard but they were smeared with dust and there was a musty smell from the carpet.

'We don't come in here much now,' said Ted, 'Not since the accident, I mean. It used to be where we'd all gather as a family but…'

'Yes, I understand,' I said, 'It's full of memories for you.'

'Well, yes it is. But the reason I brought you in here now is so we can't be overheard.'

'OK', I said, 'What's this all about?'

'I want to make you Commercial Manager,' said Ted, smiling broadly at me. I must still have been looking blankly at him. 'I'm offering you promotion, you know, a better job? A bigger job? The opportunity to give the business a big kick up the backside,' Ted added, increasingly frustrated at my lack of comprehension.

My thoughts, and my heart, were preoccupied with the sadness of this house and Edward's isolation and it took a while for me to connect back with the outer world but, once I did, ambition reared its powerful head. 'Ohhhh,' I said getting excited, 'You want me to give the shops a facelift?'

'Yes, I do, among other things,' said Ted while my imagination went mad thinking about all the changes I'd like to make.

'That's one of the reasons why I've been taking you to the market – so you'd have a better understanding of the business – and now I think you're ready to make the changes.'

'Oh Ted, that is absolutely wonderful!' I said, 'I can't wait to get started. There are so many things I want to do!'

'Within reason and within budget and subject to the directors' approval,' said Ted reining in my reckless enthusiasm.

'Of course, of course, subject to all of that,' I said soberly, cutting my mental budget by fifty per cent, 'I took all of that as read.'

'I bet you did,' said Ted, laughing, 'We'll talk more about it tomorrow. I'd like you to come to the office first thing so that we can start putting things in place but for now, congratulations!' Ted kissed me on the cheek and, for a moment, I wished that my own father valued me as much as he did.

Lucy came running in from the garden. 'The others are

going now. Can I open my presents?' she said and Chrissy, following her, laughed and nodded. Ted asked me if I wanted a glass of wine to accompany the gift opening and I felt honoured to be allowed to stay for this family event. I hadn't asked Ted what Chrissy thought about my promotion but I felt I could assume they'd discussed it and he'd agreed; my sales figures spoke for themselves and I thought that even a man as preoccupied as Chrissy would recognise the difference in profitability I'd brought to the business.

Lucy opened my present first and gave a loud, high 'whoop' of delight followed by a very sticky kiss on the cheek. She stuffed the towel into the knapsack and put it on her back and wore it while she opened the rest of her gifts. Edward appeared and sat next to his sister as she tore at wrapping paper and ripped parcels open, sometimes with her bare teeth. The contrast between his quiet reserve and her manic energy was huge and it occurred to me that you could never know how loss would affect people.

I didn't want to outstay my welcome so at about five o'clock I said I needed to be going. 'I'll see you on Thursday then,' I said to Edward and Chrissy's head shot up.

'Rowena's going to help me with my fractions,' he said in answer to his father's raised eyebrow.

Oh, good....good, good idea,' Chrissy said but I thought I detected a hint of resentment. Did he think I was encroaching too much on the Johnson family? Did *he* want to help his son with his homework?

I left before these thoughts could dampen the joy I felt at having a real job for the first time in years.

18

A Table for Two

I ran next door to tell Bubbles my news as soon as I'd parked to car in the drive. She hugged me and we jumped up and down a few times before she said, 'This calls for a bottle of wine,' and we sat in her cosy room drinking it and chatting about my plans for the shops. She asked me how the party had gone and I told her about Jessica Foster's catty remark. Bubbles pointed out that Jessica was probably a trophy wife, well used to her husband's roving eye and well versed in deflecting other women. I thought of Gerald Foster, the superficial world he inhabited, the over-styled hair, the over-bleached teeth, the year round tan and the designer clothing and I knew that I disliked all of that now as much as I hated everything else Tony stood for. Give me Ted Johnson – with his honesty and his lack of pretence – any day, I told Bubbles. She laughed and said that she was sure that Ted Johnson would prefer me to Jessica Foster any day too.

I spent Tuesday morning at the Johnson & Company office at the industrial estate where I'd gone for my 'interview' for the job but this time, when I got to the door, I didn't wait to be let in, I went straight in.

Nothing had changed. The polyester clad ladies all swivelled to look at me and they were no friendlier than they'd been before. Except Olive.

Olive came to greet me with a genuine smile and asked if

I'd like coffee. I said coffee would be great and she showed me into Ted's office. He rose to greet me and I sat opposite him, staring into the sunlight, in the same chair that I'd occupied what seemed like a lifetime before but was only about six months previously.

'You'll have to help me here, Rowena,' Ted said, 'This is the first time I've done this, so I'm not sure where we begin.'

'We begin with the budget', I said, 'Everything flows from that,' then Olive brought in the coffee and we began to get down to the details.

By the end of the morning, I had a clearer idea of where I was going with the update of the company and, in particular, the shops. We'd discussed what could be done in terms of refurbishment and I'd insisted on a fair chunk of money being invested in an up to the minute website with ravishing visuals. We also needed a logo and a 'house-style' so that we would acquire a known presence and a 'go-to' name and reputation in the areas where we had shops. Ted huffed and harrumphed at some of this, thinking that it was all 'black arts', but I explained that most people used the internet to source things these days and that Search Engine Optimisation really did have a role to play in the modern marketplace. This was all dry, fairly dull stuff but, when we got onto the transformation of the shops, I got really in to my stride.

I'd been thinking about this for months – waiting for my moment to pounce – and so I'd done quite a bit of research in my own time and was able to present Ted with colour charts and drawings. He liked my idea of the dark green paint for the shop-fronts and he liked silver for the sign-writing but I had to argue quite strongly for paying out what seemed to him like a lot of money for the rights to use a really stylish, sans-serif font.

Then we began to talk about the shop interiors and I mentioned staff uniforms and Ted gave me a look of disbelief and called a halt to the discussion so I kept my arguments in favour for our next meeting in a week's time. I promised to come back with costings for all we'd discussed that day and a fully worked out timetable and was about to leave when Ted called me back.

'What about money?' he said.

'What about it? Haven't we discussed the budget enough today already?' I asked.

'No,' Ted said laughing, '*Your* money. Your new salary.'

'Oh yes, I forgot about that,' I said, coming back into the room, sitting down and leaning towards Ted, all ears.

'How does thirty five thousand suit you?' Ted said.

It was less than I'd earned in my high-flying job but it was handsome in comparison with my current wage and I knew that the company couldn't afford to pay me any more at that time.

'It suits me fine,' I said, 'Thank you. It makes me feel I've achieved something'.

'You have,' said Ted, 'You've given us the kick up the backside that we needed.'

It was getting too warm in the room so I thanked Ted again and went over to the Chipstone shop where Chrissy had been holding the fort. I was flushed with happiness when I got there.

'How's it been', I asked, leaning on the counter, looking across at Chrissy sitting on the big stool.

'Quiet, you know, just like a Monday morning,' he said. 'How did you get on with Dad?'

'Oh it was great, thanks,' I enthused, 'We had a really productive meeting. I'm going to work out a detailed plan and present it next week,' I said.

Wondering how much Chrissy really knew about the plans, 'Will you be there?' I asked, 'Ted said that it's all subject to board approval.'

'I suppose he did, I mean it ought to be subject to board approval. But Dad's the one with the creative eye and, to be frank with you Rowena, I have enough on my plate just being a father, buying the stock and cashing up,' said Chrissy, looking tired and harassed.

'I'm sorry,' I said, 'I didn't mean to intrude between you and your Dad.'

'I know you didn't,' he said, looking me in the eye but not in the least sympathetically, 'But I just haven't the energy to get excited about changing things. That's why Dad's given you this job; I'm so exhausted all the time.'

'I see that, I really do,' I said, 'And I hope that I'll be able to repay Ted's trust in me by making the business more profitable.'

'I know you mean well,' said Chrissy and my heart sank because that phrase usually introduces something the listener doesn't want to hear, 'I know you mean well but the thing is; I just want to be left alone.'

There it was. The big smack across the face. The 'don't try to get near me or help me because I don't want you or your meddling' speech. I straightened up and went to walk away.

'I understand,' I said, 'I totally understand. But you're not the only one who knows about pain and hurt and grief and loss and I *know* I can help Edward with his maths and he needs help so I *will* be coming on Thursday whether you like it or not.'

Then I went into the back of the shop and made myself a cup of tea. When I came out, Chrissy had gone.

Ted came to cash up that night and open up and cash up on Wednesday and I didn't see Chrissy again until I went to the house at six in the evening on the Thursday as I'd arranged with Edward. I'd spent much of the day steeling myself for this encounter so, when he opened the door, I was ready with a bright confident smile.

'Hi,' I said, as he pulled the door wider to let me into the narrow passage. I had to pass quite closely in front of him and could smell the animal manliness of a guy who'd been up since before dawn humping heavy boxes and packages and hadn't had the chance to take a shower since. It was an honest smell, the smell of genuine hard work and, despite our sour exchange of earlier in the week, I felt a big surge of understanding for his problems.

'Edward's in his room,' he said.

'I know where it is,' I said and went up the stairs.

Edward was sitting waiting for me, his books lined up on the desk next to his tidy bed.

'Hello Rowena,' he said, 'I'm all ready for my lesson.'

'Hi there,' I said, 'Let's hope it's going to be a bit more exciting than a lesson,' and I pulled up a chair next to him.

We began by looking at the calculations he was to perform for his homework but, rather than show him mechanically how to do them, I took him right back to the beginning and asked him to try to think why it might be important to know how to work with fractions. He couldn't see any reason at first but then I asked him to think about the jobs his Dad did about the house. Would it be useful to know about fractions for DIY, carpentry, decorating, etc.? He thought about that for a while and agreed that it probably would be useful. Then I said that ladies are usually very impressed by a chap who's handy with a screwdriver and a hammer and he laughed. He actually laughed and said, 'Yes, OK, I see why we need to learn about them,' and we moved on to the nitty gritty of the sums.

Three quarters of an hour later, Lucy appeared with a cup of tea for me. 'Daddy asked me to bring you this,' she said and sat on Edward's bed playing with his game console while he and I finished his homework.

Chrissy appeared fifteen minutes later. He'd showered and changed his clothes and, as he bent down to hand me a glass of red wine, I smelled his freshly washed hair and was treated to a glimpse of nicely muscled chest under his white T-shirt. I crossed my legs.

'Seems everybody's in here,' said Chrissy.

'Oh, it's nice in here', said Lucy, 'I like it. Robina's here.'

I wanted to laugh but thought better of it. 'Well, we've finished now so I might enjoy this better downstairs,' I said, holding up the wine-glass.

'But you will come back next week and help me again, won't you,' said Edward and Lucy jumped on me with pleasure at the thought, nearly spilling red wine down my new blue dress.

'Careful now,' said Chrissy, keen to contain his daughter's enthusiasm for this female cuckoo in his nest.

I left soon after, determined that Chrissy's antagonism wasn't going to prevent me from helping Edward and, if I could be something of a female figure for Lucy while I was at it, so much the better. It was only nine o'clock when I got home and I had another glass of wine while the news was on followed by a leisurely bath with lovely lavender oil. It was while I was soaking in there, thinking dreamily about how the shops would look in their new livery, that it happened.

All of a sudden I felt hugely horny. I gasped with shock; my body had for so long been used to duty sex and then none at all, that I hadn't felt the rush of desire in ages but here I was lying naked in the bath fantasising about Chrissy Johnson. I thought I must be mistaken so I tried on for size the idea of actually being in bed with him, skin to skin, and the response was overwhelming. Yup, I really had the hots for him – bathwater notwithstanding. I hoped the feeling would go away or diminish at least when I got out of the bath but, if anything, it was worse.

I got into bed but all that did was make me think about being in my bed with him. I put the light out and tried to sleep but he kept crowding my thoughts and, this is no exaggeration, my body ached for him. On the one hand I was pleased by this return of my libido – it was a welcome reminder of being back to my old self – but on the other hand it was quite uncomfortable – that weird feeling of being all dressed up and nowhere to go and nothing to be done about it. I needed a strategy to cope.

Normally, I would have discussed my problem with my wise counsellor, Bubbles, but I didn't feel I could broach this subject with her even though she'd probably know what to do.

No, I'd just have to tough it out and hope that it was a temporary blip in my non-existent sex life.

Chrissy came to open up the following day and my stomach lurched when I saw him. As my heart pounded and mouth went dry, I felt like a teenager. When I said 'Hi,' it came out like a squeak and he shot me a look so I had to pretend that I had a sore throat. He didn't stay for a cup of tea and I was grateful because I thought I'd just have had to pin him to the counter there and then and have my wicked way with him.

Luckily both Friday and Saturday were busy in the shop and that stopped me thinking about him and about IT but Sunday was my day of rest and I spent it mooning about the house watching as many romantic movies as I could lay my hands on while daydreaming about how his mouth would taste and other things too graphic to mention.

I had to put my business head on for Monday morning because it was the day for my meeting with Ted but I wasn't as well-prepared as I'd like to have been because I'd been obsessed with his son for most of the previous week.

I needed to get a grip; the chances of my having anything other than a business relationship with Chrissy were slim to none so I had to find a way of putting my treacherous hormones back in their box.

But then, why shouldn't I want to get into bed with him? We were both single, heterosexual adults in good health and it was natural for me to want him. I alternated between these two views having long talks with myself as Chrissy and I pussy-footed round one another for a few weeks. I was going regularly to his house to see both Edward and Lucy and he was civil to me but no more than that, but the children, I could tell, really enjoyed my visits and now Edward was able to smile at me all the way up to his eyes.

Then Chrissy asked me out to dinner.

What happened was that I'd been helping Edward with some more geometry and was just drying Lucy's hair for her (a weekly ritual) when Chrissy appeared in the doorway of her bedroom. 'Can I have a word with you before you go?' he said and I followed him to the kitchen where he closed the door and turned to face me.

'I've been unfair to you,' he said and, although I was inclined to agree, I just gave him a questioning look.

'I've been a bear with a sore head and you didn't deserve it,' he said, 'And I'm sorry.'

'Well that's a handsome apology,' I said, smiling with pleasure.

'So, I'd like to make it up to you by taking you out to dinner,' he said and my jaw dropped.

19

Oops!

'There's a new tapas place near the shop, I'd like to take you there,' he said and I had to close my mouth first before I could open it again to speak. My voice came out strangely.

'Yes, that would be very nice. I like tapas,' I croaked.

'Good, if you're free on Tuesday evening, Dad'll look after the children and I can pick you up at seven-thirty.'

I made to think about whether I was free that evening – a short but definite pause while I reviewed my crowded social diary – and said, 'Yes, I am free on Tuesday so that'll be great.'

'OK then,' said Chrissy, opened the kitchen door and let me out of the front door.

I drove away without doing a victory jig on the way to the car but had to stop before I got home because my heart was doing some sort of tattoo and it wasn't conducive to safe motoring. I parked in a little lay-by outside a chip shop and (madness, I know) felt that I needed hot salty, vinegary chips to help me calm down.

The chips were fabulous – crispy on the outside and steamy on the inside – and soothed me enough to get home in one piece. Once inside the house, I did the victory jig all the way down the hall and started planning Tuesday evening in my head.

Was it a date? I hoped it was. I went into the sitting room and sank down on the sofa. My mind and my emotions were raging all over the place. I went to the garage and got one of the few remaining bottles of *Louis Roederer* down from the shelf. This was an emergency; I needed the kind of help only upmarket alcohol can give.

Back on the sofa, drink in hand, I tried to analyse my feelings in the light of Chrissy's invitation. I was elated, obviously. I was excited, obviously. I was anxious that it would go well. All of that was to be expected, but what was different was the way that my stomach melted when I thought of him and I realised I felt deeply protective of him, would kill anyone who hurt him, unselfishly wanted only what was best for him, and then I knew that I was deeply, passionately, irrevocably, head over heels, in love with Chrissy Johnson.

Shit, shit, shit! Overwhelming lust I could cope with – I'd been coping with it for weeks now but love – that was altogether different. I began to cry; tears fell down my cheeks, taking a layer of foundation with them and landed, plop, on the lap of my new dress leaving a puddle of glistening beige emotion on the taupe fabric. This was serious. There was only one thing to do at this moment. Go for another bottle.

I got the fizz, a larger glass from the kitchen and some ice and went back to the sofa. I tried to analyse the situation and searched in every part of me for all the thoughts and feelings that were lurking in dark and distant corners and I brought them all out into the open and, with the significant assistance of the champagne, I had to conclude that I wasn't just in love with Chrissy, I was in love with the whole Johnson family; I adored Ted as the father I would have liked for myself – strong, generous, kind, supportive and funny – and I adored the children – the brave little children who were trying to make the best of a terrible blow and who still had life and love in them.

I was lost beyond rescue. How could I fight these feelings? Should I fight them? Should I look upon Chrissy's dinner invitation as the beginning of a process which would see me incorporated into the family I loved? Should I just think of it as an invitation for sex from a man who'd probably been celibate for over three years? It was all too confusing and, by that time, I was too far into the *Louis Roederer*, so I just finished the second bottle and went up to bed.

My hangover was a blessing. It was of such epic proportions that it was Sunday before I got over it and it helped get me through Friday and Saturday at the shop in a daze courtesy of a throbbing headache and acid stomach. Ted asked me several times if I was OK and I pleaded a tummy upset.

By Sunday I felt well enough to work out what I'd wear for the big date. What look was I going for? Sexy? Definitely not – too obvious – but I didn't want to look like Mary Poppins either. I felt that I could easily pull off sheer black tights with my lovely black suede court shoes and the mid height heel would show off my neat ankles and lengthen my legs without making me too tall in relation to Chrissy. So far so good. The white wool skirt could be teamed with the fitted black silk cardigan I'd bought recently which had a 'V' at the front and at the back and, if I wore the right bra, gave me a very definite bosom and hinted at hidden delights without being at all revealing. I'd read somewhere once that a failsafe test for if a guy fancies you is that he looks at your breasts – however fleetingly - so I would need to be on the lookout for this. If I wore a scarf at the beginning of the evening then I could take it off during supper when we'd had some wine, it would be a subtle sign suggesting availability and, depending on where his eyes wandered, I'd know if he were interested. A bottle green leather mock-croc clutch bag I'd had for years would add colour and be suitable for the evening without being too dressy. With freshly washed hair, gold earrings and redone make-up, I reckoned I'd feel happy in my own skin and that I'd done my best to look good.

That was the easy part. Now came a much more fundamental decision. To wax or not to wax? That was the question. I couldn't put this off – I needed to make my mind up there and then so I went straightaway to my bathroom and waxed my legs telling myself that this wasn't a preparation - it was a good thing anyway as it would soon be warm enough to be bare-legged under Capri pants. I didn't take the wax strip to my nether regions though as Tony hadn't liked that 'bald as a plucked chicken' look and it wasn't the time to experiment with a new look for my delicate parts.

When I got back downstairs, there was an e-mail from Chrissy asking for directions to my house. It was the first e-mail I'd ever had from him and my heart soared when I saw his name on my computer. It was a brief, businesslike request for information and, obviously, I didn't expect it to end with kisses so I answered it in the same tone, briefly giving him the directions and ending with a simple 'Rowena.'

On the Monday I had my meeting with Ted and I was still trying to persuade him that it was a good idea to introduce a staff uniform; I'd done 'secret shopper' visits to the other outlets and was not impressed with the get-up of some of the assistants. Some of them were fine but others were grubby and ill-kempt so the only thing to do to bring them all up to scratch was to get them into uniform. I'd done my research and concluded that if we asked them to wear black trousers, white polo shirts and long green aprons inscribed with 'Johnsons' over the top left hand side, they'd look really smart. I thought that the assistants who were well-turned out wouldn't mind having a uniform as it would save their own clothes and the ones who were a mess would be pleased because it would mean they didn't need to think about what they were going to wear for work.

When I put this to Ted he took a deep breath and sucked his teeth in disbelief. 'I don't know, I really don't know,' he said. 'I don't know if I could say that to any of them. I don't think I could stand up in front of them and say that we expect them to conform.'

'Well, I think it would be very good for the business and it would foster a feeling of belonging to something worthwhile,'

I said and then, in a mad moment, 'And if you don't want to tell them, I will,' I added and the words were out of my mouth before I knew it.

'There's brave for you,' said Ted, 'Do you know some of these women? They'd have scared Napoleon witless.'

'Well, they don't scare me,' I said with more conviction than I felt but I was sure that I was right about the uniform. If we got the design right, and I thought that I had, then any woman would be pleased to be relieved of the early morning dilemma of what to wear.

'OK, Lady Nelson, go forth and preach the gospel of the staff uniform,' said Ted with a dramatic gesture.

I loved it that Ted had such confidence in me and trusted my judgement but how I was going to 'sell' the concept to the sales assistants. Would it be best to have a sales training and team building day and introduce it then? Would Ted think this was a step too far? Then again, I remembered my first brush with Johnson's and the stroppy girl with her mobile phone and 'sod you' attitude and wondered whether a mere one day course on the joys of customer service would be enough.

Then I remembered my date with Chrissy and the problem of persuading a handful of women into uniform faded into insignificance – my heart and my body became alert to the prospect of happiness and pleasure and I looked forward to it with an odd mix of dread and joy.

Tuesday came. A bright, blue sky, late spring day. I hoped that Chrissy wouldn't come to the shop as I wanted him to see me in my glory later, untrammelled by memories of the workaday me and I got my wish – it was Ted who opened the shop and cashed up and I was away by five forty-five so I had plenty of time to get ready.

After my shower, I blow- dried my hair just how Mr Robert had taught me and I knew, I *just knew*, it had never looked better. I put on my silk knickers in honour of the occasion and the lacy, underwired bra that made my bosom a force to contend with. Then I put on my sheer black tights and skirt and, lastly, the form-fitting silk cardigan and the strategic scarf. Pulling in my stomach and pushing out my chest, I looked in the mirror. Not bad, not bad at all – once I'd got my make-up on and, my shoes and my earrings, I'd be looking, if not hot, at least deliciously, attractively warm.

Finally, I was ready. I decided on *Mitsouko* for my perfume as Chrissy would not be as familiar with it as my usual *Chanel No. 19* and I wanted *him* to feel there was something different about this evening – I wanted him to think of it as a date. I put my keys, wallet, phone, lipstick and compact in the clutch bag and I was ready. My heart was pounding with anticipation. I felt like a cat on hot bricks, walking up and down in the kitchen so as not to be waiting behind the front door. I looked at my watch. It was seven twenty-three. I had the sudden urge to pee and, cursing, hurled myself into the downstairs cloakroom and did the deed just in time to hear the doorbell.

I was all of a dither and could hardly pull up my knickers and tights because my hands were shaking so much. Was Chrissy feeling the same? Had his legs turned to water? I checked that I hadn't stuffed the back of my skirt into my tights by mistake and left the loo. I could see Chrissy's outline through the mottled glass of the front door. I swallowed several times and cleared my throat in the hope that my voice would sound normal when I spoke. He pushed the door bell again and then I was there, opening the door, smiling.

'Hi,' he said, gesturing to his car, parked in front of the house. He'd obviously showered and changed after work. His hair shone like a new conker and I smelled his cologne – something brisk and fresh – and very welcome since it meant that he'd made an effort too. He was wearing a very bright white T-shirt under a dark jacket, black jeans and casual black leather shoes. He looked good enough to eat and I hoped I'd be able to get through the evening without making a fool of myself.

'You look nice,' he said and I glowed – all over.

'Oh, I still scrub up quite well,' I said laughing as he held the car door open for me. I felt like a princess. Tony never held doors open for me, saying that if women wanted equality then they could effing well open doors for themselves.

I got in the car but couldn't find my seatbelt so Chrissy had to show me where the seatbelt clip was located. This meant he had to come very close to my prominent bosom and it was a gloriously intimate moment as, in handing me the seat belt, he deftly but deliberately skirted my chest and we each knew what he was doing and that the other knew.

'Nice house,' he said, as he drove off. 'Have you lived there long?'

I decided I should get this bit out into the open and get it over with so I said, 'About seven years. My ex-husband and I bought it together but, as part of the divorce settlement, I got the house.'

'Dad told me you were divorced. It can't have been easy for you,' he said.

'No, it wasn't, Tony went out of his way to make it difficult. Funnily enough, he knows your friends the Fosters – Gerald and Jessica? It seems that they all met at some company do and Tony was with his new wife,' I said, wishing I hadn't as the earlier playful mood was evaporating fast and the last thing I wanted was to sound bitter and twisted.

'They're not my friends, not really,' said Chrissy, pulling up at the tapas bar, 'I only have them round now and again because their little girl is in Lucy's class at school. Frankly, he's a bit of a bore and she's just a pain.'

'Agreed!' I said laughing with relief and then, wanting to change the subject, 'I'm hungry, I hope they have *albondigas*.'

'You speak Spanish along with all your other talents?' said Chrissy, taking me by the elbow and ushering me into the little bar area. I was on cloud nine. I guessed Chrissy got his somewhat old-fashioned manners from his father and imagined him as a boy, watching Ted being courtly towards him mother and it had rubbed off. I loved all these little gestures which made me feel like a cherished piece of china.

I also loved the banter Chrissy and I were having. His barriers were down and there was no sign of an elephant anywhere.

'Actually, my Spanish is confined to menus and wine lists,' I said, 'But within those parameters, it's fluent.'

'OK, well it's going to be your job to order then!' said Chrissy as the waiter brought the menus.

'I think I'm up for that,' I said looking at the long list of tapas and choosing my favourites. I gave the waiter the order and Chrissy said I had to choose the wine too as I would know what went with the food so I ordered a bottle of white *Rioja* which impressed him when it came as he thought that *Rioja* was always red.

'Wow, you know your stuff,' he said and we chatted amiably about holidays and languages and national stereotypes. He was fun to be with and, as we got half way down the second bottle and it was getting dark, they lit the candle on our table and I suddenly felt hot.

It was time to remove my scarf. Being as casual as I could, I untied it and put it on the back of my chair. As I turned back to the table Chrissy's eyes were resting on my chest. It wasn't a fleeting glance either. It was a full on, have a really good look, stare.

He collected himself and brought his eyes back to my face. He suddenly looked serious.

'I asked you here tonight because I wanted to thank you,' he said.

'For what?'

'For helping my children…and my Dad.'

'Oh?' I said.

'Yes, really helping them. Edward especially. He's a much happier boy. He's stopped wetting the bed now.'

I had the sudden urge to cry.

'It was school…you know the writing…being left-handed,

and the maths. The thing is, you saw what he needed and you were able to get through to him...and to Lucy. She's got a woman who's her friend and she's more settled.'

'It's so nice of you to say this to me,' I said. 'Not everyone would be so generous.'

'And Dad, you've given him a new lease of life. And I just wanted to be able to say that I've noticed and thank you.'

'Wow, erm, I think I might cry,' I said, tears welling up and threatening to ruin my carefully applied make-up.

'No, don't. Please don't cry, don't spoil that face,' Chrissy said smiling and the mood changed again, back to boy-girl banter.

We left the bar at about ten. It was a mild, late spring evening and I felt full of good food and wine and happiness and gratitude for Chrissy's words. As we walked to the car I realised that I felt something else – the sudden return of that overwhelming desire I'd struggled with. Chrissy was in my life but I wanted him in my bed.

We drove back to my house in comfortable silence, I felt he must be, as was I, reviewing the evening's events, revelling in our new found intimacy. Then Chrissy parked outside my front door and we each unclipped our seatbelts. He turned to look at me. He leaned forward, his chest coming very close to mine, his face close to mine.

'It's been great,' he said and came closer.

'This is it,' I thought, 'This is the moment when everything slots into place, the moment when Chrissy and I acknowledge our feelings.' I closed my eyes and, turning my face to his, opened my lips ready, eager – oh so willing – to receive his kiss.

His lips brushed my cheek, slid over my mouth and slipped off.

Chrissy gave a polite cough whose meaning was quite clear. I'd got it wrong. He wasn't going to snog me – he'd been trying to give me a social kiss goodnight.

I wanted to keep my eyes closed. I didn't know how I

would meet his eye. I didn't know how I was going to get out of the car and into the house without screaming. How would I live with myself? How could I have got it SO wrong? So much, so bloody much for the wisdom of the body language experts. I'd misread it all.

'I, I, I'm sorry,' Chrissy said and I had to open my eyes. 'I didn't mean...'

'No, it was my fault,' I said, opening the car door and gulping in the cool night air, 'Thank you for a lovely evening.'

I heard his car start as I walked up the path and he drove away just as I got into the house. I locked the door behind me and slid down the wall, landing on the cold floor with a bump. I turned on my side into a foetal position and groaned like a wounded animal. How was I going to face him after this? How could I bear the shame? Years from now I'd still wake up in a muck sweat thinking about the horror of that moment when Chrissy made it clear he didn't want me; he didn't think of me in that way.

Dawn came to the rescue. 'Get up Ro,' she said in my head, 'You've got work in the morning. Have some cocoa, go to bed. Try to sleep.' I knew she was right so I did as she said.

20

Desperate Measures

As soon as I woke the next day, I knew what I had to do. I made the appointment for Thursday and just hoped I could survive until then. Mercifully, Ted came to open up and cash up on Wednesday – I thought that Chrissy must have arranged that to avoid seeing me so I was still in one piece when I got to the hairdresser at eight o'clock on Thursday morning.

Robert gave me his usual effusive greeting but looked quizzically at me. 'You're looking fierce today,' he said.

'Cut it off, cut it all off,' I said, And dye what's left bright red!'

'Whoa there, little lady,' said Robert in a fair approximation of John Wayne at his most irritating. It worked. I stopped thinking about my hair and looked at him in shocked surprise.

'OK, that's better,' he said. 'Now, something's happened, hasn't it?' I nodded.

'Something to do with a guy?' I nodded again.

'Something so bad that you want a completely new look, so you can feel different?'

I nodded again. There was no need for therapy in my dire situation; my hairdresser knew it all.

'OK, I understand,' said Robert, 'And I will cut you hair shorter and I will colour it but I'm not going to cut it all off and I'm not going to colour it bright red.'

'Why not? It's my hair,' I said defiantly.

'Because you'll hate it by lunchtime and you'll think it's all my fault and, anyway, in order to sell flowers, you don't need to look like one,' said Robert firmly. I glared at him in the mirror.

'What we'll do is get you a cup of coffee and a nice blueberry muffin while I mix the colour and then I'm going to give you a semi-permanent auburn rinse so that it'll wash out over the next few weeks,' said Robert calmly and authoritatively. I looked at him with respect.

'I've been through this with so many clients, you wouldn't believe it,' he said. 'Some bloke upsets them and they think it's all down to them and they want to change themselves. I tell you, men and women were designed not to understand one another. I mean, did you ever meet the bloke who wants to change his look after a bust-up with the girlfriend?'

'No,' I said, 'No, they probably go to the pub with their mates,' but I knew that Chrissy wouldn't be doing that, not least because I wasn't his girlfriend.

Robert went to mix my colour and Kylie brought my coffee and muffin. By ten thirty when I left the salon, I had a feathered cut with a longer piece which fell, stylishly, I thought over one eye and my hair was reddish with lots of highlights and lowlights. I liked the cut but I wasn't sure about the colour so I was very grateful to Robert for having been firm with me. In another mad moment, I'd asked for a manicure and now had bright red nails which clashed with my usual lip colour so I had to dash to the nearest chemist to buy a coral lipstick before my lunch date with Bubbles.

I met her at the little Italian place and her jaw dropped when she saw me.

'Oh my goodness, dear,' she said, 'What brought this on?'

'I needed to do it,' I said and then I told her everything, *everything*. Well, alright, I didn't tell her about Chrissy staring at my breasts but I told her about the misunderstanding over the goodnight kiss and she listened to me all the way through, not interrupting, giving me her full attention, nodding now and then and giving my hand a pat, until I'd finished. I took a sip of wine and waited for her verdict.

'It's not your fault, dear,' she said. 'Why wouldn't you want him to kiss you? He's young and single and attractive and so are you. It's quite natural and if the timing wasn't quite right then it's not the end of the world.'

I smiled and felt some of the shame leach away.

'And just think, dear,' she said, 'Just think of the lovely things he said to you. He told you that you'd helped his children – the most precious things to him in this world – and he was grateful to you for that. I think that was a huge compliment.' Bubbles paused to let this sink in.

'And the children are still the most important thing in all of this, aren't they?' she went on and I nodded.

'So, you'll go there later today and go on as if nothing's happened because you want them to feel safe and secure, don't you?'

'Yes, of course I do,' I said, 'I wouldn't dream of giving up Edward's maths lessons just because his father doesn't want to kiss me.'

'Doesn't want to kiss you *yet*. Remember what I said to you before; never say never,' said Bubbles filling up my glass and raising hers to me in a toast to the power of positive thinking.

I got home from lunch feeling a lot better but I still wanted to ring the changes so, as the weather had suddenly become warmer, I swapped my long trousers and boots for pedal pushers and wedges and my jumper for a checked shirt with a cotton sweater thrown over my shoulders. With the new hair, lips and nails, I really did look different. Good. The final touch was a liberal spray of *White Iris* by Trish McEvoy so that I'd smell new and fresh too.

Chrissy opened the door to me and blinked quickly several times. I shot him a look which said 'Don't *say* anything' and shuffled past him into the house. Lucy came running out of the kitchen to greet me and stopped in her tracks.

'Robina! You're not my Robina any more!'

'Of course I'm your Robina,' I said bending to kiss her.

'You even smell different,' Lucy said.

'Don't you like it?' I said.

'I like it but I don't like things to change,' she said and her father sniggered in the background, muttering to himself something I couldn't quite catch but it was to do with babes and sucklings.

'Well, I think I'll go and find Edward,' I said and went upstairs, shaking my head at the obstinacy of the Johnson family.

I needn't have worried about Edward though; he pronounced my new look 'Most becoming,' in his grave way and then we went back to the long division.

Lucy came into see us about an hour later. Her hair was wet and I knew it was an invitation to me to offer to dry it so we went into her bedroom and she sat quietly while I wielded the dryer and brush.

'Robina,' she said, after what seemed like a long silence. She said my name in a way which emphasised the syllables and added more to the final one; 'Ro-bi-n-a-a-a,' she said and I recognised the precursor to a big question.

'Yes, my darling,' I said clenching my stomach muscles in anticipation of what was coming.

'You're not going to change anything else, are you? Cos if you are, I'd like to know before. Before you do it, I mean.'

Why?' I said, perfectly reasonably, I thought.

'Because you're my Robina and I like you the way you are,' Lucy said and I dropped down on my knees beside her.

'I promise,' I said, 'I promise that I'll discuss it with you next time I want a new hairdo.'

'Good,' said Lucy firmly then rewarded me with a wide grin and a sticky kiss on the cheek.

'Glass of wine before you go?' said Chrissy appearing in the doorway. It would have been churlish to refuse so I nodded and followed him to the kitchen where he poured us both a large glass. He picked up his glass and raised it in my direction and said, 'Here's looking at you,' which, for some reason, really annoyed me. I snorted.

'Is something bothering you,' said Chrissy. 'Don't you like the wine? It's that white *Rioja* you ordered the other night, I got it specially for you.'

The mention of the setting for the most embarrassing event of my whole life in this casual manner made me see red.

'No, there's nothing at all wrong with the wine. I, on the other hand, am royally pissed off.'

Chrissy looked dumbfounded – whether on account of my mood or my potty mouthed words I didn't know, nor did I care. 'Why?' he said.

'Because I've had the temerity to have a new hair cut and colour and you and Lucy are behaving as if I've committed a terrible crime,' I said.

'Well we're entitled to our view,' said Chrissy, wrinkling his brow in a way which indicated that he was the one who was being fair.

'And this has *what* to do with *you*?' I hissed.

'Whoa,' he said, putting up his hands in a gesture of thus far and no further. I wondered why no-one had ever said 'whoa' to me before and then they'd said it twice in one day but, whatever the reason, it was bloody annoying.

'I cannot believe that it's any of your business,' I said, pulling myself up to my full height and willing Chrissy to stare me down.

He dropped his eyes first and said, 'You're right, you're absolutely right, it's nothing to do with me but Lucy's different. She needs you. She loves you…she loves your visits, I mean, and she seemed a little upset, that's all.'

My defiance disappeared. My shoulders sagged and I put my hand on the table for support. 'I understand that,' I said, 'And I've already promised her I'll consult her before any drastic makeovers in the future'.

'Good', said Chrissy and gave me a smile which came from

his heart, reached all the way to his eyes and made my knees melt.

Back at home, I sank onto the sofa again and reviewed my situation. Still in love with Chrissy Johnson? Tick. Still in lust with Chrissy Johnson? Tick. Still in love with the Johnson family? Tick. Still hoping for a good outcome? No tick.

It was best, it was much the best thing, I decided to get on with my job and get on with my life as a single woman rather than live in hope. I half remembered a quote from somewhere and felt that it perfectly described my feelings – the despair I could cope with, it was the hope that was killing me.

I couldn't flick a switch and fall out of love with Chrissy but I could get on with the rest of my life which was, actually, looking promising; I owned outright a nice house in a good part of London, I'd got my health back, I had a really interesting job which I loved, I'd lost weight and I had something of a social life. These were all really positive things on which I could build and the first thing to concentrate on was my job.

21

Business Not Quite As Usual

I was ready for my next meeting with Ted. I had brochures and drawings and costings for the uniform and I could see he was actually beginning to think it was a good idea. We agreed we'd invite the sales assistants to Sunday lunch at a local hotel followed by my presentation in their conference room. I liked this as it offered them chance for some team building over lunch and we'd all have had a glass or two before I got up and spoke to them. I was used to making presentations – I'd done a lot of it in my previous career but I hadn't done it for some time and I hadn't presented to an audience of women before. The thought of it made me quite nervous as I imagined that some of them, at least, would think I had a nerve wanting to change things when I'd been in the company less than a year.

Ted and I agreed we'd set the date for the Sunday lunch three weeks ahead so the assistants would have time to arrange their family life around Mum not being there for once and in the hope we'd have a hundred percent attendance rate. In the end, it was more than a hundred percent since Olive decided she'd like to come too and then several other women from the office joined in and, finally, Chrissy said he'd like to come as well. 'It's turning into a blooming works outing,' said Ted, 'Why don't we all go to Blackpool?'

'Haven't you done anything like this before?' I asked and he shook his head.

'That's why everybody wants to come,' I said. 'And it's good because it means they're interested.'

'Sunday lunch for fifteen it is then,' said Ted.

I spent ages thinking about how I'd broach the subject of a uniform and whether I needed slides or a Powerpoint presentation but, in the end, decided they'd all be full of roast beef and Yorkshire pudding and that I should be brief and purposeful. In the meantime, I'd had an idea about the uniform but I needed to act quickly.

The appointed Sunday came about quickly enough and Ted came to pick me up so I'd be able to enjoy his hospitality to the full. I opened the front door to him and he gave me one of his winning smiles, 'That's better,' he said.

'What is?' I said.

'Your hair, it's back to normal now,' he said, 'Or is that another of my unacceptably sexist remarks?'

'No, it's quite acceptable, as it happens,' I said, 'You're entitled to think that red hair doesn't suit me and I'd be inclined to agree with you.'

'I like the dress though', he said and I smiled.

It was a new dress, specially bought for the occasion – thick cotton, blue background covered in big yellow and white daisies, semi-fitted, elbow-length sleeves and a Peter Pan collar. It made me feel young and pretty – what more can you ask for in a dress?

When we got to the hotel, Lucy made a beeline for me and threw herself at my legs.

'You look pretty,' she said.

'So do you,' I said and she grabbed hold of my left hand while Ted put a glass of wine into my right. Some of the other guests were milling around, drinks in hand, but a lot of the sales assistants, my target audience, were sitting on big sofas grouped around little round tables. They kept stealing glances at me and I held on tightly to Lucy's hand as a kind of security blanket in the face of the unknown.

I sat between Lucy and Edward at lunch and didn't have

much to do with the adult conversations going on around me but I could hear that they were all going well and any initial uneasiness was dispelled by the good food and plentiful wine. No-one dared order a pudding after the huge main course so it was while they were having coffee that I excused myself and went to the 'Ladies Powder Room' to change.

Ted knew what I was up to and shepherded his guests from the dining room into the small conference room we'd chosen as being intimate enough but not too poky. Ted was standing at the head of the large table with everyone seated around him when I came in. They all turned to look at me and there were a few dropped jaws.

I went to stand next to Ted and smiled at the rest of the room.

'Well, ladies, you've not come to listen to me, you've come to listen to Rowena, our Commercial Manager, and I'd like you to listen carefully to what she has to say. Over to you, Rowena.'

I stood in silence for just a second to let them look carefully at my uniform but I didn't say anything about it. Instead I talked for a while about the economy and how businesses had to change to keep pace with new challenges. I talked about inflation and said they'd know all about it as their weekly shopping basket got more expensive and the winter fuel bills became ever more frightening. I saw that some of them were a little hostile to me at the beginning, sitting with closed faces and their arms folded in front of their torsos, but I knew I hit home with the stuff about their own struggles with inflation. Then I asked how a business becomes more profitable. Is it all to do with price? Not exclusively, I said; in a luxury business like flowers, customer service was equally important.

How could we improve customer service, I asked.

'You can smile at them', said Edward, breaking the silence after my question.

'Too right,' I said, 'I absolutely agree with you Edward, a smile is worth a lot on a grey day or any day. Anything else?

Can anyone think of anything else?'

'Say 'please' and 'thank you'?' said a little, mousy looking woman who, Ted had told me some time before, had a husband in jail for armed robbery.

'Quite right, 'please' and 'thank you' go a long way to oiling the wheels of commerce,' I said. 'Anything else?'

'Look smart', said Olive.

'Yes, that's a really good idea, isn't it?' I said.

'Now does anybody here think I look smart? Put up your hands, please, if you think I do'.

Edward put up his hand, Ted did the same, Lucy followed, then Chrissy then Olive, wonderful Olive, put up her hand and several of the shop assistants put up theirs.

'Good. This, ladies and gentlemen is the new uniform for Johnsons's shops. Just think, ladies,' I said, gesturing to the shop assistants round the table, 'Just think how this will give you more time in the morning – you won't need to waste a minute thinking about what you're going to wear and you won't be ruining your own clothes in the shop any more.'

There were some smiles, some of the women readily accepted my arguments in favour of the uniform but there were still several who looked unconvinced.

'Is there any choice?' said a large woman with blonde hair and several inches of dark root.

'I'm glad you asked that question. Yes, there is, you can choose either a white polo shirt or a yellow one and you can have either a dark green apron or a black one,' I said, happy that some of the other women smiled at this.

'No, I didn't mean that. I meant, is there any choice about wearing this or not?'

'Er, I, um…'

'No, there isn't,' said Ted, 'And it's a good thing. You'll be provided with three sets of your colour choice and all you have to do is keep them clean and wear them when you're at work. It's a good deal.'

'I never said it wasn't Mr Johnson, I just wanted to know

the score, that's all,' said the woman.

'Can we have two yellow shirts and one white one and two green aprons and a black one?' said the mousy woman.

'No', said Ted.

'Yes', said I, at the same time as Ted said 'No.'

Ted and I looked at one another and then he said, 'Yes.'

'I think it's a good idea,' said the mousy woman.

'Me too,' said Olive, 'I only wish they were handing out uniforms for the office.'

'That's next week,' I said and they all laughed.

The firm's outing repaired to the bar shortly after and when I came in, back in my daisy dress, Chrissy strode over to me, handed me a glass of champagne, and said, 'You handled that really well. Putting on the uniform was a stroke of genius.' I smiled at him and sipped my champagne. It was wonderful to know that he appreciated my brain and my business skills but his closeness and the fact that he was whispering in my ear made my traitorous body ache for him.

We all chatted in the bar for about an hour and, if Ted and I had planned it as a team building exercise, it couldn't have gone better. People started to drift away at about 5 o'clock and Ted and I were about to leave when he took me to one side.

'I wanted to ask you something before we go,' he said.

'What is it?'

'Well, we've just heard from one of Chrissy's late wife's cousins in Italy,' said Ted, pausing to let me decipher the relationship. I nodded indicating that I was with him so far.

'His name's Massimiliano Falcone and he's coming to over here to do a business degree this autumn and he wants to come early to brush up his English,' he paused again and I nodded again.

'Well, I wondered if I could sort of billet him with you, during the daytime, that is? I thought you'd be the best person to teach him the business words.'

I considered it for a few seconds and couldn't see too much of a downside. I didn't speak Italian but I assumed that

Massimiliano Falcone spoke reasonably good English and I imagined he'd be keen to learn the rest so I didn't really mind baby-sitting a student. It might be quite fun, actually.

'No, I don't mind, I don't mind at all,' I said, 'I'd be glad to.'

'Oh, that's a relief. Thank you. I'll tell them that he can come then. He'll be staying with us, obviously. He's arriving at the beginning of July so I hope you don't have any holiday plans for then,' said Ted.

I hadn't given a holiday a moment's thought and it caused me a pang that there probably wasn't anyone I could go with but I smiled and said, 'No, I haven't any plans for then. I don't like to go in the school holidays.'

'Good. And well done for today, jolly well done,' said Ted giving me a hug.

22

A Taste of Italy

Ted and I worked out the detailed plan for the refurbishment of the shops and agreed my Chipstone premises would be first. The painters, carpenters and sign-writers would work in the evening and at weekends to minimise disruption to the business and I couldn't wait to see the results.

Bit by bit, the old, tired shop disappeared under fresh new paint and smart new laminate flooring. When my Farrow & Ball Hardwick White painted tongue and groove counter with its faux-marble top was installed I thought I'd cry with joy. I went out into the street and tried to look at the shop with a customer's eyes. The exterior looked chic and inviting and the cool interior would provide a perfect backdrop for a display of blooms; I felt that in making the flowers the stars of the show, we'd got it right. I imagined the shelves filled with Ted's choice of gorgeous, colourful, architectural flowers and couldn't wait for opening time the next day when I'd welcome the first customer to my new shop.

It was Bubbles who was first through the door.

'It looks fabulous, dear,' she said, 'You are a clever girl.'

I handed her a stunning bouquet of delphiniums and green chrysanthemums mixed with grey velvety scencio maritime leaves as a gift from me and she made me a cup of tea while I sorted out the piles of tissue paper on the counter. We chatted for a while and, when she left, I watched my friend walk down the street and had one of those surging moments when you feel everything is fine, that things will work out and the world is really a nice place.

My shop's profitability climbed on the back of the refit and, as the other shops were transformed, their profits slowly followed. Ted and I met regularly on Monday mornings and my next challenge was to persuade him we needed a handbook of bouquets so we were offering the same service across all the shops. He didn't quite follow what I meant at first but I explained it needn't be costly and all we had to do was take photos of the bouquets I made and put them in a laminated book as examples for the other shops of what could be done with the flowers.

Ted stroked his chin for a while then said, 'Supposing they have their own ideas?'

'Well, they haven't yet,' I said, 'I've checked and, anyway, we'll say the photos are only examples.'

'That's what I'm worried about,' said Ted. 'Suppose they get ideas and make up something of their own? Suppose they make up a bouquet of pink lilies, blue lisianthus and orange dahlias?'

'Well that would look terrible,' I said.

'Exactly, so we need to make the book a standard, don't we?' he said.

'It'll have to come from you, then,' I said, 'I don't want to be blamed for being little Miss Hitler, making all sorts of rules and regulations.'

'You make up the book and I'll sell it to the troops,' said Ted.

So I spent a week or two taking pictures of the bouquets I'd made and sourced the right kind of folders so we could add and subtract pictures as the seasons and the stock changed. I enjoyed all this bustle and activity and seeing the results meant I went home at night tired but happy.

Spring ran into summer. Chrissy and I were more at ease in one another's company – the elephant had gone – but he was at pains to hold me at a distance; even when I was at the house seeing the children, he stayed in the kitchen and didn't join in our games. As June gave way to July, I worked with Ted on the company's website. It was not easy. Ted was no-one's idea of a silver surfer and had no truck with computers or the internet; he just didn't understand that they were essential in modern day life and to the future of his business. Ted and I usually worked well together but we were at loggerheads over this.

The thing was he couldn't understand why it's so costly to put together a really effective website. I explained that we needed good web design, eye-catching graphics and Search Engine Optimisation in order for the site to work and he followed my argument until I made the mistake of talking about 'SEO' whereupon his eyes went glazed and he said, 'Rowena, if you want to spend twenty five grand of the company's money, on top of all this refurbishment, then please have the courtesy to speak to me in a language I understand.' He said it in a nice way but the meaning was clear – there were limits to what I would be allowed to do and I knew then to abandon my idea that we should have a laptop or tablet in every shop so that I could instantly update the bouquet designs based on that day's delivery.

One Tuesday at the beginning of July, I was busy making bouquets with new stock and photographing them when I saw Ted's van pull up outside the shop. I wasn't expecting him and was in the middle of dealing with a tricky bit of foliage so went back to what I was doing.

I heard footsteps outside the shop and the jingle of the bell as the door opened. Out of the corner of my eye I could see two pairs of male feet – Ted's in the steel toe capped boots he wore to the market and another pair in immaculately clean, expensive, black loafers. The woody fruity aroma of *Hugo Boss Baldessarini* hit me just as Ted said, 'Rowena this is Massimiliano Falcone, from Milan. You said you'd look after him for the summer.'

I looked up from the shoes, past long strong legs and a wide chest clad in what looked like Armani and a brilliant white shirt, open at the collar, past thick, black, wavy hair to dark eyes which were dancing with amusement. I'd expected a gawky teenager but this guy was at least mid-thirties and drop dead beautiful – think Rufus Sewell as Aurelio Zen but with more hair and eyes like big, shiny chocolate buttons and you'll get the idea.

I dropped my shears on the counter and hoped that my hands weren't all sweaty from their labours. I toyed with the idea of wiping them on my apron but decided against it. I held out my hand and said, 'How do you do.'

'I'm pleased to meet you at last,' said Massimiliano, 'I've heard a lot about you.'

'Oh really?' I said, 'I hope most of it was good.'

'All of it was excellent and please call me 'Massi', it's less of a mouthful,' he said and I shouldn't have done it but I looked at his mouth when he said it.

'Well, I'll be off then,' said Ted, 'I'll leave you in Rowena's capable hands and pick you up when I come to cash up'. He left and I was left wondering what to do with Massi for the rest of the day. He looked as if he'd be more at home on a catwalk than a suburban shop and, insofar as I'd thought about how to occupy Ted's Italian visitor, I'd assumed I'd be looking after a boy in his late teens rather than a mature, handsome man. I had to be honest with him.

'Er, I haven't got a programme worked out,' I said. 'When Ted asked me to work with you over the summer, he told me you were coming to sharpen up your English before you went to University.'

'And you thought I'd be an undergraduate. An eighteen year old?' said Massi laughing and showing off his blindingly white teeth. I wondered if I should fall to my knees and worship this amazing creature there and then.

'Well, yes, I did,' I said.

'Ah, I understand. Well, my story is a little bit different,' said Massi pronouncing 'little' as '*leetle*'. 'You see in my family we think that you need to study the practice before you find out about the theory so I went to work in the family firm, in the factory, when I was eighteen.'

'That sounds wise to me. What kind of business is it?' I said.

'It's a sweet factory. We make *torrone*, I think you call it nougat,' he said.

This made me want to laugh. Massi, this god from Olympus worked in a sweet factory! I didn't laugh though, I merely smiled and said, 'Oh, that's interesting. Your business is a bit like ours in that you're selling a luxury item – something people buy as a treat rather than a necessity.'

'Yes, that's right,' he said, 'And it's seasonal too. We sell most at Christmas and Easter.'

'Ha!' I said, 'They're busy times for us too but we also do well at Valentine's Day and Mothers' Day.'

Suddenly, I could see that, apart from Massi's extreme capacity to be easy on the eye, there were aspects of our businesses which were common and we could possibly be helpful to one another and it was not going to be a hardship to 'mentor' him for a few weeks.

'So you worked in the family factory for a while and then what? I said.

'I worked at many jobs. I swept the floor to begin with, then I operated machines for a while, then I went out with my uncle buying the ingredients and then I worked in the sales office and the accounting office and only then did my father let me go to University.'

'Wow,' I said, 'So you really learned the business from bottom to top?'

'I did,' he said, pronouncing 'did' as '*deed*'. 'Then I went away to study *beesniss* in Rome and when I graduated my father and my uncle appointed me to the board. I was thirty years old by then and they felt I was mature enough to make sensible decisions.'

185

'And what now?' I asked.

'Now I come to do a postgraduate degree in international marketing,' Massi said.

'Why?'

'Because we're selling more and more product abroad and we need to know how to maximise our sales in places like the States, the UK and the Middle East,' he said.

'Oh, that's interesting. I was in international sales myself. I was Head of European Sales Section for one of our big manufacturers, my degree was in Economics and Business Studies,' I said.

'And now you're Commercial Manager for Johnson's Flowers?' said Massi, meaning, 'Isn't that a bit of a comedown?'

'It's a long story,' I said, 'But basically I needed a 'little job' when I was getting divorced and Ted kindly took me on as a Sales Assistant but it's grown a lot from there and we're really going places. The business had been allowed to drift for some time and was losing profitability...' I tailed off, realising we were straying into delicate territory involving his cousin's death.

'Yes, Ted told me all about it. He said you'd given the company the jolt it needed,' said Massi.

'I, I, er, realise how awful it must have been for you all,' I said, 'To lose three generations of your family all in one horrible accident. It must have been unbearable. I was so sorry to hear about it,' I said.

'Thank you,' said Massi, 'It was a dreadful time for us all but you have to move on. What do they say? Life has to go on.'

At that moment I became aware of a phenomenon which I was to see time and again over the following weeks – a woman going past the shop, catching sight of Massi, her jaw dropping and her very nearly losing her footing as she strained for a better look at him before smiling and striding on with a spring in her step.

'I think you're causing a bit of a stir in the neighbourhood,' I said, pointing to the woman and Massi smiled at me in a conspiratorial manner.

'I guess it's the suit,' he said.

'Sure it is,' said I. 'And we need to do something about that because you can't possibly work here in a suit. I'll ring Ted and get him to bring you a uniform shirt and apron. Do you have any black trousers or jeans?'

Massi nodded. 'Good, they'll do fine under the apron. Remember to wear them tomorrow,' I said.

Ted brought the garments and some lunch for us. Massi removed his jacket and hung it up in the little kitchen at the back of the shop while I was eating my sandwich. Then he started to unbutton his shirt showing a tanned chest lightly covered in black hair. I didn't know if he was doing it on purpose but it was very unsettling so I excused myself and went back into the shop while he changed into one of the polo shirts.

It turned out that Massi had a good eye for design. He was helpful in putting the bouquets together and we often had a window full of gorgeous arrangements made by him and me. We became quite competitive over it, squabbling light-heartedly over the more outlandish flowers and hooting with laughter at the antics of some of the customers.

Massi was a gifted mimic and sometimes he'd do impersonations of people for my amusement. Obviously, he always did this out of sight in the back of the shop. Our sales figures went up again – partly due to the refit, partly due to there being more bouquets but mostly, truth to tell, because Massi himself was attracting people into the shop.

The number of new customers we gained during that time was enormous. They were nearly all women of a certain age and socio-economic class – early middle aged, well-preserved, rich, possibly trophy wives types – who came ostensibly to buy flowers but really to flirt with Massi and he gave them very good value for money, playing up to them like a pro. We also gained a few new gay customers – immaculately dressed metropolitan guys with perfect teeth, hair and nails who came to salivate over the god in the black apron and were more outrageous in their appreciation of his charms than the trophy wives club. It was these flirty customers, male and female, whom he impersonated and I was often crying with laughter at his antics.

One afternoon we were waiting in the back of the shop for Ted to come and cash up and Massi was giving a virtuoso performance as a particularly insistent woman with a large, most likely silicone, chest and I was helpless with laughter when the doorbell went. Massi was pretending surreptitiously to hoist up his huge bosoms but also to draw attention to them while studying the floral displays and I was hanging onto the little fridge for support because I was finding it hard to breathe through all the laughter.

'What the bloody hell is going on in here?' said Chrissy, 'I can hear you two in the street.'

I still couldn't speak so I waved my hands in protest at his misreading of the noise.

'I am making Rowena laugh,' said Massi. He pronounced my name as '*Rovina*.' I hadn't tried to teach him to pronounce it correctly. I found his mispronunciation charming.

'Well can't you do it a bit more quietly?' said Chrissy, 'People will wonder what the noise is all about.'

I'd recovered my voice by then and was just a little bit angry that our innocent bit of fun was being frowned upon by the self-appointed Headmaster.

'I think you'll find that it hasn't affected the takings. You'll find that they're at record levels. Why don't you go and check?' I said.

'Why don't I?' said Chrissy stomping off into the shop.

I tidied up the kitchen while Chrissy checked the till and the takings. I knew he couldn't argue with me about the money we'd taken but as I entered the shop I saw from the set of his shoulders, even from the back, that he was angry.

'All in order, then?' I said, coming round to the front and raising an eyebrow at him.

'Perfectly in order, thank you,' he said, putting a sarcastic emphasis on the 'thank you.'

'Good, I'll be off then. See you tomorrow.'

'See you,' said Massi, 'I'll be looking forward to it.'

Chrissy glared at him and said nothing to me.

At that moment Ted appeared, humming gaily. Chrissy gave his father a cutting look but Ted ignored him.

'I thought you'd want to know that I've got the figures and last month's sales from this shop were a record. They were the highest sales we've ever had for all the shops even at Christmas' said Ted, raising his palms upwards as if he were encouraging an audience to applaud.

'Wow, oh wow! I said, 'That's fantastic Ted. I'm so pleased!'

'Congratulations,' said Massi, 'And I'm sure a great deal of it is down to Rovina.'

'No, a lot of it is down to you too,' I said.

'I think I'm going now before we get to the group hug,' said Chrissy sourly.

'Oh, stop it,' said Ted, 'This is really good news. And I came to say that I think it's time that Rowena went to market on her own. Unless Massi wants to go with her, that is?'

'I'd be delighted,' said Massi, 'It would be a great pleasure.'

'Good,' said Chrissy to Massi, 'That means you have to get up at one in the morning tomorrow instead of me and I can lie in bed.' He didn't look pleased about it though.

I was pleased. I was delighted, even though I'd have to be up just after midnight to be able to pick Massi up in time from Chrissy's house. I was on a high and felt full of energy.

23

Meals On Wheels

It was high summer and not really a hardship to be getting out of bed almost as soon as I'd got into it. The prospect of being able to choose my own flowers was alluring and, let's be honest, several hours of Massi's company away from the shop also had its attractions.

By this time, I'd lost so much weight that I was back in jeans I'd not worn for years and so I poured myself into a nice skinny black pair and teamed them with a dove grey marl T-shirt and strong trainers (fashion footwear was a no-no at the market) at about forty five minutes after midnight. It was dark so I had to put my make-up on in artificial light but I'd allowed myself the time to do it carefully. After a quick spritz of *Chanel No. 19*, I threw my trusty grey boyfriend cardigan over my shoulders and left the house.

Massi was already waiting outside Chrissy's house and jumped into the van with more energy than I felt at that early hour. We didn't speak much until we were getting close to the market and I explained to him what to expect.

We parked the car, put on our hi-vis jackets and entered the market. What I hadn't expected and so hadn't warned Massi about were the wolf-whistles and cat-calls which our appearance attracted; as we walked down the aisles between the various stalls both men and women whooped and hollered and whistled and shouted as though we were strippers performing to a group of guys who'd been marooned on a desert island for years.

'Is it always like this?' said Massi, 'When you come here?'

'Not when I come with Ted, no,' I said, 'I think they must think you're a male model or something and they're having a little joke.'

'Ah, the famed English sense of humour,' said Massi before putting his hand on his hip and mincing down the aisle to the delight of the stallholders. He then took off his jacket and trailed it behind him on the floor just like a supermodel and, even though it was still only three a.m., I thought I'd die laughing. He was amazing.

Once the stallholders had calmed down and we started talking business, Massi proved he was as intelligent as he was handsome by asking questions showing he'd learned a lot about the business and was interested in it. We agreed on most of the purchases for the day and then went for a bacon butty and cup of coffee.

'So Rovina, this is your life?' he said.

'Well, it's part of it. There are other things in my life,' I said but I was hoping he wasn't going to ask me about them as I wasn't sure what I could say.

'But there is no husband, no children?'

'No, I'm divorced, quite recently really, after ten years' marriage and we didn't have any children,' I said, blushing for no apparent reason.

'You didn't want children?' said Massi. He pronounced 'children' as '*cheeldren*'.

'No, yes, no…what I mean is we *did*, I *did*, want children but we didn't manage to conceive,' I said, blushing again and hoping that Massi hadn't noticed his companion had turned into an embarrassed fifteen year old.

'And that broke up the marriage?' Massi asked.

I didn't know quite what to make of this. I would have expected these questions from a woman whom I'd known for a few weeks but it was unusual in my experience for a man to delve into personal details in such depth and I wondered if it was a cultural thing or whether he was just much more sensitive than might be imagined. I thought for a few moments before answering.

'I'm sorry Rovina, I didn't mean to pry. I shouldn't have asked. It is none of my beesniss', said Massi, 'It's just that a lovely woman like you deserves a husband and a family.'

This made me want to cry and I had to blow my nose and take several sips of my coffee before I could meet his eyes.

'Thank you,' I said, 'You're very kind.'

'I'm not kind. I mean it,' he said.

We finished choosing our flowers, loaded them into the van and drove through the streets of London as the day was just getting under way for the rest of the city.

'I like this time of day,' said Massi. 'It's full of promise. When you are awake and alert so early, there is nothing you cannot achieve. What is it you say in English – the early bird catches the worm?'

'Ah yes, we do say that but my father who likes to stay in bed puts it the other way – he says that the early worm gets caught by the bird,' I said.

'I never thought of it like that. Your father, he is a philosopher?' said Massi.

'No, my father is a selfish pig who left my mother when she was terminally ill but he had a stack of good one-liners,' I said and Massi must have thought that he'd cross-examined me enough because he was silent until we got to the shop.

I noticed a difference in Massi's attitude towards me after that. Where he'd been funny and teasing before, making me laugh at every opportunity, he became considerate, kind, thoughtful and very helpful. He'd offer to go to Starbuck's to get me a Frappuccino or he'd offer to take my car to the carwash, he'd open doors for me and, several times, I just caught him looking at me and when I looked up and saw him doing it, he'd smile that devastating smile and my stomach would do somersaults.

Our sales figures continued to rise much to Ted's delight but I was finding it more of a chore to keep on photographing the arrangements and sending the pictures out to the other shops.

'Why don't you just e-mail the pictures?' said Massi one day.

I gave a laugh heavily laced with irony. 'Because Ted won't have iPads in the shops. He doesn't get it that it would save so much time and effort,' I said.

'But you're making a lot more profit here now and it would improve efficiency,' said Massi.

'You're singing my song,' I said. 'But I've tried telling Ted and he won't listen.'

'Perhaps he will listen if we both tell him,' said Massi and we agreed we'd make a joint case to Ted.

Our joint case was made the following Monday morning at the weekly meeting with Ted. Massi was allowed to come because he was being mentored by me and because he was family to the Johnsons. We sat facing Ted, looking into the strong morning sun. Ted was in a good mood – as sunny as the weather.

'OK, well it's been a record month, Rowena. The shops look great, the bouquets are doing really well and I think Massi here has helped boost sales,' said Ted.

'We're going great guns,' I said. 'But there are still improvements to be made. The website isn't ready yet and even with Massi's help photographing the arrangements and then getting them out to the shops is a distraction. It's not taking the pictures that's the problem it's the printing them off and then distributing them.'

Ted gave me the beginning of a stern look.

'And often the pictures are out of date by the time the other shops get them,' said Massi and Ted gave him a look which meant 'Are you joining in this too'?

Massi took this in his stride and said, 'Well it makes it a waste of time and the other shops then make up their own bouquets.'

'With mixed results,' I added and Ted raised a questioning eyebrow.

'Red carnations, yellow chrysanthemums, gypsophila and elephant grass tied with a blue bow', I said. Ted looked unhappy.

'What do you suggest?' he said.

'It would be best if all the shops had iPads or equivalent,' said Massi while I held my breath. I couldn't see Ted's expression in the sudden shaft of brilliant sunlight which blinded me.

'How much?' said Ted. Massi brought out our spreadsheet from his messenger style man-bag and put it on the table. We'd priced iPads and cheaper alternatives and included the cost of the most useful programs, training and anti-virus protection.

'Anti-virus protection?' said Ted. 'Don't tell me these bloody things catch cold?'

'No but they get invaded by all sorts of stuff you don't want – like a virus,' I said.

'And we could link with the website. We could upload the new arrangements to the website so that it would always be up to the minute,' said Massi.

'It'd avoid expensive mistakes,' I said. 'The carnation, chrysanthemum and gypsophila thing didn't sell'.

Ted was thinking. It was best, I'd found, to remain silent while he was doing that. Olive came in with the coffee. I wondered how Massi, brought up no doubt on wonderful Italian brews, would deal with gritty dishwater from a machine.

We were sitting in silence, sipping our hot beverage when Chrissy came in.

'Blimey, you're all looking serious,' he said.

'I'm thinking, that's all,' said Ted. 'These two want me to buy some of those tablet things and put them in the shops.'

'And?' said Chrissy.

'And I think they've made a good case for it,' said Ted, 'But we'll have one of the cheaper brands and I'll tell Olive to issue a note that the assistants aren't to spend all day doing their shopping on the damn things.'

'Thank you,' I said, smiling.

'Thank you,' said Massi, smiling.

'Another victory for the Two Musketeers,' said Chrissy but he wasn't smiling and he left without saying goodbye. Ted gave his son's disappearing back a mildly amused look and we went back to the spreadsheets.

The next few weeks passed quickly in a flurry of getting the website up and running, getting the tablets installed in the shops, the staff trained how to use them and told not to abuse them and all the while we were trying to keep up our sales figures. It was tiring but exciting and Massi and I worked very well as a team. He was due to leave for his postgraduate course at the end of August and I really wondered how I'd get on without him; I'd become so accustomed to his easy humour and good business sense. And, if I were honest with myself, I just loved having him around – it was good for my ego to have this totally beautiful man hanging on my every word and gently flirting with me most of the day.

Two weeks before he was due to leave, we were talking about food – a topic we often discussed. I was asking Massi about the speciality dishes of Milan and he was telling me about a seafood risotto his grandmother used to make. His face lit up as he recalled as a small boy being at her villa with all the family around and how he and Lucia who was in her early teens but had a great sense of fun would make faces at him across the table while the risotto was being served from a huge pot. It sounded idyllic.

Ah, I wish you could taste my grandmother's risotto,' he said. He pronounced 'wish' as '*weesh*' and I smiled thinking that I wished I'd been able to see them all sitting happily at their big table. Then Massi jumped as if he'd just been struck by something.

'I have it!' he said. '*I will cook it for you!* I will buy the ingredients and I will cook it for you at your house. I will cook it for you!' He was ecstatic at the thought and who was I to argue if a lovely man wanted to cook dinner for me in my own home?

We agreed Massi would cook for me on the Saturday so we'd have time to enjoy the meal without worrying about washing up and work the following day. I bought a new, copper-bottomed pan in readiness and cleaned the house from top to bottom. I changed my sheets, waxed my legs and had my roots done on the Thursday. I was on a high and Robert said I was glowing. When I got home after my hairdo, I removed the spotty wellingtons from the hall and put some of the more outrageously feminine things away – wouldn't want the man to feel he'd strayed into a teenage girl's bedroom by mistake, would we?

I was like a bitch on heat, wondering what would happen, dreaming of being in Massi's arms and more intimate caresses. He was very attentive and almost kissed me in the little kitchen on the Wednesday but someone came into the shop and the moment passed.

I couldn't wait for the Saturday evening and was preoccupied by all my preparations so wasn't firing on all cylinders when Ted turned up half way through Friday afternoon. 'Can I have a word with you Rowena, in private, please?' he said and we went into the kitchen.

'What's happening?' I said.

'Well, the thing is, there's a big dinner coming up in August, in Birmingham. It's the annual get-together for the floristry industry – growers, wholesalers, retailers, you know the kind of thing?'

'Yes,' I said, 'I expect it's black tie and it's a room full of badly dressed people having a second rate, lukewarm dinner and too much to drink while the charity raffle takes half the night and everybody's bored to tears.'

'Oh, so you won't want to come then?' said Ted.

This stopped me in my tracks and I was suddenly all ears. 'Why would I be going?' I said.

'Because I'm inviting you,' said Ted. 'As my 'plus one' I think they call it and because you're this company's Commercial Director. And because, frankly, this is the first year in a while that we've had a lady executive we could take and I want to show my face again.'

'On that basis, I'd be delighted to come,' I said.

'Good. It's at the Majestic Hotel and the company will pay for all the expenses including your room,' said Ted.

'I'll be honoured to accompany you,' I said.

'And you might want to enter the competition?' said Ted.

'What competition?' I said, sensing that Ted was manipulating me, in the nicest way possible.

'The competition for the most innovative arrangement,' he said and left the challenge dangling in the air. 'I'll get Olive to send you all the details about the date and stuff.'

'Fine, I'll look forward to it,' I said, thinking that, in terms of excitement, it didn't hold a candle to the prospect of a private dinner with Massi and…whatever might be served for pudding.

24

Risotto Alla Milanese

We agreed that I would go home on Saturday evening and change while Massi went to the supermarket to get the ingredients for our dinner and then I would pick him up and bring him back to the house. This plan charmed me because it was so thoughtful and like playing happy families; it was a brief and tantalising taste of the happy relationship I so wanted but hadn't yet found.

Saturday at the shop could not go quickly enough for me and I know I was short and possibly a little rude to Chrissy when he came to cash up. He may have sensed my excitement and disapproved of it because he was surly in return. Finally, it was over – the door was locked and I got in my car while Massi set out on foot for the supermarket. Massi called out 'Ciao' to Chrissy and I assumed he'd told him he was going to be out for the evening but I didn't know if he'd said that he was coming over to my house to indulge in a little culinary showmanship and I didn't care too much either way – Chrissy had made his feelings quite plain.

I raced home in record time and was under the shower within a minute of getting through the front door; the house was immaculate and I wanted to match it. I managed not to ruin my hair in the steam by donning one of those ghastly shower caps which you see mature ladies wearing in old Hollywood movies – it felt odd but it did the trick. I slathered my arms, legs and feet in *Clarins* bodycream and put primer on my face so my make-up would be flawless. Next was the super-whitening toothpaste for the smile that would get me noticed and my choice of *Shalimar* as my perfume for the evening as it made me feel very feminine and just a bit dangerous. Then I put on my 'best' bottle green silk knickers and the gorgeous new dark green lacy bra I'd bought recently; since I'd lost weight my boobs had regained their former perkiness and didn't need the kind of heavy-duty support they'd required in the IVF years. Under the black silk cardigan the bra gave me enough support to be comfortable but still with a very natural outline – so far so good.

I pulled on my new white jeans and slipped my feet into my black suede wedges. Gold hoops were my only jewellery apart from my watch and then I did my face. I kept it simple – just a light covering of foundation, a bit of powder to set it, some lilac eye-shadow to bring out the grey/green of my eyes, black liner and a slick of deep pink gloss; it wouldn't look right to be done up like a dog's dinner for supper in my own home. I brushed my hair and looked in the full length mirror – not bad, not bad at all. The outer and the inner me matched – an attractive, mature woman who knew what she wanted and didn't mind going out (or staying in!) to get it.

The doorbell rang just as I was coming down the stairs. Excellent. I opened the door and in came Massi and several bulging carrier-bags. 'Where to?' he said and I pointed the way to the kitchen. He plonked the bags on the table and looked round. 'Nice house,' he said, 'But I don't see my friend Rovina in here. Where are you?'

'It was decorated more to my ex-husband's taste than mine,' I said.

'Poor baby,' said Massi and kissed me on the cheek as he passed by to get to the sink. He put the Arborio rice into a sieve and ran it under the cold water tap. His bum wiggled slightly as he jiggled the rice. I had a vision of his naked bottom and wondered how his skin would feel under my fingertips. It was a delicious thought but it was too early in the evening to think of jumping him.

'Drink?' I said and he nodded while he removed a little packet of saffron and some Normandy butter from one of the carrier bags.

Then he brought my heart to a standstill. 'I'm cheating here,' he said with a guilty look and I thought he was going to tell me about his lovely wife and beautiful cheeldren in Milan and I'd have to swallow my desire and disappointment and be gracious and say that of course I'd guessed he was married.

'How, how are you cheating?' I said, as coolly as I could muster.

'Well, I'm going to use a ready made beef stock and my grandmother would *keel* me if she knew. She always boiled the veal bones herself,' he said and I smiled indulgently at him across the table.

Massi took the new copper-bottomed pan and started the risotto by melting a big knob (my mind made the connection with what was nestling in Massi's trousers – dirty mind!) of the butter, adding the rice and the stock and letting it cook very gently. It smelled good and we chatted while it bubbled gently for about five minutes. Then Massi added some fresh garden peas to the mixture and the aroma changed again. He explained that the classic dish doesn't use peas but his grandmother liked them so she added them as her variation. By this time, we were most of the way down a bottle of Pino Grigio Blush and I was feeling very amorous.

But I was also hungry. 'How long?' I said and thought again of a double meaning for this innocent question; it was amazing how filthy my mind could be when my baser instincts were engaged.

'Oh, another twenty minutes or so,' said Massi adding some precious strands of saffron to the mixture in the pan and the aroma changed yet again. It occurred to me that this kind of slow cooking, of melding very simple ingredients into a masterpiece which tasted subtly of them all but in which none of them dominated, was a kind of alchemy and it was a pleasure to watch Massi bring it to life in my kitchen. I opened the second bottle of Blush and poured a generous slug of it into our glasses. Massi took a big chunk of Parmesan from one of the carrier bags and gave me an interrogatory look asking where he might find the grater. I gave it to him and put two large warmed white china soup plates on the table. I was ravenous by this time and the risotto, which had acquired a deep yellow colour, smelled wonderful.

'Coming up!' said Massi, ladling steaming mounds of his grandmother's fabled dish onto my plate and similar amounts onto his own. He deftly grated a nice mound of Parmesan on top of my rice and the same for himself and then this god, this perfect man, sat down at my kitchen table and invited me to eat.

I took a forkful and put it in my mouth. It was soft and yielding but had a definite texture equally based in the smooth, round peas and the more gritty rice. The flavour was complex and multi-layered and I loved it so much that a small moan of pleasure escaped from my chest.

'It's good, isn't it?' said Massi.

'It's very good,' said I, thinking that this evening might be the most pleasurable of my whole life.

We ate in comfortable mutual appreciation of the dish. I had seconds and a small third portion and Massi ate all the rest. We finished the second bottle of Blush and started the third with the orange and rosewater polenta cake he'd cleverly found at the supermarket deli counter. After all of that, coffee was needed and I made strong espresso while Massi loaded the dishwasher.

'Shall we have our coffee in the sitting room?' I said, trying to make my voice sound normal.

'Good idea,' said Massi, allowing me to leave the room first and show him the way. I went and sat on the sofa – very much at one end of it so there was plenty of room for another person.

Massi came and sat next to me. My heart beat

uncomfortably hard and fast and I thought I'd stop breathing with excitement and longing for him. He put his arm along the back of the sofa behind me, the textbook move of the guy who's going to make a move on the woman. He turned towards me and I looked at him, my heart in my mouth and pounding so much I knew, if he didn't kiss me, I'd have a heart attack there and then.

He brought his face closer to mine and moved in. I closed my eyes as he put his mouth to mine. I was just getting that lovely sinking feeling of giving myself up to an overwhelming passion and pleasure when doubt began to crowd in as Massi filled my mouth with saliva and practically dribbled over my face. Imagine being drooled on by an enthusiastic St Bernard and you'll get the idea. I was wondering whether I could cope with this and then he did it. He did the thing that killed my ardour stone dead; stopped my hormones in their tracks. I don't know what it is about the female psyche and our attitude to sex but, from teenage fumblings onwards, I've been capable of raging passion one minute and stone cold nothingess the next just because the guy in question has done something tacky like crack his knuckles.

Massi didn't do that. He did something worse. He did something unbelievably crass and utterly juvenile and afterwards I couldn't, I just couldn't, regard him as a person suitable for access to my intimate parts; it was as though he'd flicked a switch and the woman who wanted him with every cell of her body suddenly wanted him to leave.

It was such a fleeting thing, a thing of just a few moments but it revealed a whole aspect of Massi that I didn't want to know; while he was giving me his slack, sloppy kiss, he took my hand and crooked his middle finger and tickled my palm, back and forward, his finger tracing a path across my hand.

Such a small gesture. Such a smutty, silly thing to do. Maybe it was a cultural thing – maybe only the best people in Italy did this. Maybe it was a great compliment. Maybe. But to me it smacked of schoolboys with inky fingers trying it on with the girls and using their fingers as a means of communicating what they'd like to do with their inexperienced dicks. If only he'd just been open and honest and kissed me and taken me by the hand and led me upstairs it would have happened, we'd have made love in my bed. But no, he had to go and do that grubby little thing to my hand and it all disappeared, all the passion, all the longing, went.

Just as my ardour disappeared, my mind switched in and went into overdrive. What was I doing here on the sofa with Massi anyway? How could I disentangle myself? 'You can't drive,' said Dawn appearing like the Fairy Godmother, 'You've had too much to drink and you're in love with Chrissy.' She was right she was always right. 'Either get him a cab or let him sleep on the sofa and go to bed yourself. It's over.'

While Dawn was lecturing me, Massi must have cottoned on to the fact that all was not well with his foreplay. He broke off from wet hoovering my face and held me at arms' length.

'Not good?' he said.

'Not really,' I said. 'I shouldn't have led you to think I was up for it. There's someone else. Someone I'm in love with who isn't in love with me but it still means I can't do it. I'm sorry, I'm really sorry.'

'Oh my poor girl,' he said, cuddling me and kissing the top of my head. It occurred to me then to want him as my brother who'd shield me from the world of hurtful men. How wonderful to have him come to my aid with his strong arms and soft hands doing kind things – It was a darn sight better than his attempts at lovemaking.

'I can't drive you home. I'm well over the limit. I can call you a cab or get you a duvet and make you comfortable here,' I said.

'Here is good,' said Massi patting the sofa and so he stayed the night downstairs while I fell into a drink sodden stupor liberally laced with guilt and self-recrimination for having got it *so wrong*.

I woke at about nine on the Sunday morning to the sound of the radio and the smell of bacon and coffee. I brushed my teeth, ran my fingers through my hair, pulled on my tracksuit and went downstairs.

Massi was frying bacon and the coffee pot was full. He turned when he heard me come in and gave me a dazzling smile.

'I brought bacon and eggs and sausages for us, I thought we'd deserve one of those big breakfasts,' he said, making me feel even worse than I did.

'I'm sorry, I'm so sorry,' I said coming towards him. 'I wish it could have been different.'

'It's Chrissy isn't it? He's the one you're in love with. I'm right, aren't I?'

'Yes, you're right. Is it so obvious?' I said.

'No. I only worked it out this morning but he's a lucky man,' said Massi. I shrugged. 'You think he doesn't love you?' he said, turning the bacon carefully.

'I know he doesn't,' I said, 'And I've got to learn to live with it.'

'Well, my Grandma, who obviously knew a great deal about cooking, was also a wise woman and used to make me feel better when I was little by telling me that things often turn out differently from what you expect but turn out better,' said Massi and I wanted to cry because he had been thwarted but was still full of kindness and I made him put down the spatula so I could give him a big hug.

We had a lovely breakfast; he was a good cook and would make some girl whose tastes in foreplay were different from mine, a lovely thoughtful, affectionate, drop-dead gorgeous husband. Massi read the paper while I showered and then I drove him back to Chrissy's house.

I parked in the road outside and Massi gave me another big hug before getting his things out of the back seat. 'Don't give up,' he said, 'My Grandma always told me to believe in myself.'

'She *was* a wise woman, there's a lot of you to believe in,' I said blowing him a kiss before driving off.

25

Surprise, Surprise

It wasn't at all awkward being in the shop with Massi after our failed attempt at passion; he was still charming, amusing, helpful and attentive. In fact he was positively solicitous. I think he felt sorry for me that my love was not returned and he went out of his way to make me feel that I mattered to *him*. I was dreading his leaving at the end of August – it would create a big gap in my working day; I'd miss his presence, his help and his being a sounding board for my ideas.

We were collaborating on the company's entry for the most innovative arrangement. I'd had an outrageous idea and discussed it with Massi thinking he'd say it was too weird to work but he clapped his hands with delight and encouraged me to go for it. I didn't tell Ted about my idea as he'd specifically said he wanted to be surprised by it at the dinner. This meant I'd be making my own way to Birmingham in the company van with my piece de resistance in the back and Ted was planning to go either by train or in his own car. I wasn't looking forward to the dinner as such but I was looking forward to the competition.

I didn't have a dress which was suitable – it was such a long time since I'd been to a black tie 'do' that anything I had was old-fashioned or didn't suit my new hairstyle so there was only one thing to do. Buy a new outfit.

I went shopping with Bubbles and my intention was to buy

a little black dress which I'd accessorise with pearls and we looked at loads of little black dresses which were either too short or too low-cut or split to the thigh and I didn't want to look as if I was touting for any kind of business other than floristry. I was getting tired and downhearted and a bit worried that Bubbles' energy was flagging when, in one of those shops where the number of dresses on the hangers is in inverse proportion to their cost, she suddenly whooped with delight and, blue silk hanger in hand, said, 'What about this?'

It was not a little black dress but it was a humdinger of a dress. Nun-like at the front it dipped so low at the back that a bra was out of the question but it was lined from top to bottom so modesty would be preserved. It wasn't black – it was an amazing mid blue silk printed with irises and it flowed in pleats from a high neck accented with a big ruffle, down to a low waist and then to mid-calf. I looked at it and it made me smile; it was a joyful dress, it had style and a kind of humour and I wanted to look good in it.

'Wow,' I said to Bubbles. 'Give it to me *immediately*! I love it. Let's just hope it fits.'

It fitted but I felt a bit odd wearing it without support and was worried about too much wobble if I had to cross the room or walk down a long corridor. The sales assistant understood my dilemma and produced some strange sticky things which you attached to your rib cage and wound round each breast to keep them in place. She swore blind that all the Hollywood actresses rely on these things for red carpet appearances. I loved the dress so much that I bought a pair.

Bubbles and I left tired but happy with one of the shop's beautiful understated heavy white carrier bags with black rope handles and my gorgeous dress nestling within swathed in black tissue. I was delighted with my purchase even though it had cost the best part of two week's wages.

On the Sunday, I went out again and bought royal blue suede court shoes, ten denier black tights, a gold clutch bag and a chunky gold cuff. 'Less is more' Dawn told me as I was tempted by some chandelier earrings. 'Let the dress speak,' she said and she was right. She was always right.

For the week leading up to the dinner, I was in one of those schizophrenic moods when I was looking forward to wearing my dress but dreading meeting a lot of boring old farts and their golf-playing wives so it was helpful to be busy with sorting out the arrangement to take my mind off things. Chrissy came and went once or twice but was curt with me and offhand with Massi. It occurred to me that he resented our success and I thought it was unfair as it brought in the profits which fed him and his children.

Friday came and I was at the market early to make sure that I got the blue hydrangeas and huge, deep purple calla lilies I needed for my arrangement and then I had to go to the fruit and vegetable market to buy my secret addition – the thing which would make my bouquet stand out from the rest. They had it, I bought it and took my purchases back to the van before going home for a couple of hours' sleep; Olive was minding the shop that day so I didn't need to go in to work.

I woke at about ten thirty which felt like the middle of the day so accustomed was I by then to early starts but I was rested and refreshed and it was a great pleasure to be able to have a long soak and time to do my hair and nails without having to hurry. I had a bit of lunch, packed the van and was on my way to Birmingham by one o'clock – the flowers and my wonderful dress keeping close company in the back.

Birmingham being an unknown quantity, I had the satnav on and only made two wrong turns but they sent me into the one way system at the beginning of Friday rush hour and it wasn't until just after five that I finally arrived at the Majestic hotel, dress-carrier and overnight bag in hand.

The Majestic is a new hotel, all metal and glass and a reception area the size of Grand Central Station. It's carpeted in something hideously swirly in too many colours so that if you dropped a packet of *Smarties* on it, you'd never find even one of them. I wasn't impressed but I made my way boldly up to the desk at the far end of the vast expanse of carpet. There was a queue of people, all carrying evening dress in various types of bags, and it was clear they were attending the Gala Dinner.

I looked at my watch wondering if Ted had arrived and if we'd be able to have a drink together before the formal dinner. Out of the corner of my eye I saw a familiar figure crossing the busy carpet.

Chrissy.

'Oh, I wondered if we'd run into one another before the dinner,' he said.

'Where's Ted?'

'Oh Dad's got some sort of tummy bug – a dodgy curry I think – I'll spare you the details, but he said he didn't feel well enough to come and so he sent me instead,' said Chrissy looking about as happy as was I at the prospect of rubber chicken in the company of boring strangers.

'I'm sorry to hear that your Dad's not well,' I said.

'I expect he'll be fine, he took something and went to bed,' said Chrissy. 'Do you need a hand with the arrangement – is it still in the van?'

I didn't want Chrissy of all people to see my entry in the competition ahead of everyone else so I said, 'No, it's OK, thanks, I'll get someone from the hotel to help me.'

'I'll see you in the bar then,' said Chrissy and I nodded as the receptionist gave me my key and directions for how to get to Room 511.

As I rode up to the fifth floor in the lift, I thought how much more considerate both Ted and Massi would have been of my situation had either of them been present. Neither Ted nor Massi would have casually said 'See you in the bar.' Neither of *them* would have allowed me to walk unaccompanied into a bar filled with strangers – they would have come to my room and escorted me to the bar. Chrissy seemed to have lost his manners – or had he just lost whatever interest he had in me? I squared my shoulders as I left the lift and thought, however hard it was going to be, my gorgeous dress and I were going to make the best of this evening.

I unpacked then rang the front desk and secured the services of a busboy to help me unload the van and take the components for my arrangement to the ballroom where the competition entries were to be displayed during the Gala dinner. The busboy looked askance at my choices and was smirking when we got to the ballroom. I ignored him and the stares of the other people (mostly women but there were a few men) as I got to work. It took me about three quarters of an hour to get it exactly as I wanted it and one of the hotel staff helped me put it on the podium alongside the other entries.

After a quick shower (wearing the shower cap) I put on my make up – more eyeshadow than usual and some eyeliner – and sprayed myself liberally with the perfume Bubbles had lent me. She said it was for luck. It was new to me but I loved the square black glass bottle and that it was called *Bandit* and had been Marlene Dietrich's favourite. Bubbles said it was really hard to get nowadays and she had to order it from Fortnum & Mason. It was a dry, smoky smell, something like the interior of a very expensive vintage car, and I liked it because no-one else in that big room would be wearing it.

Then came the complex task of applying the sticky plasters to my boobs. It wasn't easy. It would probably have been simpler if someone else did it for you but I didn't fancy ringing Chrissy and asking for help…or maybe I did but I wasn't going to do it. The rejection would have been too hard to handle.

Eventually my boobs were secured in their strange glue-on cups and I put on my dress. I tested the strength of the cups by bouncing up and down on the side of my bed. No *jiggle*. Thank goodness. After tights and shoes I put on my statement piece of jewellery – the gold cuff and picked up my bag.

There was one of those horrible full length mirrors beloved of hotel chains on the wall just inside the door and I paused to look in it. I never looked better, even though I said it myself. The dress was inspired and made me feel truly lovely, my hair was just right and my face looked rested and glowing. I puffed out my chest and left the room.

The bar was full to bursting with all kinds of people: some on their way home from work in the city, couples out for dinner, families with teenage children and, conspicuous in their evening dress, the guests for the Gala dinner. I fought my way to the bar, registering scowls from several women who obviously liked my dress better than their own, on the way. I ordered a gin and tonic and then asked for a double as I wanted to relax a bit after all the hustle and bustle of getting there and getting my competition entry installed.

My drink arrived and I was standing at the bar having that very enjoyable first long pull at it when a voice at my elbow said, 'Might I be allowed to buy that drink for you?' and I turned and looked into deep blue eyes set in a tanned face. He was about forty, a bit taller than me, square set and dressed from head to foot in *Brooks Brothers* Fifth Avenue preppy style business clothing – trousers just a little too short for a European, button down collar, silk tie Oxford brogues.

I smiled and said, 'No, I don't think so, thank you. It's very kind of you though.'

'It's very kind of you to be wearing that dress,' he said, 'I'm Henry J Bendell the third,' holding out his hand.

'And I'm Rowena Boxer,' I said, holding out my hand which he grasped in a warm dry embrace which made me think that I'd rather be spending the evening with him.

'What brings you here, Rowena,' he said in one of those cultured WASP voices which scream money and privilege.

'Oh, um, I'm here for a Gala dinner in the ballroom. I'm in the floristry business and this is the annual shindig.'

'Sounds like a lot of fun,' said Henry, holding my eyes as he spoke and grinning in a way which indicated that he didn't really think it sounded like fun.

'Well, it is, kind of, because I've entered a competition,' I said.

'Wow,' said Henry, 'Talented as well as beautiful,' and I

laughed and he laughed and then Chrissy appeared with a face like thunder.

'Rowena! I've been looking all over for you. We'll be late for the pre-dinner drinks.'

I smiled at Henry and, taking his hand said, 'It's been a great pleasure to meet you. I hope you have a pleasant evening,' before turning towards Chrissy.

He was in black tie, snowy white dress shirt, silk cummerbund and a proper, wool barathea suit. He looked wonderful and I drank him in with my eyes while trying to appear unaffected by either his appearance or his bad temper.

'I'm sorry,' I said, 'I didn't know about the pre-dinner drinks, Ted didn't say anything and you said to meet in the bar so that's where I went.'

'Yes, you're right. I didn't mean to be sharp with you. Was that guy trying it on with you?'

'No, I don't think so, he's American and he was probably a bit lonely so far from home. He only said that he liked my dress,' I said.

'Bloody right,' said Chrissy with feeling. 'It's a gorgeous dress and you look.....beautiful in it.'

My face went hot and I found it hard not to grin from ear to ear but I needed to remain cool and calm so I just said, 'Well you don't look so bad yourself,' as we entered the ballroom where they were serving drinks from a long table at one end of the room. We had to walk past the competition entries to get to the table.

'Good God Almighty! ' said Chrissy pointing at one particular entry. 'Who on earth submitted *that*! Fancy putting rhubarb with hydrangeas and calla lilies!'

'I think you'll find that it's the entry of Johnson & Company,' I said, 'And I like the rhubarb – the leaves are big and dramatic and the stalks make a colourful contrast to the flowers and, obviously, I put them in that huge glass vase so you'd see the bright red stalks. It's meant to be innovative and it is.'

'Well good luck with that,' said Chrissy but he said it with a smile that went all the way to his eyes.

We went to the drinks table but were too late as the Master of Ceremonies was banging on his table telling us it was time to sit down. We were at a table of eight and found our place cards. Chrissy was opposite me and I was between a chap from Hull on my left and one from Penzance on my right. They were both in late middle age, comfortably married to the women who were next to Chrissy and, dare I say it, smug and patronising. When they weren't staring at my chest (thank heavens for the sticky thingies) they were talking over me about how profit margins had dropped. At one point, one of them said something about my being Chrissy's wife and he overheard.

'Rowena isn't my wife. She's our company's Commercial Manager,' he said, 'And she's increased our sales by forty five per cent in the last eight months. She has a first class degree in economics but she's also very creative with flowers.'

I smiled my thanks at him and he smiled back, across the expanse of white tablecloth – a shy, boyish smile that melted my heart and made me forgive him his earlier boorishness. The dinner was less awful than I thought. It wasn't grey chicken, it was slow roast belly of pork with colcannon mash and glazed carrots. Chrissy and I shared a bottle of Soave and a half bottle of Rioja with the cheese.

As the coffee (served with the obligatory mint which then melts against the hot cup) was cleared away, the Master of Ceremonies rose to announce the results of the competition and introduced the Chairman of the panel of judges, a woman from one of the major wholesale companies. She took the microphone and explained that the judges were looking for entries which would make people think about flowers in a different way or which took familiar blooms and used them in a new way. Chrissy gave me a sympathetic look from across the table which said, 'Don't be upset if you lose.'

The Chairman had envelopes with the winners' names in

them – just like the Oscars – and she invited the guest of honour, a TV Chef, to come to the podium to read them out. They were announced, like Miss World, in reverse order. Fourth place went to a woman from Shrewsbury who'd made a delicate heart-shaped arrangement from peonies, black centred anenomes and lily of the valley which was very pretty but not that different. Third place went to someone from Bedford who'd entered something post-Apocalyptic that looked as if it had escaped from the set of *Waiting for Godot* and then the envelope for second prize was opened. I held my breath. The TV Chef adjusted his reading spectacles and announced the winner of the second prize was Johnson & Company's highly original arrangement. He went on to say that the judges liked it very much and would have made it the winner but it included something which wasn't technically a flower and so they didn't feel they could award it first prize.

I swallowed hard and hoped I could make it to the podium to collect the silver cup. I wished that Ted could have been there, he would have been so proud. Getting up the steps to the podium with jelly legs was difficult but I managed it without mishap and to smile and take the cup from Mr TV Chef and accept his kiss on the cheek without kneeing him in the groin even though he gave my bum a good feel with his other hand. When I got back to the table, Chrissy came over to my seat and kissed me on the cheek and whispered, 'Well done. Dad will be delighted.'

The first prize went to a woman from Sheffield who'd made a very bold arrangement with exotic bird of paradise, big white roses and huge amounts of gypsophila cut to different heights. It was an unusual mixture of blooms but it didn't do that much for me.

I had a large brandy to celebrate my win and then it was eleven o'clock and I suddenly felt very tired so I said 'Goodnight' to the people at the table and told Chrissy I was going to bed. I took the silver cup with me.

In my room, I took off my clothes and hung up my dress.

When would I wear it again? My social life wasn't big on glamour so probably not any time soon. I was thirsty so I rang room service and asked them to bring me a big bottle of fizzy water. Then I went to the bathroom and peeled the sticky things off my breasts. Unfortunately not all the glue came with them so I spent a good ten minutes picking bits of sticky stuff from my chest. There was a knock at the door. Good. I needed the water so I put on the soft white bathrobe and went to answer it.

It was Chrissy.

26

More Surprises

'I've been a fool,' he said, standing there in the corridor in his shirtsleeves.

'What's the matter? Have you locked yourself out? Can't Housekeeping to let you in?'

'No, it's not that! I've been a bloody fool! Can I come in?'

I wasn't all that sure I wanted visitors as I was tired but I opened the door wider and let him in without saying anything. He passed close by me in the narrow passageway into my room and started pacing up and down.

'I shouldn't have let it happen,' he said as if he were talking to himself. 'I saw it coming and I didn't do anything to stop it.'

'I don't know what you're talking about,' I said.

'I'm talking about you and Massi,' he said and I looked uncomprehendingly at him, shrugging my shoulders to emphasise that I still didn't know what he was talking about.

'You know,' he almost shouted, 'You and him! Having an affair!'

'What?' I said.

'Oh come on Rowena, don't try to deny it. I'm not blind and I'm not stupid. He's been all over you like a cheap suit and...you've encouraged him. I saw him in your car, kissing and stuff, the morning after he spent the night at your place.'

I didn't know whether to be angry or amused or delighted

so I was a bit of all three.

'And, putting aside that it isn't any of your business,' I said, 'Why shouldn't two single people enjoy one another's company?'

Chrissy started to say something, stuttered and blustered and looked as if he would have apoplexy. I'm sorry to say that I was enjoying his discomfort.

'Huh! Him and his poncy man-bag and his Armani this and his Gucci that,' he managed after a few seconds and then, triumphantly, as if this were the answer to his dilemma, 'Huh! He lives at home, you know. Thirty-three years old and still lives with Mummy and Daddy. Pathetic.'

'Lives at home with his parents in a palazzo,' I said quietly.

'Huh, and I expect he's invited you there to meet the family!' said Chrissy.

'No, he hasn't and I don't suppose he will,' I said. 'Why would he when we've enjoyed being colleagues and friends but there's nothing more to it than that.'

Chrissy stopped pacing and looked at me as though he didn't believe me.

'You mean you didn't....?'

I shook my head and said, 'Nope.'

'Really?'

'Really. He cooked dinner for me, and very good it was too. We had a bit of a kiss and a hug or two and I knew that we could never be more than friends,' I said. 'But he is one hell of a friend and one hell of a nice man.'

'Oh,' said Chrissy, all the fight going out of him. 'Oh, so you're not in love with Massi?'

'Definitely not,' I said.

'Not even a bit?'

'NO, not even a bit,' I said and Chrissy's face broke out into the widest grin I'd ever seen him wear.

'Oh, well, in that case,' he said, starting to walk up and down again while I sat on the edge of the desk and watched, 'In that case...I, I, I, oh sod it, there's no other way to put this.

I love you Rowena. I've been a bloody fool trying to ignore it and deny it, but I can't. I absolutely bloody adore you and I'm in love with you. You're an amazing woman and I've been stupid not letting myself see it and not allowing myself to admit that I do, I really do, love you.' He stopped pacing and turned to look at me, wanting to gauge the effect of his words.

I was dumbstruck. I didn't know what to say. The very thing I'd dreamed of for months had just happened and I didn't know what to say.

The time for words was gone.

I opened my arms and Chrissy fell into them, putting his lovely head against my neck where he rested for quite some time as we each drank in the exquisite pleasure of our bodies resting one against the other. I felt his breath against my skin and the softness of his hair under my fingers. His hands rested against my back and I felt his heat under my robe. It was a time of extreme tenderness and my whole body relaxed as though I'd come home after a very long, difficult journey. But after a few minutes we had other things to attend to and soon Chrissy brought his lips to mine and there was nothing of the enthusiastic puppy about his kiss – this was the kiss of a mature man who wanted to show the woman he loved how much he wanted her.

I don't know how many other women have had the experience of their first coupling with the man they love having to be preceded by his applying baby oil to her chest in order to remove glue and bathrobe fluff from her breasts but I'm one of them and can vouch for the fact that it doesn't hinder proceedings at all; it was highly enjoyable and erotic and tenderly funny all at once and, afterwards, Chrissy and I got into my bed and made love. I use that word very deliberately because, looking back, it occurred to me it was the first time any man had actually made *love* to me. Tony gave a performance and it was my job to be properly appreciative of his efforts but with Chrissy it was different; a totally mutual thing, deliciously wonderful and very addictive. We slept in one another's arms between sessions and I didn't want the night to end. At about seven in the morning Chrissy woke.

'I'll go back to my room now to preserve your reputation,' he said kissing me. 'See you at breakfast?'

'About half past eight,' I said, sleepily, feeling very happy that we were about to have our first breakfast date.

I had a snooze after Chrissy left, then showered and dressed and did my hair and face. Standing at the window, slathering foundation onto my cheeks, I realised, in the light of day, I needed to think with my head and not with my heart or anywhere lower down.

I didn't want to 'go out' with Chrissy, I didn't want to be his 'girlfriend,' I didn't want even to be his live-in lover. I had to face the reality that I wanted to be his wife and I wanted to help raise his lovely children in a settled home. If it wasn't going to work out like that then I did not want to torture myself with trying to settle for anything less and I needed to broach this subject as soon as possible.

'You look serious,' said Chrissy as I sat opposite him in the bright, busy restaurant where people passed to and fro to the breakfast buffet bar carrying plates of stewed fruit, croissants and overdone scrambled egg.

'I'm trying not to look like a woman who spent most of the night on her back,' I said. 'It's either this or a smirk so satisfied other women will hate me.'

'Is that a compliment to my skills?'

'It certainly is,' I said, 'But…'

'Oh no, not a 'but'. Is there a problem?'

'No, but I just wanted to say that, for me, last night was really important. I mean, it was a lot more than just a roll in the hay or several, very wonderful rolls in the hay and I want to know where we're going with it…' I tailed off.

'OK, I understand. I get it. I don't want to talk about it here. Let's go for a walk after breakfast and blow the cobwebs away and we can talk then.'

So we did. As soon as we got to the street, Chrissy took

my small hand in his large, warm one and my heart filled with delight that he wanted us to appear as a couple – it didn't matter that we saw no-one we knew, it mattered only that he wanted to hold my hand. We wandered about the streets looking at shoppers and families and, now and then, Chrissy would give me a reassuring smile. I wondered when he would begin the conversation on which my future happiness hinged but I had said my piece and I must wait until he felt ready to speak.

'Let's sit here,' he said, indicating a wooden bench in the sun. I sat beside him and waited. I could feel the tension in him. He cleared his throat and, taking my hand again, squeezed it quite hard.

'This is really difficult, Rowena.' He cleared his throat again, 'I mean, it's not often a man has to make a speech like this and, frankly, I'm out of practice, but what I want to say to you is that, I don't mess about. I mean, I'm not one of those blokes who go in for wham, bam, thank you ma'am.' He looked at me and I smiled and nodded to let him know that I was following his train of thought.

'The thing is, the thing is, I love you.' Chrissy scratched his head. 'And really that's pretty much all there is to it. I love you and I want to spend the rest of my life loving you and making you happy. I've loved you from the first time I set eyes on you, you blew me away but I was too scared to think I could find happiness again and now I can't bear to think about a life without you.'

'I love you too,' I said, 'But what about the children? How will they feel if we become an item?'

'We *are* an item! I hope we're more than an item. I hope we're engaged,' said Chrissy.

'If you want me to marry you, then I think you need to ask me,' I said, grinning widely.

'Will you, will you marry me?' said Chrissy, 'As soon as possible?'

'Yes, I will,' I said, 'but what about the children?'

'My children want nothing more than to be normal,' said Chrissy. 'And that means having a mother. They both adore you and will be delighted to have you as their new Mum.'

'Am I moving in, then?' I said.

'Yes, before the children pack up their stuff and move to your house, anyway. And in case you're worried about what Dad might think, we'd better get married soon, before he adopts you!'

I began to cry. Chrissy put his arms around me and, in the comfort of his embrace, I allowed myself to believe that this was all true – that he loved me, his children accepted me and his father approved of me. It was all too much to take in. One minute I was a single career girl whose only responsibility was herself and the next I'd inherited a whole family.

Chrissy stroked my hair and patted my back. 'I know, I know,' he said. 'It's all happening at once but sometimes life's like that.' He bent to kiss my neck and then he kissed my cheek and then he kissed me on the lips and we had a proper snog on the wooden bench in the middle of Birmingham in broad daylight.

Chrissy held me at arms' length. 'Er, Dad isn't expecting me until the evening,' he said.

'Are you thinking what I'm thinking?' I said.

'Yup.'

We ran back to the hotel, obtained a half-day rate for his room and went back to bed to celebrate our engagement in time-honoured tradition.

Chrissy drove the van and me back to London and we talked all the way home about our plans. We agreed that I would come to the house with him and we'd tell Ted and the children straightaway.

'Ted's not feeling well, though,' I said.

'This will cheer him up, then, won't it?' said Chrissy but, when we got to the house, Ted was romping around the kitchen making Lucy laugh and appeared to have no ill-effects from his stomach bug. When we told him our news, his first words were 'Thank God,' as if he'd known it would happen all along and we'd taken our time about it. Lucy flew across the room to me and screamed with delight so loudly I thought she'd deafen me while Edward came and put his arms on my shoulders and said, 'I am so pleased. It will be wonderful to have you in our family.'

I went home for a few days to pack my things but it didn't feel like home any more. I took all the spotty, dotty, girly stuff with me and left my house as uncluttered as it had been when Tony was in residence so the letting agents could market it to yuppies. A couple of visiting Japanese theoretical physicists rented it from me for a year and I was happy they wouldn't abuse my property. My only pang of regret was that I would no longer have Bubbles as a neighbour but Chrissy agreed Thursday evenings would be hers and I was free to dine out with her or to have her come to the house to eat with the family. She and Ted soon got on like a house on fire (irritatingly, they shared a passion for The Goons).

We all settled into a routine quickly and easily. It was as if there had long been a Rowena shaped hole in their lives and I filled it perfectly whereas, for me, they were all the family I'd have chosen given the chance.

Chrissy wanted to buy me an engagement ring so we went to see Mr Shapiro whose face was a picture when I showed up with my new fiancé. Chrissy insisted on a beautiful 1.5 carat diamond and Mr Shapiro added pave diamond shoulders to the setting as his gift to me.

There was so much going on with wedding plans, decorating the sitting room at the house for the wedding, keeping track of the children's homework, attending to the business, etc, etc, that I didn't notice at first. I was losing weight because I was so busy and living on adrenaline and happiness so it didn't occur to me for quite some time that I hadn't had a period. In fact, it was Chrissy who mentioned it, in a slightly embarrassed way, 'Er, shouldn't you, er, you know…be having a period, sometime? Or am I wrong?'

'No, you're right. I should. I'll go and have a look at the calendar and see what's what,' I said thinking that I might be a little bit late and it was all down to the excitement.

The calendar told me I was three weeks late. I shook my head at it. No. Couldn't be. Not me. Not the woman who'd had five rounds of IVF and failed to conceive. I left it for a week but by then I was feeling quite queasy and spilling out of my bra so I went to the chemist (one of the ones I used to frequent and the assistant gave me a pitying look) and bought a tester-kit.

I hardly dared take it into the loo. I'd done this so many times and been disappointed. But, hey, I had a gorgeous family anyway, now, so what as there to be afraid of?

I peed on the stick and held it in my hand, waiting, with my eyes closed. I opened them after three minutes. Oh my God! Bloody hell!

Pregnant. Definitely pregnant. I fell back against the cool porcelain of the low cistern for support and tried to slow my breathing down. Phew. I quickly did the maths in my head. Four weeks since I should have had a period. Six weeks since Chrissy and I became lovers. We hadn't taken any precautions as I hadn't thought it necessary. The irony was delicious.

I told Chrissy that evening when he came to close up the shop. There was no point in waiting until we got home and, anyway, I'd waited a long time to be able to give this news to the man I love.

'I'm pregnant,' I said, as soon as he came through the door. Chrissy took a moment to digest this announcement and then his face broke into a broad, boyish grin. He bounded over to me and gave me a big hug.

'Clever girl,' he said, into my hair. 'How far on?'

'About six weeks, but it's definite, the stick was very clear about it,' I said.

'So… you probably got pregnant that first time?'

'Probably, or the second time or the third time or even when we went back to bed after our little walk around

Birmingham,' I said.

'Well, how about that?' said Chrissy, pleased at his own virility.

We told Ted next and there was a tear in his eye as he kissed me in congratulation. The children were cock-a-hoop with joy and my dear friend Bubbles dusted off her knitting patterns and started on gorgeous little garments for our new baby while my trusty *Mulberry* bag filled with paperwork for ante-natal appointments and wedding details.

Chrissy and I were married soon after. Lucy and Laura were flower girls and Edward and Adam jointly carried the ring on a velvet cushion. Bubbles was a maid of honour and Jane did her best sisterly bit by crying almost all the way through the Register Office ceremony.

As I got bigger, Chrissy said it wasn't good for me to sit on the high stool behind the counter so he got me a lower one and there I was one grey winter's afternoon, six months' pregnant, doing the company's books, when the shop doorbell rang. I was adding up a column of figures and didn't look up straight away as I thought whoever it was would be browsing the flowers but the customer coughed to attract my attention. It was a male cough.

It was Tony.

'What do *you* want?' I said.

'The Japanese bloke told me where I could find you,' he said. He was tanned as if from a very recent holiday and when he spoke I could see he'd had his already bright teeth further whitened. His hair was gelled to perfection, his gym-worked chest muscles strained at the tight, black T-shirt under his shearling flying jacket. A scarlet cashmere scarf artfully knotted at his throat completed the style points of his outfit. He looked as if he'd come straight from a casting session for *The Only Way Is Essex*.

'You didn't answer my question,' I said. 'What do you want?'

'I want you,' said Tony.

223

'You want me to what?'

'I made a big mistake,' said Tony, 'I should never have left you.' He gave me what he no doubt hoped was a winning smile but all I saw was the inside of a shark's jaws.

'Well, it's a bit late now,' I said. 'You've got a new wife and a baby to consider.'

'Actually, no,' said Tony looking less confident and, for the first time ever, a little bit defensive.

'Don't tell me she's left you already,' I said.

'No, I left her,' said Tony, shuffling his feet.

This was getting interesting. 'Why? I thought she was your ideal woman,' I said. 'She was supposed to be a better bet than me. She was carrying your baby. Something *I* failed to achieve.'

'It wasn't mine,' he said, quietly. 'The baby wasn't mine.'

For a moment, my curiosity got the better of me and I couldn't stop myself from asking, 'How did you know? How could you tell?'

Tony misinterpreted my interest for sympathy and became more animated, 'It came out looking a bit yellow and a bit puffy around the eyes. She said it was jaundice at first but it didn't go and it wasn't jaundice. The baby was half Chinese.'

'*What*?'

Tony obviously thought he was getting onto solid ground. 'Oh yeah. It was half Chinese alright. She had to admit it in the end. Kid looked nothing like me. She'd had a fling with Douglas Cheung. Remember him?' he said. I nodded. 'Well, it was his.'

I couldn't help myself. It was too much. I started to laugh and couldn't stop. Tony's face set solid and hard.

'That is *so* funny,' I said, 'Because it was Douglas Cheung who said Tasha was so thick she'd have to look down her blouse to count to two and, obviously, he was down there helping her do it'

I started laughing again. Tony's face was a picture of rage.

'You were always a bitch Ro and you're still a bitch,' he said in a raised voice.

'Is he bothering you?' said Chrissy coming into the shop from the back kitchen with two mugs of tea in his hand.

'What's it to do with you, pal?' said Tony, puffing out his chest in a display of male power.

'Because you're bothering my wife,' said Chrissy putting the tea on the counter and squaring up to him. Tony was lost for words. I stood up and faced him with my pregnant belly and put my left hand with its gorgeous real diamond on the counter.

'You made two mistakes,' I said. 'One was leaving me and the other was thinking I might want you back. You're as phony as the ring you bought me.'

'So clear off,' said Chrissy his real, work-hardened muscles showing through his plaid shirt as he pointed to the door.

'Tosser,' said Tony, 'I was going anyway.'

'She's mine now,' said Chrissy. 'So don't come back. We don't want you here.'

Tony slunk away, his tail between his legs. I expect he went out that night to a bar, dressed to the hilt, found a girl, impressed her with his looks, his talk and his designer labels, took her back to his place and began a new affair with her. It wouldn't have mattered who she was as long as she fitted into his cut-out model of the perfect female accessory. God help her.

Amelia Grace Johnson and Rafael Henry Johnson were born thirty eight weeks after Chrissy and I became lovers. They're with me here in the kitchen at home now, two perfect little faces peeping out from their white *Babygros*, as they lie asleep in their matching Moses baskets while Lucy parades up and down wearing the brown knitted radio tea-cosy as a hat and Edward takes pictures of her using my smartphone. They're both giggling. I'll shortly begin to prepare the Spaghetti Bolognese we're having for supper when Chrissy comes home and Bubbles arrives. Ted is in the garden, digging in the onion sets as we've decided to grow some of

225

our own vegetables now we're such a big family.

And my Bayswater bag? It lies open on the kitchen table - it's really handy for baby wipes and nappies.

THE END